PUNK
SUNK
LOVE

PUNK
SUNK
LOVE

DHIRENDRA TIWARI

Srishti
PUBLISHERS & DISTRIBUTORS

SRISHTI PUBLISHERS & DISTRIBUTORS
Registered Office: N-16, C.R. Park
New Delhi – 110 019
Corporate Office: 212A, Peacock Lane
Shahpur Jat, New Delhi – 110 049
editorial@srishtipublishers.com

First published by
Srishti Publishers & Distributors in 2016

To my father, my hero
and
To my son, who wants to be a superhero.

"While falling in and out of love, a young devil-may-care man accidentally untwines the causality of love through a murky battle between self-retribution and true redemption."

Acknowledgements

Writing is simple. We write almost every day at work, at school, at home. However, writing a novel is serious business. A writer needs to be committed to the characters and their journey. Like a surrogate, drowning in their sorrows, brimming in their joy; but then there is also real life to deal with. In my case, that means a twelve-hours-a-day job, family and everything else that is called life. At times I wonder what it would've been like if it wasn't for my wife's confidence in my ability to deliver and her rock solid support. I don't think I can ever thank her enough, but I'll try.

Thank you Ashi for all your support, your unabashed critique, and spending many nights playing invent-the-title game before settling on this one. My baby, Vihaan, thank you for singing "Didn't your heart just break" so beautifully!

There are some memories that always live with us in the shadows, inspiring us, driving us, as if they are a part of us. I want to thank all the wonderful people whose memories I still carry with me.

A really big thanks to team Srishti Publishers for believing in the story and helping bring it to the readers. Thanks to Wasim Helal for a wonderful and thoughtful cover design.

I'd also like to thank Writer's Side for a constructive critique and wonderful suggestions that have made the plot tighter and juicier. Thanks to Siyahi for providing another round of critique and very valuable initial edit of the manuscript.

viii ‖ *Acknowledgements*

A heartfelt thanks to all of the focus group readers for your suggestions. It has made the story so much better.

A big thanks to both of my brothers (Hirendra Tiwari and Virendra Tiwari) for always sticking by and providing me with unrequited support. My nieces (Jiyaa and Shagun), my nephew (Veer) and both of my sisters-in-law. I'll always be thankful to Satya Pandey and Anand Pandey (my in-laws) for their kind words and encouragement.

Mr. R.S. Garg, my housemaster, my mentor and the actor who was the life of TV serial *Neev;* thank you, Sir.

A special thanks to Shyam Sunder, Nalini Parmeshwar, Gowri Shankar, Amit Bhat, Saurabh Jain, Rishi Kwatra, Joe Kennedy, Stu Dolleck, Susan Dolleck, Abhishek Sharma, Dinesh Baldawa, Deepak Mittal, Praveen Mehta, Sachin Gupta, Abhishek Ratnakar, Amit Roshan, Amit Upadhyay, and my music teacher at Scindia School for making me understand that I can't sing and that writing may just be the thing for me!

And above all, a big thanks to my parents. I wouldn't exist without you, and I wouldn't be the person I am without your care, guidance and abundant love. I love you!

What is love? *I'll know it someday, or maybe I already know. Perhaps I've experienced it, lived it, and died in it. Or maybe not...* Philosophical thoughts daubed Roy's mind as he trudged up the spiral staircase.

Life behind this façade is a storm of changes; you can see some coming and some hit you like a train, making you think, "What am I doing? This, today, tomorrow – does any of this matter?" Isn't that 'the' question...the Holy Grail, the infinite search?

Maybe today I'll get all the answers. Today I'll come to terms with life and love.

But this is not love. This looks umm...a little different. There's the love of my life Pia, the oh-so seductive fragrance, my own bed... but who is that with her? That ain't me. It can't be. I am standing here looking at him.

"There's nothing that can't be explained." Pia's soft husky voice rolled in Roy's ears only to be decimated by the obscenity of her actions.

I want to fly out like Superman. I can also web out like Spiderman. Wait a second! Occam's razor – All things being equal, the simplest solution is the best solution. That's right. I should just walk out the main door. Without saying a word, Roy turned around and like a stiff pre-programmed robot, descended down the staircase to quietly exit the house.

The Maharaja of Air India, with his folded hands, smiled away to a torpid Roy staring at the built-in TV screen of his first class seat. The Maharaja smile wasn't helping much. He looked out of the window. *Look at that Red fort! All its grandeur is lost in this space-time continuum. All that is left of it is a depressing view like it's a tiny model on a canvas surrounded by matchbox-sized houses*, thought Roy, as he loosened his tie, rolled up the sleeves and lay flat on his reclined, cushy seat thousands of feet above mankind.

The events of the day seemed like a dream that Roy hoped would die with the flight turbulence.

There goes another one! I have been shown my place. Love and I are just not to be. Is it really that simple? You know what, I won't even try to analyze it now. It's not worth it. Just focus on what's ahead. You are twenty-nine years old, have a new job, and would hopefully live long enough to figure this shit out.

The deep sea of pathos within him was safely tucked away under the blanket of his superficial smile, a smile that he wore even in his sleep. But today, his smile was secretly preparing to betray him, strip him of his chameleon camouflage, baring the wretchedness of his soul.

I wish I could sleep, even if just for a few moments. Damn insomnia! It's back from the grave. Sewn to my soul. What else sticks with us? That first kiss, first break-up, the smell of sand after rain, and at times, little words someone said to us.

Words – Words are so deceptive, so fatal. It's amazing how a few words can shake the very core of what makes a person.

His eyelids moved frequently under the blinders, for his mind was racing. *All the thoughts must go; I should not dwell in the past. You can't change it, because you made it. Your actions drew the skeleton and words filled in the color.*

The soft announcement bell stabbed through his trance. "The plane is in the final leg of descent. Please pull your seats in the upright position, and ensure that your tray tables are locked."

Roy took his blinders off, pulled his seat up and looked at his chrome Tag Heuer watch. He had been sitting there for fourteen hours, deprived of a single wink of sleep. His tired dark black eyes lingered over his own reflection in the dark TV screen before him. His square-cut face was devoid of any happiness, and thin stubble covered it. In sharp contrast to the numerous compliments he received that likened him to a tanned Brad Pitt with black hair and eyes, he saw his reflection to be as barren as a hundred-year-old tree. Self-pity was even more staggering today. *This isn't good. I can't let this happen to me.*

Now is the time to pull yourself out of this dark hole you keep getting pulled into, for if the darkness persists, god must be a myth.

The big Boeing 777 aircraft pierced through the cloud like a giant whale cutting through the deep sea. As the plane lowered altitude in the wee hours of a dark early morning, Roy looked through the window at the spectacular view of Manhattan and its tall, sparkling high-rise buildings through a clandestine transparent layer of cloud.

Roy had seen this multiple times, but it looked different today. It was almost poetic and philosophical in a very abstract way. *Look at that calm placid Hudson River running along the skyline...the yang to its yin - New York City.*

There is no good without bad and there is no god without evil. Like there is no happiness without heartbreak.

I was happy though, for a long time, and now I am sad. But I am the writer of my destiny and I, only I, have the power to alter my destiny if and only if I chose, remembered Roy from one of his life coaching sessions many years ago. *Why am I getting these thoughts in my head? I am glad no one can hear my thoughts, else the only job I could get would be flipping burgers. Pull yourself together Roy...get mature...think like the world sees you...a hot-shot Wall Street guy. But the world doesn't know me; how could they? How could anyone?* Somewhere in his chain of thoughts, Roy was beginning to tread down a battle within...that he had fought one too many times. *It is easier to let go. Think of last year as a sabbatical. As time away from the sixteen-hour workdays, the heightened sense of anxiety of trading, and the barking of fat, impatient brokers. Hmm, that actually sounds refreshing now. Maybe I am ready to go back in the Pit.*

It was perhaps a good thing that after a brief hiatus Roy was coming back to the city he had spent a decade in, and now he was also ready to embrace it – not with a loser's spirit but with the very spirit of joy and excitement that was the lifeline of New York City.

While a shattered and wounded Roy boarded the plane, a healed Roy would get off. Let this be a new beginning.

$\mathcal{A}$ cell phone vibrated on a polished classic red oak side table, colliding with an untidy stack of torn out playboy magazines.

A hand lazily snaked up to the side table and cancelled the call. The nasal sound of light snoring filled the air only to be interrupted by the resonating sound of the vibrating phone again. A bare arm came out of the comforter, grabbed the phone and skittered it out. The phone slid and with a bam, struck Bumpy on his head.

On the bare floor, Bumpy lay flat on his fat stomach, his bare waist sure to disgust everyone who could see it. He rubbed his head, looked up to the bedroom in dismay, picked up the phone and sleepily said, "Yeh, hellooo…"

Bumpy got up when the call ended. He looked around, wondering why he was not in his hostel and why in the world was he sleeping on the floor? Hung over but wide awake, he walked into the enormous bedroom and started pulling the comforter.

Bumpy was around five feet three inches tall, with a chubby, hairy apish body and long unkempt curly hair. "Shammi, wake up. Anuja is in our college hospital," he said.

The sound of ruffling sheets broke the placidity as Shammi turned sides. Bumpy stood there, waited for a couple minutes and then pulled at the comforter again.

"Who?" A sleepy reply came from under the comforter.

"You don't remember? Okay, go back two or maybe three months…slightly healthy figure," Bumpy paused. "You said you will hook me up with her, but when you slept with her for two weeks, you realized that I was too good for her. Remember that?" He genuinely questioned.

"Let me sleep and you do that too. Slightly healthy, my ass!" Shammi said from under the comforter, clearly irritated.

"I would understand under normal circumstances, but this is serious yaar. She is in the hospital. You cannot be that stone-hearted," said Bumpy.

Moments of silence followed, and then a pair of legs fell from the California-size bed on to the red oak wooden floor.

"This better not be a fuckin' joke," said Shammi rubbing his dreamy light brown eyes groggily. With a long pliant stretch, his lean toned body puffed up, carving a chiseled veneer through his black polo t-shirt, he looked at himself in surprise, wondering why he had slept with his jeans, t-shirt and shoes still on.

His grumpiness melted away as his eyes fell on a painting on the wall. "Look at that painting. It's so beautiful now," Shammi remarked contently. The beautiful 'Reclining Odalisque' by Henri Matisse for some reason was now clothed with a smudgy black bra.

Bumpy looked at it admiringly, lost in his deep analysis of the modification. "Genius!"

Shammi still wasn't very keen on going to meet Anuja – supposedly a girl he had slept with – who was now in the hospital.

"What if she is pregnant?" Shammi asked, alarmed by the possibility.

"It is even more important to go then. You can perhaps convince her to take care of all that, you know."

A quick Listerine gargle later, Shammi sprayed some perfume over the same set of clothes, and they were ready to roll.

A pair of slim legs wrapped in faded Armani Exchange jeans walked swiftly down the corridors of Ricochet hospital.

"I think I am getting a heart attack," Bumpy plodded his way up to Shammi, huffing and puffing.

"This floor, man...I need to go take a dump," said Bumpy and darted straight to the bathroom. Shammi had gotten used to his incoherence. He just shrugged and turned, scanning the maze of the Ricochet Medical College.

"Ma'am, would you know where B243 is?" Shammi stopped a nurse passing by.

The nurse slowly turned, gave Shammi a cold hard stare, and walked away.

Nice. Is everyone in this world just fucked up or what?

Strolling along the winter style garden, his prying eyes rested on someone. *See this is what I like - 'cute and girl' in the same sentence.* A smile adorned his Ranbir Kapoor-like charming, boyish face.

Shammi was no slouch. Even though not bathed, his dirty spiked hair, stubbly oval face, sexy carved lips and those dreamy inviting light brown eyes were always ready to woo. Loaded with swag, Shammi walked closer to the girl, who was seemingly being eaten alive by what looked like a very horny, sleazy doctor.

The tall, middle-aged Dr. Dhoort had his back to Shammi, leaning against a support beam. He was completely engrossed in his conversation. "You are lucky. First year medical student and already gettingavisittotherealpatientward.Tellme,likedyourfirstvisit?"said Dr. Dhoort, murdering the word visit by pronouncing it as *vijit*.

"Don't lie, haan. Remember, I am your mentor."

The girl was as confused as a kitten on a treadmill. "I didn't know of this mentor-mentee program. Is this something we get auto-enrolled into?"

Dr. Dhoort had started drooling by now. "This is an invitation only program. I reserve it for the bestest of best medical students of mine." He paused, "...and also the most beautiful ones." His creepy gummy smile rolled out.

The conversation was turning sleazier by the second.

This guy is, hmm, frustrated. Nah, weird. Nah...depraved and weird. Wait what is that? Is that a toupee?

Shammi tapped his shoulders. Dr. Dhoort completely ignored Shammi's interruption and continued his conversation with the girl. "What do you like better - hospital or morgue?" The girl suddenly turned bug-eyed, speechless at the morbidity of the question.

Shammi being the persistent fella cleverly tapped on Dr. Dhoort's neck with just enough maneuver to clip out his toupee. "Sir, do you know where room B two-four-three is?"

An agitated Dr. Dhoort turned around and rudely shot at Shammi, "Can't you see we are having an intelligent conversation?" Dr. Dhoort had totally flipped out as he scrambled to put his toupee back, and the girl found a chance to sneak out of his sleazy clutches.

"I can help you." She told Shammi before turning towards the doctor. "Thank you, sir. This tour was really helpful. I'll see you in college." She slid out before Dr. Dhoort could even comprehend what had happened.

Shammi and the girl walked away, leaving Dr. Dhoort sulking with a forced smile on his face.

"Hi, I am Shammi," Shammi introduced himself.

"Hi, I am Sona Gill," said the girl.

"You are a very kind person." Shammi gave a loose puckered smile, countered almost instantly by a gracious nod from Sona.

Sona was a delicately beautiful girl with big eyes and pouty lips. Dressed in a very casual tank-top, jeans and flat sandals, she looked shorter than her everyday look, but cute nevertheless.

Shammi had all but forgotten about his sick ex-girlfriend or of his fear that she might be pregnant. Instead, he was digging in his arsenal of the three-step process, designed for success and customized for every category of girl. For cute, homely girls like Sona seemed to be, his playbook was to crack a funny joke, pretend to be a good listener and speak very softly. This would make the girl feel he is funny and can be trusted to be the good friend. The whole speaking softly thing would firm up his image as a guy with a humble upbringing. Now he was in, the goal was to get them talking – the homely girl will start babbling about her dog, dolls and other boring shit. But, once they start talking about stuff in their bedroom, it's only a matter of time before he would end up in the bedroom too!

A smile appeared on Shammi's face.

"You know, that doctor is so out of whack," said Shammi.

Sona was hooked.

"There is this story about him. He was playing with his pen. A nurse walked up to him and asked to borrow a pen. He said which one? One pen-is in my mouth, the other pen is in my pocket."

Sona broke into laughter. "You are crazy…"

A victorious feeling ensued as Shammi courteously held the door open for Sona, who paused and said, "This is your building." She turned around to take off when a strange-looking man in a hospital apron walked by. His gaze was fixated on Sona.

Shammi was puzzled by his leer. Just then, the guy hopped a step towards Sona, folded his arms in an erratic pattern, turned and twisted his fingers and droolingly said, "Will yoooou beeee mmyyyy girrlfrrrienddd?" All things including the slow drag in the man's tone rebuffed Shammi. *What the fuck is this? Is this some new way of hunting? And Sona is smiling? What the fuck is going on? I'll do it too.*

"Shhhee iisss youuurr sissstteerr, remmmemmbbbeerrr?" jumped in Shammi with an equally slow drag tone. Shammi put his fake smile and looked at Sona, expecting accolades for his stellar performance.

"Why would you make fun of people with special needs?" Sona was visibly upset.

"Did you say special needs?" Shammi's voice was still soft. "Hmm," he paused. "This is not a looneyland. Is it?"

He looked at the weird man and then at Sona. "It was a rhetorical question. Really."

"Sir, let me help you." Sona held the man's hand and helped him sit on the bench.

A nurse was passing by in a hurry and stopped on seeing them. "Oh thank you, kiddo. I was looking for him."

Sona nodded to the nurse with a smile and then walked out of the building without even looking at Shammi.

Shammi was still reeling from the shock of what he had just heard. *What the fuck is my supposed girlfriend...ex-girlfriend, doing in fuckin' looneyland? And why am I here? And, where the fuck is Bumpy?*

Shammi had turned around to walk away when he noticed that he was right outside 243. Battling his nineteen-year-old overwrought delirium of skipping the madhouse with his curiosity to find out more about the girl whose face he didn't even remember, he chose the latter. He nervously stepped closer and peeped through the frame of the door.

A man acting like an ape was jumping around and scratching his tummy with both hands, an old man was playing with his own dentures, an old lady was dancing like Madonna, and somewhere in the corner, a young woman hidden behind the ape man was murmuring – "he loves me...he loves me not..."

A blurry image of the past was beginning to infringe upon him. Anuja's face started to look familiar. The heartfelt dedication of her love was beginning to confuse him. The emotional toll and empathy was about to rain through his eyes when the ape man jumped away and Shammi saw Anuja's hands. While chanting "he loves me, loves me not", she was plucking hairs from the head of this frail old man.

Shammi's whole emotional state mutated. *What the fuck?* Taking small discreet steps, he backed away from the room.

$\mathcal{A}$ yellow cab zoomed through the scarce morning traffic of Queens Tunnel opening into the heart of Manhattan. The monumental top of Grand Central station stood in the corridors of the skyscrapers like a Greek god, analogous to a guardian of the creativity and the enormous wealth that the city had stacked in its underbelly.

The cab pulled over next to a high rise on Park Avenue. The doorman rushed to open the door. Roy stepped out of the cab, stood up straight and lazily stretched his entire body.

"Welcome home, Mr. Roy," said the doorman.

Roy gazed around the skyline of the plush neighbourhood. "I am home, Willis," said Roy. "I am home."

The door of the apartment opened and Willis advanced the luggage cart. In the darkness of the apartment, the stunning thirty mile view of the city looked like a modern art painting stuccoed on the wall.

Willis turned the lights on and the view disappeared, only to be filled with reflections of the mundane empty apartment.

Roy looked around his apartment and a faint smile appeared on his face. If Roy ever felt like he was home, it was in this apartment that had nothing but a couple of bean bags, a small side table, a small TV and the vastness of empty space.

"Will there be anything else, sir?" asked Willis.

Roy shook his head sideways, smiled and generously tipped Willis, who left with the emptied luggage cart, closing the door behind him.

Roy strolled towards the kitchen, opened the drawers below the sink, and took out his neatly organized tray of cleaning supplies – yellow cleaning gloves, Windex, Tilex, Pinesol and cleaning towels. He put his yellow rubber gloves on. "Let's get to it!"

Two hours had passed. The lemon fresh smell of Pinesol wafted through the apartment, complementing the pristine visual of the roomy, clutter-free apartment. Dressed in a pair of shorts and t-shirt, a scrubbed and bathed Roy dropped on to the large beanbag. *Gosh, it feels nice. I feel ten pounds lighter.* Roy lifted his legs up, relishing the feeling of weightlessness even as his eyes battled a coma-inducing jetlag. Just after a short while, he stood up and walked to the window, opening the blinds to the breathtaking view of Grand Central.

The foot traffic in and out of Grand Central was swelling up already. He stood at the window, gazing through the swarming crowd. Each one's dressing and appearance bore touches of individuality, but every one of them was following the same regimen, the same routine, the same commute. *Who knows what the girl in that weird dress is going through, her personal baggage, her own ordeal, maybe a tragedy or perhaps a celebration.*

The coffee in his cup had dried up. Roy looked at his watch. It was five past seven. He closed his window blinds. *It's time to put on the Joker mask.*

Roy was no different than any other New Yorker. His persona at work didn't carry the slightest hint of his personal turmoil. Smartly dressed in a navy blue suit, bright blue tie, white shirt with collar buttons and chrome cuff-links, he stood in the E line subway train as it swiftly clunked in the dark tunnels of New York City. His smile hiding away the deep canal of personal turmoil.

After a few stops, Roy alighted at the World Trade Center station. The crowd moved along in the same direction like a giant colourful wave rising up the dizzying steep escalators.

Roy hopped on to the still staircase and quickly climbed up the steps, took a left turn, crossed the street and entered the World Financial Center; a block away from the tallest building symbolic of modern day freedom – The World Freedom Tower, built on the solemn lot of ground zero.

$\mathcal{A}$ BMW 3 Series sped through the well-lit roads of suburban Mumbai with Shammi at the helm and Bumpy on the passenger's seat. Both were deathly quiet like they had just seen a ghost. As the traffic light turned red, the car came to a screeching halt. Shammi and Bumpy jolted a bit before settling back in their seats. Both looked at each other, and after a split second of silence, they roared with laughter.

"You?" said Bumpy, "you thought you did this to her?" Bumpy spat between laughs. "Dude, thank god she didn't pluck hair or for that matter some other very important 'thing' out of you," Bumpy joked.

Shammi still couldn't believe what he had seen that morning and just shook his head.

The lights turned green and the car took a turn into the glittering lanes of Bandra Linking Road, honking through 'the' club street of the entire country.

"Remember the three steps to woo spoilt girls – Be arrogant, snub a big guy (if there is one), and wickedly smile at them, gazing into their eyes," said Shammi as they made a grand entry into the elite club. Before them was an army of hot chicks dancing to loud hip-hop music under the hazy blue flickering club lights.

Everyone seemed to know Shammi: many dudes and chicks did the chin up hello; the bartender greeted him by name and even did the whole brotherhood clapping and knuckle handshake thing.

He pulled out a bar stool next to a pretty girl. "Hi, I am Shammi. Someone just stole my balls so I apologize if I come across as a bit retarded."

"You look like a guy whose brain is in his balls," unwittingly commented the girl, her face hidden behind her luxuriant hair.

"True, my balls must be in my head then. Looks like an epic swap," Shammi replied with a straight face.

A suggestive smile creased the pretty girl's face. "That was funny." She turned around.

"Ro, a dozen tequila shots please." Shammi pulled his bar stool closer to the girl.

"You didn't ask my name," her words were laced with mischief.

"I will. Tomorrow…morning."

"Hmm, so is that what those shots are for…"

"Maybe…" he said as he bent backwards on his bar stool. "Lesson of life: Don't fall in love. It can make you crazy. I mean literally…"

Shammi stood up just when the bartender served the shots which disappeared within seconds. Shammi shook the salt shaker on the sexy girl's waist, and squeezed a fizzy lime onto her curves. Armed with his pout, Shammi slowly licked the salt off her bare waist. The girl leaned forward and with fresh impetus fell in his arms. Shammi's lecherous gaze had begun the catalysis, synthesizing spontaneous ignition of their sexual shenanigans.

The girl took a shot glass and gently parked it in her roomy cleavage. "Don't you wanna nibble on it?" she whispered in his ears.

"No…" Shammi buried his face in her breasts. "I'll devour it."

The couple took to the dance floor with the rest of the gang. Dirty dancing, alcohol and more alcohol blended into the loud foot tapping hip-hop music of the club.

In the placidity of her suburban house, the sparrow of ink raced the white paper on Sona's diary.

"Today was a weird day. I have no idea what's wrong with me. Why do I get hit on by older men like Dr. Dhoort? May be this face pack will help." She stopped writing for a second to firm up her orange peel pack. "Okay, so I met this dude-type boy. He was cute. He was funny but how could he be so insensitive? Next time I meet him, I'll give him an electric shock myself; then his hair would be spikey permanently and he will get a taste of what those poor souls go through."

"Are you coming for the movie?" Sona's mother yelled from the living room.

"Is it Rom-Com?" Sona asked as she closed her diary.

Sona's mother walked into her room and smiled. "C'mon! It's just a movie. And I as a mother am giving you permission to watch this *khatarnak* action movie."

"Okay, I'll watch it...some other day." Sona had no interest and she went off to wash her starched face pack. "I'll go to Aarti's then. Maybe I'll have a sleepover. I have to study for mid-terms."

"Okay, as you wish." Sona's mother paused. "We will drop you."

"Thanks Mommy, and can you please put that DDLJ DVD in there please? We will watch it after studying."

"Come out of your Shah Rukh Khan world, my little baby!" Sona's mom walked into the bathroom and looked at her face in the mirror. But nothing could budge Sona out of her comfort land.

"You must be Roy," asked the office attendant Rosie, greeting Roy in the waiting area by the front desk.

"Yes ma'am," he politely replied. "I didn't quite catch your name."

"I am Rosie and I have been working here for the past thirty years," Rosie said with her everlasting smile. "Yup. Thirty long years. You were probably doing poo-poo in your little diapers when I first started and now when you expected a red hot smokin' blonde, all you got is me. Don't worry kiddo. I'll give you pictures of my younger days and you can pretend it's the young me." The non-stop blabbering was something Roy thought he must get used to.

Rosie stood up to walk Roy to his new private office. On the way, Roy learnt everything about Da Vinci Capital and its association to Rosie. As a bonus, Roy also got to know that Rosie was twice divorced, was an avid karaoke singer and recently had a colonoscopy done which she had weirdly enjoyed and that event had now brought a whole new dimension to her stagnating sex life.

"I know you are sad, but I gotta leave ya here," said Rosie in her Yankee Italian accent as she walked out of Roy's office. "All the meetings should be on your calendar. And Hilton said he'll find you when he gets a minute to breathe." Rosie walked away, closing the door behind her.

The glass window next to the door had Roy's name printed on it. Roy was amazed. It had been less than two days since he had accepted the offer and the office already had his name printed on the wall.

He leaned back on his retro style plush office chair. The chrome frame shone as the ribbed leather seats pressed with the rocking motion of the chair. He leaned forward and slowly walked towards the glass wall overlooking the New York/ New Jersey Waterway ferries steaming back and forth from Battery Park to Hoboken. To many, this view was truly therapeutic; something about watching water flow calmed the mind.

Roy shifted his attention to the bookshelf and flipped through the pages of the books placed there. He took a few books out – applied mathematics, quantitative trading, Japanese technical indicators, and Hedge fund trading – and dumped them on his table.

The term 'hedge fund' had become exotic around 2008. When all the big multi-national banks were either going bankrupt or running on the lifelines provided by federal reserves, a niche group of traders that generally worked in the shadows caught the attention of the entire nation. These savvy investors had a monster appetite for risk and the foresight to see the impact that technology would bring to traditional shout-in-the-pit trading. Ninety percent of the employees working at these hedge funds were alumni from Ivy League schools. And breaking in to the inner circle of this group meant pledging oneself to the secret societies of the worlds. For an outsider, it was more probable to be hit by a flash of lightening than to enter the inner ranks of these firms.

Despite no Ivy League degree or rich dad, Roy had earned his right to be a part of this privileged group by his record-breaking multi-million dollars profit earnings for the last few years, before he left everything and moved to New Delhi to be with Pia. *This is a leftover privilege from my legacy days. I must bring back my game or it will be bye bye Roy.*

Da Vinci Capital had earned its name on Wall Street as the Goldman Sachs of hedge funds. With its small army of just fifty traders under the leadership of founder CEO Hilton, the firm traded everything from stocks, to orange juice, to currency to oil. The firm shot to fame during the 2008 crisis when it made hundreds of millions of dollars betting that the market will plunge into a deep recession.

Roy had met Hilton at an investor's conference in late 2007. Hilton had later confessed in a printed magazine: "...I was looking at the market conditions, and figured that it would be bad. But there was this young man I met in 2007 who convinced me that shit was about to hit the fan. What was meant to be a five-minute conversation actually went on for four hours and when I got back to New York, I looked at my portfolio and cleaned house of positions that exhibited optimism. I gradually built my portfolio around the assumption that the entire world economy was about to face a collapse of epic proportions."

Hilton and Roy had been in touch all along, but it was only for the last couple of months that Hilton had been personally calling Roy, rallying him to join Da Vinci Capital to lead Equities.

There was a rumour in the market that Da Vinci Capital was getting ready to go public and Hilton was looking to get established market names to better position the firm for the public offering.

As the clock ticked 9.00 a.m., Roy's day started with a string of meetings. All meetings focused on a two-point agenda – to understand what the firm currently does, and to assemble his team of trusted experts and earn their confidence. *I am here to make money and your job is to enable it. If I make money, then we all make money.*

After meeting with several specialists, including quantitative analysis expert Dr. Zhao and expert programmer Mr. Srini Swami, Roy entered the conference room for his last in the series of endless meetings.

Roy looked at his watch as it ticked eight minutes past the scheduled time of 3.00 p.m. He tapped his pen on the folder and flipped through pages.

"Zhao may have some communication issues, but his mathematical concepts are solid," Roy looked at his notes.

He flipped a page and saw a smiley drawn next to a name – Srini Swami. Roy smiled. The chain of thoughts had already formed in his head. *Why it is that wherever you go, the technology geeks are Indians, the Math folks are Chinese, the attendants are always blondes (young or old), the security guy is always dark, the landscaping guy is always Hispanic and the guy with the most money is always white? Maybe I am being a racist, or maybe I am just being an analyst.*

Roy was curious to know who would emerge from the door as his deputy head. This was the last one-on-one meeting that he couldn't get on his calendar and had no idea who the person was. Roy started doodling on his notebook.

Seeing that it was already forty minutes past three, he stood up and straightened his jacket to walk out of the room. Just then, the door opened and a stunner walked in. The mundane conference room was suddenly electrified. In part by her energy, but largely by her attitude fitting her five-feet-five-inches high stature. Monica wasn't a typical conservative half-Indian girl. She was more Irish than Indian – in her looks, in her behaviour, and in her attitude.

"I am so sorry. You know, I was trading and it ain't 4.00 p.m. yet," her attitude swelled up with her words and actions as she sat down with her legs crossed under her knee-length grey pencil skirt. Roy was miffed at her attitude, but a part of him was also pleasantly surprised. While he had been expecting a typical Ivy League stereotype male, before him was a beautiful woman. His charitable heart had already forgiven her for the sarcasm.

Though he didn't like to profess it openly, but having made all his money without even a college degree, he had earned the right to despise the Ivy League types.

"Hi, I am Monica," Monica introduced herself.

Roy's gaze was fixed on her batting eyelashes playing hide and seek with her pretty eyes. Roy shook his head and introduced himself. "Hi, I go by Roy."

"Nice to meet you, Roy," Monica said flatly and then quickly dug her eyes back into her Smartphone.

"So," said Roy, trying to ward her off her phone.

"I am sorry." Monica looked up with a fake smile. She straightened her blonde streaked hair, revealing her radiant and smooth olive skin.

Roy smiled. "No worries."

Monica knew how to be a straight shooter, and how to play the game of offense. She was doing everything right, straight out of the MBA toolkit of psychological warfare in business management: it was important to be authoritative in your first act, and that is what she had done. Roy on the other hand wasn't ready to give up either. But, before he could have gone too far, the door of the conference room opened again.

"Aha, here you are young man," said Hilton. "Thank you for accepting our offer. I heard you've made us a hundred million richer already."

"Haa," said Roy.

"Oh well. Tomorrow then," said Hilton still in the momentum of his joke.

Roy knew that this man wouldn't give up easily. He had to come up with a smart answer so as to not ridicule Hilton and also credentialize him. "Fifty million," said Roy, "Monica just told me that she is the co-head, so in all fairness, I just have to get half of your money."

"Nice. Did you just have Monica sign up for another fifty mil? That's wonderful," said Hilton while looking at Monica. "So this would be on top of the forty-five million you made us last year, Monica."

"Always happy to help," said Monica looking at Hilton. "I am counting on Mr. Roy too. I hear you are a self-made millionaire." Monica raised the question.

"Actually, I was on a sabbatical for the last seven months, but prior to that I did okay," said Roy.

"So, you didn't really make any money?" said Monica.

"Oh, well... I'll leave you to it. Knock each other off, guys. But," said Hilton, "save some fun energy for after-hours, and Roy, I am sure you are anxious to help us make some money too." Hilton walked out saying, "Let's celebrate your inaugural money churning trade at our Quarterly event this Friday."

In simpler words, Roy had just been told – Make money fast. The clock is ticking.

It was imperative that he mobilized his resources and came up with the low hanging fruit, i.e. a quick profitable trade. He also knew that it was a race against time to make it happen before the end of his debut week.

Monica sat back on the chair and quipped, "So, what do you want to talk about now? Do you want me to tell you how I made forty million dollars in the last seven months while you were trying to be the monk who had no Ferrari?"

Roy was tactful but also aware that she was a tricky person. There could have been a multitude of reasons behind her hostility. *Perhaps she was raised in a family that looked down on women. But then, why would her parents send her to MBA School? Maybe she just had a bad break-up? Well I just had a bad break-up too. If anyone should be acting up, it should be me. I can't figure her out. Maybe she needs a little coaching, may be a hug or perhaps coaching and a hug.* "Are you gonna speak up?" said Monica.

"Uhh, absolutely. How about we talk over drinks?" said Roy.

"What?" Monica exclaimed. "Maybe you don't understand that when people don't react well to you, it a signal that they do not want to hang out with you..." concluded Monica with her forced smile, then she stood up and walked straight out of the conference room.

Srini slid his feet in the closing door and pushed it back open. "Care for a drink, Roy?"

A Mercedes S-class pulled into the sprawling compound of a sea-facing high-rise in the suburbs of Bandra. A truck carrying a trailer followed the car into the compound.

A man quickly stepped out of the front door of the Mercedes and rushed to open the passenger's door.

Thakursaab got off the car.

"Thank you, Makhmal," said Thakursaab, lowering his eyes to the short and frail Makhmal.

Makhmal's smile was overflowing with empathy.

Thakursaab straightened his jacket and pulled an envelope out of his upper pocket. His bulky arms puffed on the outline of the jacket, glorifying his six foot stature.

"Take the car down and take the cover off," Thakursaab instructed. His sparkling eyes were at ease; adding a fresh playful perspective to the otherwise 'don't-mess with-me' look, abetted by his thick jet black moustache and shining bald head.

The watchman came rushing to them. "Sir, this way please."

Thakursaab, Makhmal and the watchman entered the private outdoor glass elevator as it zoomed up to the penthouse floor, overlooking the calm sea and the affluent Bandra neighbourhood. A flurry of memories came rushing to Thakursaab's mind; the apartment had always held a special place in his heart.

It was the first apartment that he had bought after he first booked profit, clinching a deal that expanded his liquor business from producing one malt whiskey to its present-day catalogue of more than two dozen alcoholic beverages sold in eleven countries with a total turnover of more than five billion dollars.

"Sir, the painting was installed two months ago," Makhmal said nudging Thakursaab out of his nostalgia.

"Ah, Henri Matisse!" Thakursaab reminisced the nerve-wrecking auction where he had spent twelve million dollars for that painting. "That is a good painting."

"Sir, I don't know about that sir, but M F Hussein Saab's work on the ceiling is mind-blowing," the watchman said. "I have to shoo away people who just want to come and look at the apartment," he paused. "I tell them it's not a museum. It's private property." The watchman was delighted to have Thakursaab's audience and was doing everything he could to win some brownie points.

Thakursaab smiled. "Maybe I should charge them. It will earn back some of the money I have spent on it."

Makhmal and the watchman both chuckled.

His fingers ruffled through the envelope, his mind digressing to the exciting moment earlier in the day. Thakursaab had received an unexpectedly surprising package. The letter in the package had filled him with overwhelming joy. He had cancelled all his meetings and zipped straight to his son's apartment. He wanted to be the first one to share this news with his son.

Childhood memories of Shammi gushed through Thakursaab's head.

"What is this?" A young Thakursaab had asked a toddler Shammi.

"Maa-raa-ti," toddler Shammi had replied looking at a red Maserati.

"Do you want it?" young Thakursaab asked.

"Daaa," toddler Shammi had replied.

A smile appeared on Thakursaab's face as he looked at the

shiny Maserati Granturismo unwrapped out of the cover in the parking area below.

The special private elevator came to a smooth stop. The door opened directly into the living room of the apartment. Thakursaab almost stumbled on a bunch of empty beer bottles that rolled on the floor.

Makhmal held his boss. "Sorry sir, I wasn't quite prepared for this...special flooring that Shammi saab has put in here," Makhmal said sarcastically.

Thakursaab stood up. His heart sank as he saw the multi-million-dollar apartment in ruins due to his own child. "I can't look at this."

Makhmal interrupted, "Don't worry sir. I'll guide you. Thirty-eight degrees to the left and then take one-and-a-half steps," said Makhmal.

Thakursaab took a deep breath, altered his course and stepped right on the spot.

"Very good, sir," complimented Makhmal. Thakursaab had his legs stretched but stayed put in that position. Makhmal took his calculator and calculated the angle for his next move. "This is a tough matrix, sir," said Makhmal, his voice dripping with sarcasm.

"I am glad I sent you to school," replied Thakursaab, causing Makhmal's face to break into a smile. His loyalty and ease in front of Thakursaab was perhaps because he had been taken in by Thakursaab at a very early age.

"Okay, now, obtuse angle, hundred degrees to the right," navigated Makhmal.

The new position had Thakursaab stand in a near-split position, and it was then that a disturbing force daggered through him as the sight of the modified Henri Matisse painting caught his attention. The calm face wasn't calm anymore. A few long hops later, a fuming Thakursaab stood next to the plush bed in the master bedroom, carefully balancing his legs on the rare spots of bare floor in the trash all around. Thakursaab was strangely quiet, his lips puckered with anger, heavy breaths caught in the thickness of his moustache.

Wrapped in a silky Siberian goose comforter, Shammi slept with a satisfied smile on his face.

Makhmal's voice – "Shammi baba…" started echoing louder in Shammi's head.

"Bumpy…Quit it already man. I am not going to meet Anuja. You go," mumbled Shammi in his sleep.

Makhmal looked at Thakursaab rolling his eyes in anger. "Not Anuja, Shammi baba…its Saab, your *Daddy*," Makhmal purposefully stressed on the word Daddy.

The smile on Shammi's face vanished as he lazily opened his left eye, catching a glimpse of his father.

"Oh hello, Dad…Wow…" Shammi sprung out of the comforter. "What a surprise!"

"What happened baby?" A sleepy girly voice echoed, as the plush comforter rose conically from the centre and fell on the other side of the bed. A semi-nude beautiful girl in a tomato red bra and thong emerged from the bed. Just the bra on her upper body didn't hide the big hickey. "See what you did…bad boy…" she said as she playfully caressed the hickey.

Shammi and Thakursaab locked eyes as Makhmal put on an evil smile.

"Ahh…she is…" Shammi stammered.

"I know…" claimed Thakursaab. "Anuja beta, it's time for you to go to your papa and mumma," he said very calmly.

"Who is Anuja? And, who are you again?" asked the girl sleepily.

Shammi had no clue how to handle this situation. "This is my dad," he softly interrupted the girl.

The girl looked around, clueless and still hung-over from the wild party last night. "Hello uncle," grinned the girl.

She quickly hopped out of the bed and reached for Thakursaab's feet. Thakursaab was a bit startled by the sudden jump. The sanctity of his split position stumbled even as Makhmal rushed to provide support to his master. After a quick balancing act, Thakursaab cautiously leaned forward again as the girl touched his feet and her booty popped out in front of Shammi's face.

Shammi and Thakursaab locked eyes again, waiting for this uncomfortable situation to get over with and for the real battle to begin. Makhmal, watching like an amused spectator muttered – "Very social. Baby is very social!"

Roy and Srini walked out of the elevators and then down the escalators followed by a dungeon-like path that hid the construction at World Financial Center. Rolling out of the mechanized turnstile, they walked a few yards and sat on the outdoor patio of P.J. Clarke's. The trees on the sidewalk provided just enough shade for someone to not get burned by the sun and still be able to enjoy the nice warm weather, a rarity that lasts just for around three months in the city of New York.

P.J. Clarke's was right on the water of Hudson, and was thronged by a good mix of professional and trendy crowd.

Srini wiped the frothy Blue Moon off his moustache. "You know when I was in IIT…"

"I didn't know that you were from IIT," said Roy.

Srini chuckled. He was excellent at anything to do with technology. He had mastered the art of developing trading systems that not only interpreted data from the internet but could also hack into the Twitter and SMS traffic to determine market direction. "You know, I have been working as a programmer for eight years," he said, "and I am just waiting for one thing. Guess what?"

Roy moved his head sideways and shrugged his shoulders.

"Green Card," declared Srini. "The day I get my green card, I'll start my own firm that would be called 'Intelligence of everything'. It would perform intelligent analyses for anything that a man desires – locating restaurants, finding deals and bargains, determining the best transport route, finding best stocks and also finding...the best...girls..."

The core of the idea was very personal to him. It stemmed from his multiple failed attempts to get a girlfriend for as far back as he could remember. Mostly filled with extraordinary self-confidence, Srini perhaps wasn't aware of a few things lacking: his language, for example, was still tied to the phonetics of Aminabad. Any up-close conversation and one would come out bathed in his frothy spit, and of course that natural body odour. Nothing mattered for him, because in his mind, his degree in Engineering from IIT and that rich dense moustache was all he needed to get girls weak in their knees. But despite all that, why every girl kept rejecting him was a mystery he hadn't cracked yet. "I will model the dating part of my project around Dabble," said Srini.

"What is Dabble?" asked Roy.

"Oh, it's a proximity based site that Da Vinci invested in and where I worked before. Its major selling point is that you can choose to be anonymous."

"Oh, so it's Ashley Madison."

"No, no, no, no, no. It's not a hook-up site like that. No pros. Only frustos," said Srini, letting out his donkey laugh. A second later, he got a bit serious. "So, you go to Ashley Madison, huh?" he said, shaking his smiling head like a pendulum. "How is it? I have only seen ads on porn sites. I'm not a courageous hero like you."

Roy was confused by how deep into his simple statement Srini had looked. *Why is it that everyone I come across is weird? Is it a case of like minds attracting each other, or the case of opposite minds attracting each other?*

Roy quickly switched gears to talk about work, but was abruptly interrupted by Srini.

"I am a full package, but one skill that is lacking and I want to learn is how to dress to impress," said Srini.

Roy was more than happy to share his wisdom, and began with, "Make sure no hair peep out of your nostrils! The nose is meant for breathing, not farming."

Srini took his little notebook out and started taking notes. While speaking out loud, he drew a header on the page with the date and the topic 'How to dress to get laid'.

"This is so ironic. You actually *undress* to get laid," Srini said thoughtfully.

"That's some deep shit," said Roy and they both grinned.

As their laughter melted away, Roy deftly manoeuvred the conversation towards work. He told Srini how the timelines have jumped a bit and that he needed a strategy to be implemented that would result in booked profits by the end of the week.

Roy and Srini bounced a few ideas for what could help him put stake on the ground.

"I have developed a program that can connect different apps in a device," Srini paused, "Remotely."

"Wow!" Roy was amazed at how smart Srini was.

Though Srini was a programmer at heart, he had a very analytical mind and knew all the tough questions to ask. You are only as good as the people around you, reminisced Roy. *I remember when my father said that, I was too naive to understand the real meaning of the sentence.* Later in the conversation, as soon as Srini mentioned an image comprehension algorithm that he had built, Roy was alert. He knew this was something he could use. While Srini was talking in some techno-jargon-heavy meta-phrase alien language, Roy's mind was sprinting to use that technology in his own endeavour.

"You know how they predict earnings for retail stores like Walmart?" asked Roy.

"Yes, maybe... Doesn't it depend on sales projection and historical sales numbers?" Srini hesitantly replied.

"You are right, it does. But as traders, we try to beat the market by staying one step ahead. Think of this like beating the rush hour, for which you need to know what the rush hour timeslots are so that you can plan your trip around it. And in order to know the timeslots, we need to know the data that we can analyze to make a correct determination.

"In our case, for Walmart, we will use car traffic in the parking lot and gasoline consumption by carrier trucks to ascertain whether they will actually make the predicted numbers or not," said Roy.

Srini was listening very attentively. "And that is why you need my algorithm to correctly calculate the cars in those pictures." Srini was ecstatic to find a real use for his algorithm.

"What are we waiting for then? Let's start right now!" said Srini enthusiastically.

Srini and Roy went back to Roy's office and started plotting different tasks that needed to be done in order for them to make this happen. Roy quickly searched the company he could purchase the feeds from. Srini would use his algorithm to determine the number of cars, Roy would build the equation to determine earnings based on car data and gasoline consumption, and Zhao would translate all this into a mathematical tool and run it against historical data. The steps were clear and now it was time to set the ball rolling.

Srini got on to his computer right away and started working on sample images that Roy had shared with him, while Zhao hit the computer to come up with the prediction equation.

Roy, Srini and Zhao practically locked themselves in the room. Roy had given clear instructions to Rosie that no one other than the trio was allowed to go into his office.

After three days and four nights with less than four hours of sleep, they were finally ready with the first draft of the tool. Roy's immaculate and pristine office was not so pristine anymore. The glass walls had mathematical patterns full of Greek symbols and the beige couch had lost the battle of colours to a blend of dirty brown. Empty pizza boxes had taken over the floor and garbage bags were piled up with cans of red bull and empty coffee cups.

The giant metallic entrance gate opened and Shammi's BMW 3 Series drove in onto the English paved circular driveway cemented around a Japanese garden with bonsai maple trees, a Koi pond, and a bubbling fountain.

He parked his car behind the sparkling new Maserati and looked at it with desperation and disappointment. *Wow!* He looked away from the car as he plodded on the huge brick paver steps leading straight to the French door main entrance.

The lavish grandeur of the bungalow, comparable to any luxury five star hotel was aesthetically pleasing and magnificent. Shammi walked over the designer wood bridge over the shallow fish pond by the plush seating area in the living room. As the large beautiful Koi fishes swam around, Shammi walked to the centre place and nervously greeted his father.

Thakursaab sat on a black sofa, staring at Shammi.

Mataji walked past them with the support of a walking stick. Makhmal, like a careful shadow, walked right behind Mataji, slipping Shammi a sinister and sarcastic smile. A few short steps later, Mataji sat on a grand old style rocker chair with her feet comfortably placed on the matching ottoman.

"Is that new Maserati ours?" Shammi tried to break the ice.

"No," Thakursaab said flatly.

"I had no idea that the painting was so expensive." Shammi's tone was soft, apologetic.

Thakursaab sighed. "Now that you will go to Wharton, you need to learn to be the gentleman the world expects you to be," he had completely ignored Shammi's apology.

Shammi raised his head in surprise. "Wharton...Can I?" he reached out to the letter that lay on the centre table.

Thakursaab nodded.

Shammi glanced through the admission letter. "I want to study here, close to home," Shammi spoke softly but clearly.

Thakursaab could sense a familiar stubbornness in his son, a quality he knew himself to possess. Even his unflinching gaze was failing to have Shammi break his silence of disagreement.

"Then you would have to stay in the hostel," Thakursaab said.

Tempers rose, as neither backed off from their respective stances. Shammi for the most part was trying to quietly listen to what his father had to say. He had learned long ago that it was best to let his father vent his anger first, and then try to reason with him later.

Shammi looked away, trying to focus on something else, just trying to zone out of the wrath that was raining down on him. His wandering eyes stumbled on Mataji. The table next to her rocking chair was now filled with several shooter bottles of alcohol. Mataji was merrily chugging and clanking through the samples. She would drink a sample, rub lime through her mouth and then move on to the next one. Shammi had never seen this pace before.

Mataji looked pretty stressed out. "None of this is good," she clucked in disappointment as she signalled Makhmal to get something else.

"Are you even listening to me?" Thakursaab raised his voice.

Shammi shook his eyes away from Mataji and looked at Thakursaab.

"Your grandmother and I have done a lot to bring success to this business and we did this through discipline," Thakursaab smilingly pointed towards a flushed Mataji.

Mataji looked at Thakursaab with her bloodshot drunk eyes and gave a sneaky secret smile, not meant for many.

Makhmal's voice in the background was faint and barely audible. "This is 97 proof alcohol Mataji," said Makhmal while opening the sample of a carbonated gold bottle.

Mataji exhibited an excitement that was a first for today. She pulled the bottle out of Makhmal's hands and drank it all.

"If not me, at least think about your grandmother; she is old and she needs you. These reckless habits of your will take her life one day," said Thakursaab pointing his finger to Mataji as she was finishing up the intense sample of 97% proof alcohol.

Thakursaab and Shammi both looked at Mataji. A wide smile was beginning to emerge through her wrinkles. Thakursaab waited with bated breath, looking at Mataji.

Mataji's shivering hands slowly moved up her head, one palm on top of another and she bent her fingers to form an umbrella. Making a sound like there was running water. Mataji started laughing with a peculiarly goat-like sound.

"This sample is final. Mataji liked it!" said Thakursaab joyously. He looked at Makhmal and Shammi. "She even did the Nagin dance," an emotional Thakursaab said out loud.

The Nagin dance had long been a tradition at Indian weddings, where overzealous relatives get drunk and lose all the inhibitions they have harboured for all their lives.

Thakursaab was really excited that Mataji was doing the exact same step.

"I saw that too," said Shammi.

Thakursaab controlled his emotions and quickly got back to his mean angry tone. "Nothing will change. You have decided to not go to Wharton and I have decided that you will go to the hostel." declared Thakursaab. "And that is *final*."

Shammi stooped his shoulders, turned and started walking away.

"And listen, Makhmal will give you your new car keys."

$\mathcal{J}$t was past 3.00 p.m. already. Roy rushed out of his office onto his trading desk. *Shit I only have an hour to place the bet.* He threw over multiple sheets of research papers, furiously scribbled away numbers, scratching off the ones that didn't make sense. Coming up with new permutations and combinations, finally he circled on one number – eighty-one cents. His eyes perked up.

Inhaling deeply, Roy quickly swirled his chair to his desk, batting his eyes through half a dozen screens hung on the wall of his desk.

He typed 'Walmart' on one of the screens and scrolled down the page, carefully scanning every bit of information.

Roy's eyes rested on a section of the screen – "Ensemble Earnings prediction." The number was eighty-five cents. He expanded the section that displayed individual analyst predictions.

Some methods employed in predicting Wall Street data have nothing extraordinary about them. Like in this instance, the ensemble mean was a simple average of all the individual analysts' predictions.

"There it is," Roy muttered as he moved his fingers on to an outlier line in the graph – the legend of the line had eighty-one cents inscribed above it.

This means the entire trading fraternity expects Walmart to perform better, except for me and this one guy. This is good news, Roy!!

He quickly check-marked all his findings one last time and reached out to the black turret phone box and pressed button – "broadcast to all".

Roy's order triggered a frenzy of sorts as brokers on the other end of the call scrambled to get the best match of bid and offer prices, the voice of brokers filling the order blasted through the turret box. Within a few frantic minutes, his entire order was filled.

Roy had bought a put spread option of seventy-five/seventy-two at the market trade price of seventy-five dollars for the stock, at an average price of fifty cents. In common investors' term, Roy had made a directional bet that the stock price would crash after the earnings. The trade meant that Roy stood to make a maximum profit of twenty-five million dollars if the price of the stock crashed to seventy-two dollars or below; however, he also stood to lose a staggering five million dollars if the stock went up instead of going down.

The closing bell rang, marking the end of the day's trading session, and the stage was set for a nerve-wrecking trading session for the next day.

Work to Roy wasn't about money; it was the safe haven, his solace out of the dark tunnels of his mind.

Roy lay still on the bed with his eyes wide open. He had learned to live with insomnia. *What's wrong with me? I guess the better question is: what's right with me?*

At the crack of dawn, Roy got into his workout clothes and stepped outside for a run. The cool wind caressing his face as he ran around the Central Park listening to Linkin' Park was the moment Roy savoured the most; most of all, today.

The earnings announcement was streaming live on CNBC. Traders' eyes were glued to the TV and their fingers to the trading systems.

It's make or break, Roy thought as he attentively concentrated on the TV.

"The firm has managed to earn eighty-five cents per common share," the CFO of Walmart announced on TV.

Roy could see his whole world collapsing in front of him. His prediction had been proven wrong, and with every tick, he was fast losing money. His options were already two million dollars in losses and rapidly pacing towards his loss limit of five million dollars.

Think Roy, think. You can't just lose it. This could not be the end; you are a smart guy. What would you have done if you had come across this problem a few months back?

Roy closed his eyes, took a deep breath, stifling through hundreds of thoughts and ideas, as he frantically swirled around on his office chair. Sympathetic eyes from the trading floor followed his bizarre behaviour.

"The poor guy has lost it," a distant murmur was audible.

Roy opened his eyes, opened his turret box and announced his intention to sell all of his put options.

"Sold for twenty cents," shouted the broker on the phone.

Alright. Now I need to make back my three million dollars.

"Sell one hundred thousand same day call option spread of eighty / eighty-three…" Roy announced again, but before he could complete his sentence, Monica interrupted, "Hold off on the order, Steven."

She turned the turret off. "We need to talk. *Now*," she said and stormed off into the conference room.

"Are you fuckin' insane! Selling options?" Monica blasted off.

The watchers of the floor were in motion. The call was quickly made and within seconds Hilton was seen rushing to the conference room.

"What the hell is going on?"

"He is trying to pull a Nick Leeson, Hilton. He's gonna make you into a Baring Bank Part two," Monica said sarcastically.

"Alright. Hold on!" Hilton said, "Roy, what do you think?"

"I think it's limited risk. We are wasting time here. I could have made some money by now," Roy replied hastily.

"Alright, let's go to middle ground," Hilton interrupted. "Take half the risk, okay?

"And you…." Hilton pointed to Monica. "Can you stay back for a min?"

Roy nodded and dashed back to his desk while Monica sat in the conference room, sulking.

Flaring tempers, bruised egos and a roller coaster stock market – the nail-biting trading session finally came to a screeching halt as the closing bell rang and the clock ticked past 4.00 p.m. The Walmart stock closed at seventy-eight dollars and Roy's book resulted in a net loss of one million dollars. He had bridged the gap by two million dollars.

Roy was pissed. *Only if the bitch hadn't interrupted, I would have been in black.*

Reeling from his failure, Roy felt dejected to even go to see Hilton. However, it was imperative more so than ever for him to be there. *The market fucked me, even though with a bit of lubricant. What is going to happen at the party will be rape, if the analogy were to be extended. Just the sound of that sentence makes me feel violated.*

Shammi's eyes came to a grinding halt when Sona walked into the coffee shop at the Ricochet University campus, and locked on to his prey. Shammi's eyes lit up. *I think I have seen her somewhere.*

He quickly rose, and under the pretence of getting more coffee, swiftly took the place right behind her in the line.

Where have I seen you? Where have I seen you? Shammi was trying to connect the dots without realizing that his eyes now darted at Sona's boobs.

Sona looked at him and slightly jerked her head back. Shammi gave his wonder smile, which Sona looked straight through.

Shammi was confused and thought probably the smile wasn't fully formed yet. He tried to give that deliberate manual stretch, but it didn't really do anything to get it going with Sona.

"I have seen you somewhere," he said as he cancelled his wonder smile.

"I know you hear it all the time, but seriously, I think we have definitely met before," continued Shammi with no regard to the fact that Sona was trying to say something.

"Sorry....What were you saying?" asked Shammi.

"I don't know how guys like you are raised?!" Sona said in a miffed tone.

"Like a prince," replied Shammi

"Is that a joke?" Sona shot back sarcastically.

"No, seriously, I was raised like a prince. You know like the prince in that movie *Coming to America*? I did have a rule though. I cleaned my dick myself," said Shammi.

"You would do that, being a dick yourself."

Shammi was happy. *Finally, sweet success…She is talking… Even though it's a bit insulting, I think. Let's fix this. Why does she have to be this mean anyway? She looks like a placid, harmless, love-friendly creature.*

What could I have done to piss her off? Did I date her? Let's go back. Last week – that hickey girl. Last month – nope, that was the crazy lady. A month before that – that was the girl with daddy issues. The last ten months before that was the pair of cousins, one after the other. Last year – Ah, I can't remember that. Oh wait, that was the aunty whose husband was off to ship. Oh well, that reminds me that she should call back next month. Married ladies are nice; I learned a lot from her. Anyway, hmm, who is she then and why is she pissed?

Before the navy aunty was? Can't remember, can't place her or anyone that far out. Let's play it safe.

"I didn't mean to do that," said Shammi adding ambiguity to the thread.

"Everyone says that after it's done," said Sona.

"It is when people realize, you know," Shammi kept the momentum going, "realization can actually happen anytime." *What the fuck did I do? Did I kill your cat or what?*

"How can you be so insensitive? I'll give you an electric shock and then you will see," Sona's sudden burst of anger sounded more like humming than shouting.

"You don't really want me to answer that, right?" Shammi continued hesitantly after a brief pause. "I can answer it. I just wasn't sure how to be mean to myself."

"Huh, so you are one of those one liner guys…" Sona got frustrated and just gave up on the conversation, hurriedly marching away from Shammi.

That night Sona turned sides on her bed for a while before she gave up, turned the lights on and took her diary out. "Today was a surprise. I kinda breached the picture wall my life is. It was exciting! And that poor soul got thrashed. I feel bad now. I know he deserved some of it, but maybe not all of it. He was so clueless; and even in that he was funny. He'll recover. I hope he does. I'll tell you when we cross paths again."

Roy, Srini and Zhao stood by the window at a fancy restaurant, overlooking the well-lit Brooklyn Bridge, animatedly conducting the diagnostic of the disastrous trade. The place got crowded rather quickly. Roy made sure that all the important people, or at least the people he thought were important, had noticed his presence before he slipped out into his own company.

Heartbreaks make one feel the strangest of things. For Roy, it was the beckoning of his closet filled with skeletons of the past, pouncing out, ripping through the hatch of penance.

"I heard you fucked it up today," Hilton emerged from the back, throwing his arm around Roy's shoulder.

The dreadful moment that Roy had not been waiting for had arrived. He looked up at Hilton's calculating blue eyes plugged into a big fat crack-less face. He went on with his charade of lecture laced with sarcasm. His words fell on deaf ears as Roy had zoned out and his mind was trying to solve the mystery of the wrinkle-less face. *Wow, he is 65 years old, give or take, and look at his face! There are no wrinkles whatsoever. I have no idea why people are starving to keep themselves young whereas the secret mantra for ageless looks is plain and simple – Stay fat because fat doesn't crack.*

"So, are you gonna go for it?" Hilton's words barely managed to slip in Roy's reverie.

Roy looked up at Hilton. His lips were pursed. *Ok. Now, I have to come up with a statement that wouldn't make me look like an ass who wasn't paying any attention to his boss. But what else could this crackless face talk about other than money?* "Well, how much?" said Roy with a smiling face, trying to dig out the context of the conversation.

"Ahh, I tell ya. Enough is never enough, and anything less than enough...the street is not the kindest place on this planet. But I also tell ya, treating this opportunity like break-up sex is the kinda motivation you need, son. There is no fury like that of a scarred man who had been fucked over by his girl," Hilton said passionately.

Roy was surprised. *How in the gut of hell does he know? Does everyone in the world know about Pia?*

"I have lived a long life. It was my third wife," said a nostalgic Hilton. "Anyway...Make money. Get Laid. And think of making money like it's sex. You want them big and it's gotta keep coming."

Humming his patchy laugh, Hilton moved on to the other guests, while Roy stood there thinking. *He is right. Why the hell am I so hung up? I should move on.*

Roy finished his glass of wine and sat by the bar. He looked around. Bored, he dug into his pocket for his phone and started scrolling through several pages of apps available for download. The bright blue icon of Dabble flared amongst the dull icons.

Whatever...Let's try what Srini is trying.

As the painfully slow app surfaced on his new company-issued Smartphone, a little footer navigation bar of the app lit up with an ellipsis. Roy quickly snapped his fingertips on to the ellipsis.

'Isn't this crazy?' He had a message from the screen name 'whatz-wrong-with-a-shy-girl'.

Hmm, pretty inviting or perhaps just a result of boredom. Roy typed, 'hmm' in response.

A few minutes had passed by and still there was no reply. *Curiosity. Now I get it!*

'Still there?' quickly typed Roy.

The screen was static, bereft of any response from "whatz-wrong-with-a-shy-girl".

Roy was anxious. He looked at the screen name and typed again, 'No BJ?'

Roy's owlish stare at the app refused to give up.

"Hello Mr. Ashley Madison!" Srini double tapped on Roy's shoulder. Roy hastily tried to hide his phone away but before Srini could get into any detail, Zhao pulled Srini in pursuit of a hot girl. Finding that this was the most opportune time, Roy quickly slipped out of the bar, boarded a yellow cab and hurtled through the dreary lanes of the sin city.

While still in the cab, a quick note popped up on his phone.

'What does that mean? Loser!'

Roy smiled victoriously. In speed dating, it's very important to evoke some kind of feeling in a girl. It doesn't really matter what it is, as long as you can quickly make that into a bangable situation.

Roy didn't really desire a bangable situation. *On second thoughts, I wouldn't mind.*

'Oh nothing…I wanted to say, no booze and jiggle. That is what's wrong with ur screen name, you need to have a drunk screen name,' typed Roy, smilingly wickedly.

'Like what?' replied the girl.

'Let's see…how about "booty-call-activated",' quickly typed Roy.

'Lol. don't' think so. that would be solicitation,' replied the girl.

'True…how about "save-me-tonight",' typed Roy.

'Save from what?' typed the girl.

'Save from this *sookha* in my life…come like a fresh raindrop…' typed Roy.

'You sound like a retard writing subtitles of semiporn,' her response interrupted Roy.

'I like, not the retard…wait, may be that too, but really, it's the semiporn thing,' typed Roy.

'You are insane….crazyyyyyy,' replied the girl.

'I want to kiss you.' His aggressive remark surprised him too.

'Whattttttttt?' replied the girl.

His phone screen lit up. 'You don't even know me,' continued the girl.

'Then it doesn't matter. As it is, this is all virtual so it's not like we are really kissing,' typed Roy excitedly. The anonymity of the internet was beginning to infuse confidence.

'Wait...you are moving closer to me,' the girl said.

'I like that baby,' replied Roy.

'I don't mean that silly. I mean you are actually closer to where I am,' said the girl.

'Ah, you mean this app!" exclaimed Roy.

'Yup,' the girl shot back.

'I didn't realize that, but I was really heading home,' typed Roy.

'Where do you live?' asked the girl.

'Park Avenue,' Roy punched in.

'Oh well, good night dear. nice chatting,' proclaimed the girl.

'What! You are leaving? If u want I can go back to where I was, if you think I am this uncontrollable horny dog,' asked Roy.

'No horny dog. We'll chat, but right now I gotta bolt. Bye the-guy,' typed the girl.

"Good night," typed the girl and the green dot next to the screen name went dark.

Roy reached home, threw his phone on the bed, pulled his shoes off and neatly kept them beside his bed. He looked at the phone again, but the screen name was still dark and offline.

He put his blinders over his eyes, and carefully turned the light off. In the middle of the night, Roy suddenly vaulted off the blanket; he could hear every beat of his thrumming heart. He hastily took his blinders out, looked around and sighed. *It was just a dream.* He turned to the table, drank the glass of water and lay back in bed, this time his eyes wide open.

$\mathcal{A}$ cab took a slight left turn from the main road and came to a grinding halt in front of the main entrance of the hostel. The cab door opened and Makhmal's head snuck out. "Hello Baba. Your stuff is here. Shall we?"

Shammi uninterestedly looked at Makhmal, and then towards the paint-less shabby building. He sighed as he walked up to the hostel, then he turned his eyes and looked at his Engineering college building a few steps away. "Perfect. No commute now," Shammi spoke out loud, baiting Makhmal to exhibit his sarcasm again.

Bumpy jumped out of the hostel lobby. "Welcome brother! Now you are under my roof."

A few boys walked out of the hostel muttering in some different language.

"Why are they talking in monkey language?" Shammi spoke loudly.

The boys stopped and gave Shammi a cold blank stare. Bumpy whisked Shammi away to the side. "Don't mess with them. They are cocky idiots," he whispered in Shammi's ears.

Shammi turned towards the boys again, threw open his arms and hissed with a smirk, "I am scared." The unsettling silence was broken when the watchman announced, "Your room number is four-one-four. You're lucky you aren't on the sixth floor."

"Why?" asked Shammi.

The watchman gave a toothy smile. "Rector is there. Go, if you want."

The rustic metal grill shuttered down and the old elevator ascended to the fourth floor of the hostel.

Makhmal strolled the two large suitcases and dumped them in the cagy hostel room. The pieces of furniture were toppled all over one another – two sets of beds, study tables and cabinets.

"Not bad." Makhmal was conniving.

Shammi just shook his head in dismay thrashing all of Makhmal's plans to provoke him. Makhmal had hoped for Shammi to be disturbed by the gritty reality of a common man's life.

"This is good!" Shammi said with a smile. *This will be a nice new adventure, something new, something challenging. You can't break rules if they aren't there.* Shammi opened the windows and slowly stuck his face out. The soothing breeze was cooling him off as he looked around the spectacular campus. It was bathed in rain, sparkling in spots under the dull yellow lights.

The giant clock in the lobby ticked past 10.00 p.m.; the watchman, fighting off the rain, quickly pulled on the metallic shutters and locked the giant hostel gate.

Slowly, room by room, as the lights started going off, the creeping underbelly of the hostel germinated to life.

Where the fuck am I? Shammi thought as he stood in front of a bunch of students a little while later.

Grumbling soft chatter in the room was hardly audible. Shammi looked to his side. Bumpy stood next to him along with four other guys. *Who the fuck are they?*

One of them said, "We already got ragged, this is not fair."

"Fair is only your mommy, son," said a short senior guy evoking a thrust of laughter.

Shammi stood there; his mind was working sluggishly. *What did I do? What did I do? Oh yeah!* Last Shammi remembered was downing alcohol he had smuggled in empty laundry detergent containers. *I probably must have just dozed off, but why the fuck am I in this stupid standup, and why is this peanut dick sitting*

*there like he just realized that his dick is really small and blames
me for it. Could that be true? Maybe, I should just ask him.*

"I am not responsible for your peanut dick," Shammi said out
loud accidently.

The chatter in the room was quickly replaced with an eerie
silence. Everyone's gaze was beamed at Shammi. The short guy
stood up on the bed and walked closer. "What did you say, pretty
boy?"

"He is the guy who made that smart-ass comment earlier in
the day too," a thin male voice echoed from the group.

Shammi tousled his hair, "I said I am not responsible for
your peanut-sized dick. I take it, that's the reason you are angry,"
continued Shammi.

The short guy stopped at the edge of the bed and with a shallow
jump landed right in Shammi's face. Shammi tilted his head down
and gazed right through the short guy's eyes. A smile dangled,
raising the corner of Shammi's lips but then with a sneaky skid, a
hard slap slammed his face.

Shammi stood still, his head hadn't moved a bit. The crimson
cloud had crossed through the smile on his face, his fists were
clinched and his tenacious gaze beamed through his owly stare.

"Lower your fucking eyes," said the short guy.

Shammi didn't blink. The short guy pushed Shammi, pulling
his hair and angrily said, "Who are you fucking staring at, don't
you know who I am?!"

"I don't know who you are, but," Shammi pursed his lips and
mercilessly head-butted the short guy off the floor. "I know who
your daddy is," he said as the short guy flew past the bed and
banged against the wall.

"It's like your mommy fucked a rabbit, to spit you out of her
pussy," Shammi exploded angrily.

The other seniors in the room had quickly mobilized, pouncing
on Shammi and pinning him to the ground.

"I'll give one last warning to all you dumbfucks. Leave me right now; otherwise I'll fuck each one of you. I'll start with disfiguring your face and then will fuckin' peel your dick off your fucking balls," said Shammi.

The fury of the mad mob was way past simmering as they split open Shammi's arms and pinned his face and his arms. "Alright, don't tell me I didn't warn you," muttering those words through his half-shut mouth, Shammi swivelled on his back with a brutal push from his legs as he sprung out pushing all the seniors flying in all directions, like a crazy blood spatter.

Shammi quickly calibrated his eyes and ran by the wall, putting himself in an advantageous spot to deal with an army on the other side. One by one, Shammi kicked and punched his way out of more than half a dozen senior students.

"You didn't know daddy was a black belt, did you?" Shammi said as he rained a flood of punches and blows on them.

The battlefield of the Samurai came to a standstill as Rector Pasha barged into the room. He was shocked to see what was transpiring in the room.

"Kapil," Pasha screamed at the short guy.

Kapil limped forward in light. His face was all swollen up. Pasha turned around and looked at Shammi.

"So you are a gangster now?" said Pasha.

Shammi was confused. "But sir, I was..." said Shammi when Pasha interrupted him.

"They hit us, sir," Bumpy tried to speak up softly, only to roll his tongue back up as Pasha tilted his head and threw a laser sharp stare at Bumpy.

Pasha turned back to Shammi, walked closer and smelled his breath. "I knew it."

Now I have a new routine for you and it will start at 5.00 a.m.," said Rector Pasha.

Bumpy tried to interrupt with one of his incoherent thoughts, "But, it is raining outside."

"You too," Pasha told Bumpy.

Shammi looked at his watch; it was 2.00 a.m. already.

Rector Pasha authoritatively nodded his head, and scowled around the room. Everyone was frozen in whatever position they were in, like a paused movie. He shook his head in dismay and furiously walked away.

Shammi looked around the room and saw boys writhing in pain.

"Sorry man. No hard feelings," Shammi flung open the door and plodded out to the hallway.

Traders were yelling across the turret boxes. The wall of monitors on trading desks was like an electronic separator, blinking in red, black and green.

Roy had always been a careful trader; he knew the basic fundamentals of trading – supply and demand. When you predict fluctuation in either of them before anyone else does, you make money; at times, lots and lots of money.

In the last few days since the trading disaster, Srini and Zhao had improvised the trading tool. They had also given it a code name "The Black Sheep" – a fitting name because the first trade out of the system had led to a disaster.

Geeks often come across as shy, awkward, ill-shaped guys with or without weird facial hair and smelly socks. But one thing that all geeks have in common is that they know how to whip their own asses. Perhaps it's the habit of being the butt of jokes all their adolescent lives that causes the abused to become the abuser when they step into adulthood. But Geeks are the intelligent flock, so instead of abusing real people, they abuse their own creation – their code.

The days of relentless work were cheating the wheels of time, for time flew like it was on steroids. It was past 7.00 p.m. Roy stood up and threw his long muscular arms up above his head, bent his back backwards, stretching virtually every muscle from head to toe. He lazily walked around his swanky office, to the building elevators and descended into the bustling streets of New York Downtown.

Even at this hour, the streets were crowded and fast moving like a giant thrust of water pushed out to the shore. Roy stepped in the street and quickly blended into the financial capital familial, getting ready to de-stress by hitting the neighbourhood bars.

A few blocks down, Roy turned on Pearl Street. The street was relatively empty with only a few pedestrians. Perhaps it was the time of the day when everyone was already getting drunk at the bars. Roy walked a few yards down the street and then jumped over a small stone edged landscaping area to land on to the patio like setting at the Ulysses. True to the unique personality of Manhattan, this patio was really a street, blocked and barricaded for merry times, as the bulls of the Wall Street retreated out of their stress-filled offices. Sitting at Ulysses, you could feel the city – the brick-paved streets, transformed with patio dining sets with umbrellas, park-like benches, and elegant but cosy bistro-sets filling the entire street.

Flowery summer dresses skirted along the path on stand up stools while suited men took pride in drinking those fruity, rich-coloured blue moons.

Roy sat on an empty bistro table. A buzzer sound vibrated inside Roy's jacket. He took his phone out. "Hmm. Strange. No new E-mail," Roy swiped through the app list and there was a message on Dabble.

'Your recent connection "whatz-wrong-with-a-shy-girl" is at the bar you are in!'

Alright, funny man, don't cower down. Remember, the things that disinterest us are the litmus test for us to move forward.

Roy's big almond eyes quickly started scouting every woman at the bar. The crowd wasn't too bad. Almost all the seats at the patio were occupied. Roy was still searching, with all the prudence to not come across as a sleazy sex-deprived man. His eyes stopped on a partial view of a girl sitting indoors by the bar.

Roy stood up and casually walked inside the bar. The bar was abuzz with loud music. The girl sat on the backless bar-stool right by the frosty beer dispensing fountain, sipping a bloody martini out of a sugar-rimmed martini glass. The cherry at the bottom of the drink added the fresh blood flavour to the already sinful drink.

"Hi, I am Roy...uhhh..." Roy swallowed the rest of his drab words.

The girl ignored Roy as she continued to sip her drink and look the other way. Roy mustered some courage and sat on a chair next to hers. "Actually there is a weird incident that happened a few weeks ago. I was at a party and I came across this beautiful girl with a really weird name..."

The girl sharply turned to Roy and sternly said, "Not interested." But it was the face that knocked off his lucidity. The girl in front of him was Monica.

What's wrong with my life? How fucked up could it be? It's like straight out of a cooler club fate.

Cooler club is actually a career for people with extraordinary bad luck. When there is someone in a casino who is making a lot of money, the casino dispatches these coolers to play alongside the winners. The coolers have this aura that everything they even remotely come in contact with goes to shit.

Right about now, Roy felt exactly like a cooler club dude.

Monica, on the other hand, looked like a very angry tigress, ready to eat away the very essence of Roy. It wasn't anger owing to frustration, but that stemming from awkwardness. Her first reaction had never been her kindest.

Roy was awestruck by this seductive side of Monica and the sheer allure of her tall lissom beauty and light brown eyes. Her short dress wrapping her curvaceous body had totally transformed the business suit-clad plain-faced Monica, as had her soft mellow voice with a slight hint of huskiness.

Roy was listening, but he couldn't hear a damn thing. He was smitten beyond comprehension, a little odd for him, he thought. Monica's voice echoed in the background like a lullaby causing a paralysis induced hallucination. Faint words echoing sounded like

Monica was mad, some words that Roy could hear were "...crazy... awkward..."

Having gone beyond the realm of time, when Roy finally broke out of the spell, Monica was gone.

A couple of weeks passed. Roy was relieved that Monica had been nowhere in sight. Roy had focused all his energy in working on his investment strategy built on 'The Black Sheep'.

"Alright. Let's expand this bad boy for everything – stocks, bonds and commodities," Roy clicked through 'The Black Sheep', "and here are my variables."

The tool's sandbox arrow button was still thinking. Roy pulled back and turned his attention to the TV.

The weatherman was announcing, "Everything looks dull and boring from the weather standpoint. Well, it really is a good thing, because when our section heats up, it puts a lot of people in misery."

"The Weatherman!" Roy spoke up softly. Something struck him like a flash of lightning and he pulled over the weather model news he had browsed through that morning. His grey cells were ramping up and his genius coming back to work, as Roy buried himself in dozens of articles and four monitors of weather model monitoring maps. His eyes and hands were moving swiftly and simultaneously like a well-choreographed dance, working seriously on a whole set of numbers and looking at the results in 'The Black Sheep'.

Hours later, Roy saw something on the screen that brought a glimmer of smile to his gloom-ridden face. He was looking at three boxes – First one titled 'Confidence' saying 95%, a box titled 'Projected Profit' saying $20 million, and finally the box titled 'Risk' saying $1million. *Nice!! Now I need to plan the trade in a way that the market doesn't see this coming. And I have three days to build up my position.*

Over the next three days, Roy had to take a very sensible approach of laddering and throughout the day, choosing the exact price and quantity of trades while being cognizant to not ruffle the market.

"Sorry about that. Hey, 4.95 cents is my offer. The price is firm. There has to be at least one firm out there. Look harder man," Roy barked into the turret.

"There you go, like you asked, your last trade is also with Piso Capital." Broker Steve announced on the turret box. "They got your price man."

"Thanks Man. See ya tomorrow." Roy signed off.

By the time the closing bell rang on CME Exchange, Roy had accumulated his target of a whopping hundred thousand lots of Crack Spread Call Options, betting that the market will explode in volatility by tomorrow.

Tomorrow could be big. It better be.

On the rooftop of the hostel building, two giant white and red inflatable chickens blasted 'Cook-doo-koo...' at the crack of dawn. The shallow imbecilic voices were devoid of any melody, any rhythm.

"What the fuck is this?" Shammi looked over at Bumpy with his bloodshot eyes.

"Welcome to Pashaland," Bumpy replied flatly.

One of the many quirks that Pasha possessed in his arsenal of absurdity was this silly punishment. Some psychological study had concluded that the process of humiliation by way of wearing inflatable is known to forcibly make students repent their mistakes, and Pasha was sold on it.

"I am fuckin' tired, totally hung over, and for some reason, I have a hard on!" Shammi said.

Bumpy looked at Shammi with suspicious eyes, "I didn't want to tell you, but I have a hard on too," Bumpy paused. "But, it's just you and me here."

"Fuck you," Shammi replied rebuffing the awkwardness of the conversation. "It's this fucking suit, I tell you."

A coarse voice from the ground floor resonated "I can't hear you," and Shammi and Bumpy drudgingly went back to the 'Cook-doo-koo...' routine.

Pasha looked at the roof with a sadistic smile. He looked fresh as an apple; his bushy black moustache shone like it was doused in starch.

A few boys scooted past Pasha. "Good morning, sir."

Pasha turned, smiled. "Good Morning. Good Morning."

"Fucker got laid again," said one of the boys setting off laughter amongst the group.

"C'mon. It's time to parade the campus now." The watchman emerged out of the rooftop door, armed with his repulsive contemptuous smile.

Shammi and Bumpy slowly walked toward the rooftop door and a few minutes later, appeared on the campus road, strolling as fat chicken inflatables. "Good thing we have masks," Bumpy said. "To the world, we are just chickens."

"Chickens with hard-ons!" Shammi said with a splatter of smirk.

"Take your masks off," Pasha's distinguished voice echoed.

Shammi and Bumpy took their face masks off.

"And now, turn around," instructed Pasha. "Now you can go back to the hostel," Pasha said after Shammi and Bumpy had completed the full circle of humiliation. "And, remember," Pasha cautioned them, "Every action has hard consequences!"

Shammi looked up, "Trust me sir, we definitely get the hard part." Bumpy snickered but quickly covered it up by pretending to cough.

Bumpy cowered his head lower and started pacing back to the hostel, whereas Shammi held his chin high, scouting around as pretty ladies chuckled at them.

"Hold on," Shammi said.

"You are not taking this whole chicken thing to your ego, right?" Bumpy said. "You can change and then talk to any girl."

Shammi by that time had rolled like a balloon and landed right in front of Sona. Sona rolled her eyes, a few moments of silence and then she cackled up.

"Don't worry about the suit, let me tell you this though," Shammi's confidence oozed even with the silly suit on. "I now remember when we met, and, for the record, you know I really do wanted to say sorry for the whole *paagal* thing," said Shammi while acting like a retard.

Sona tried to stay still but gave in. "It's okay. It's okay." She laughed and walked away as Shammi smilingly looked at the slim milky legs below her blue chiffon dress.

Dr. Dhoort swiftly snaked through an endless array of tall hardwood bookshelves, skilfully and cautiously trying to spot Sona. Every day he would pretend to casually come to the library and somehow bump into Sona, thinking his immature plan was pure genius.

Finally, he landed at the study area behind the pathology section. Sona casually sat with a bare foot up on her chair and the other on the floor, a sandal loosely dangling from her swaying foot. She took the pen out of her hair and started jotting some notes on an already busily scribbled-on sheet in a white notepad.

Armed with his froggy smile, he edged towards Sona under the pretence of placing some books back on the shelves.

Sona, usually on high alert to watch out for this creep, was completely buried in the books that day and did not notice him close in on her.

"Oh, Sona, better prepare for the test tomorrow," he said while inching closer. "I don't want you to get a B. You know how tough the competition is," said Dr. Dhoort as he stood right by the study table.

"Sir, I know you are very concerned, and thank you for all the help," she paused. "...and I am sure Raju would agree with this," continued Sona, pointing towards Raju, hidden behind a book.

Raju slowly emerged from behind the book only to be slightly short of getting electrocuted by the intense beams of jealousy radiating from Dr. Dhoort's eyes. Raju had no idea what was going on.

Raju had a chubby build and stood at five feet seven inches. With his pinkish-white complexion, honeydew round face, light cat eyes, sharp features and a big fat nose, Raju looked every inch a Kashmiri pundit.

"Is your name Raju or Kaju?" Dr. Dhoort asked the question on purpose, bringing alive the memory of that fateful day back in Raju's mind.

The story went that the seniors had lined up all the newcomers and Raju stood out like a shining star in the otherwise darker-skinned herd.

"So you are an American studying in India?" a senior had asked.

"Okay, then let's have you propose desi style," another added quickly.

Raju had been tasked to wear a Frenchie underwear with a long t-shirt and to walk up to a girl and ask her "Will you be my American *kishmish*?" Raju had to find a willing companion within an hour or he would have a do a full Monty in the centre of the famous lovers' coffee shop.

He had finally stopped by this girl who, as luck would have it, was in her final year of engineering.

"Ma'am," whispered Raju.

The girl had glanced at the half-naked Raju in a ripped off t-shirt and a pair of Frenchies.

"Thank you for taking the time to talk to me," stammered Raju as suddenly the entire coffee shop had swelled around him.

"Are you talking to me or writing a letter to the principal?" said the girl, causing everyone around them to laugh.

"Will you respectfully be my American *kishmish*?" asked Raju embarrassed, praying for this ordeal to end.

The girl had looked at Raju up and down with her wicked cat eyes. "What is your name, American *chhamiya*?"

"Raju, ma'am."

The girl's eyes had scanned him once more from top to bottom and stopped at his crotch. She moved forward and stroked Raju's cheeks brashly. "Kaju? Makes sense!" declared the girl, dangling her pinky finger in Raju's face.

As the laughs roared in the skies of the campus, that day had, with 'Kaju', cemented Raju's destiny in the hall of shameful names.

Back in the library, Dr. Dhoort was still smiling at Raju – *This is an easy target to take out. May be I can just give him an ATKT? No, that may be a little unethical; I can't do that. I am a respectful citizen who follows the rules of society and I don't want to come across as an unethical, sleazy professor*. The thoughts continued in Dr. Dhoort's delusional and narcissistic mind.

Sona found this as an opportune moment to slip away from the library. Raju quickly followed her.

The drizzled street of Ricochet campus was thronging with students.

"Hello," yelled Shammi.

It looked like today wasn't her day. She had gone from the frying pan straight into the fire, for now she had to deal with Shammi, who she had been cordially avoiding for a few weeks. She kept walking down the street, while continuing her intense pathology-related discussion with Raju.

"Long time," said Shammi as he appeared right in front of Sona's face. Shammi walked alongside, chattering about irrelevant topics. "Did you know that Salman Khan is actually an alien who had come down to earth to find mango seeds so that they could grow mangoes on his planet?" said Shammi with a poker face.

"Really?!" Raju exclaimed.

Shammi continued his concoction taking the tale to a dark cold night in 1988, when Salman's ship had landed in the desert of Rajasthan. Salman had alighted and the ship had taken off. Walking through the desert alone, Salman had spotted a guy with a camel who agreed to give him a ride and even shared some alcohol with him. Salman had been absolutely delighted by his experience of alcohol. His mission was still his first priority and he casually asked the guy where he could find mango seeds.

"I can't believe this. Do something, Raju," Sona said in utter frustration.

Raju was so engrossed in the tale that he didn't even hear Sona.

Shammi's narrative went on. "The guy told Salman, 'Near mess ward', referring to the food mess in town.

"Salman Khan understood that to be 'Near Miss World' and begun a tiresome journey of ten years to find *the* Miss World. When Salman finally met Aishwarya, he pretended to fall in love with her, for his goal was to retrieve those mango seeds.

"He searched everywhere in her house, her car, her apartment, but found nothing. He couldn't find those seeds anywhere. However, he had found something else – his feelings for Aishwarya. He had fallen in love with her and in that weak moment had told her – 'I am an alien'. Aishwarya had gotten mad and shut the doors of her apartment on him and didn't let him in all night."

"I remember that," Raju chimed in. "It was all over the news," said Raju with a serious straight face.

Shammi professed his appreciation to Raju and continued, "Salman had no choice but to be human, 'Being human'. Anyway, after extensive research, Salman found that if he peed on a sleazy and horny filmmaker, the allergic reaction from his pee touching that body would take all the alien powers away and leave him a mere mortal human, ready to be embraced by Aishwarya. A few nights later, Salman Khan met Subhash Ghai at a party and the rest, as you know, is history!"

"Shut up!" Sona screamed at Shammi.

"Do you want me to go up and shut something, or you are talking about the phrase 'shut up' that means stop this nonsense and keep quiet," said Shammi. "...But that really doesn't fit here, right?" Shammi went on with little shame.

Sona was hopelessly sad at not being able to do anything, but somewhere in her heart she felt just a tiny bit flattered too. Shammi's unrelenting persistence made her feel special.

Even with all the flattery, it was pretty obvious from her frowning expression that she was equally weighing on the side of being annoyed with Shammi.

"I can't believe this!" said Sona. "I don't know if you are mad or what," said Sona exhaling deeply.

"Calm down, Sona. I'll try to take care of this," Raju jumped in. "This guy is good at Karate, so violence won't be possible, but let me see if I can resolve this peacefully," said Raju in his typical nerdy mumble.

Sona couldn't believe the level of insanity this conversation has reached. "Okay, baba, if I agree to go to dinner with you, will you let me go?" Sona pleaded to Shammi.

"Dinner and a movie," said Shammi.

"Don't push your luck," said Sona.

"Ok, so a movie and dinner then?" said Shammi.

After a brief silence, Shammi conceded his demands for a movie, and put on his killer smile.

"Did someone tell you, that smile of yours…" said Sona.

"Yup. Wonder smile," interrupted Shammi.

Sona gave him a sarcastic smile and gestured to Shammi to walk away. Shammi recanted his smile and asked, "But we didn't fix any time. 8.00 p.m. works for you?"

Sona nodded in agreement with her arms still held up, shooing him away.

The subway line had been shut down because of a disabled train. *One disabled train can cost this economy millions of dollars. I hope the city realizes that.*

Roy threw his bag in his office and rushed straight to the trading floor. The trading floor was more chaotic than usual. He stepped down the mezzanine level to the pit area. As soon as he was in the pit, the chatter dimmed and a herd of straight faces gleamed down at him. *What in the gut of hell happened now?*

CNBC channel was running a commentary on the usual topics. The stock market was okay, nothing like a home run. Channels on all TV screens changed, and in his over-animated tone, the weatherman was urging the world to get ready for the biggest hurricane of the season, hitting straight in the eye of the biggest refinery in New Orleans. The news was filled with people boarding up their homes, and bumper-to-bumper traffic towards inland cities like Dallas and Austin. Devastation in the aftermath of hurricane Katrina may have faded away in the memory of the world, but for the people of New Orleans, that was an experience they would never forget.

"And the effect this hurricane is having on gas prices is astronomical," said the weatherman in the TV discussion panel. "If the past is any indication of the future, this is just the beginning…"

The entire trading floor broke out of their New York poker face routine and a thunderous applause welcomed the new money that Roy's trade would make for the firm. Roy blushed as he shyly acknowledged the accolades. *It's strange. It's sad. These folks are leaving everything they hold dear and running away from their homes, which may not even be there tomorrow. And here we are, clapping and singing because we put our chips on the side that the city will be screwed by a natural disaster. What am I? A sadist? Well, I am just a minion doing my thing.*

Hilton stood on the mezzanine level. He looked at Roy and nodded, silently acknowledging it to be a 'job well done'.

Coffee is known to be the daytime fuel for traders and alcohol the night-time fuel. Roy stepped into the break room to get a coffee when he stumbled upon Monica. There was this awkward moment between the two. Monica did everything possible to avoid him. Roy on the other hand was equally embarrassed.

"Hey, I know what happened that day was odd, and I really, really, want to apologize," said Roy.

Monica looked straight up waiting for her coffee to pour out of the coffee machine.

"I had no idea, plus, you looked so different than you do here," Roy said with a fading tone.

Monica looked at him. "It's okay. Don't sweat too much."

"Don't think of me as the weird psycho who follows you everywhere. I know you may think like that, but trust me. You can look at my apartment; I don't even have a basement," said Roy

"What basement? What are you talking about?" Monica was confused.

"I don't have a basement to store dead bodies," said Roy "Psychos....dead bodies," Roy tried to clarify while moving his arm up and imitating the stabbing shower action from the movie *Psycho*.

Monica looked at Roy, and for the first time she genuinely smiled at him.

Roy was happy and relieved. "Alright, this is the part when I get really excited and make a sex-laced joke, so now I will shut up and go. And hopefully, like humans, we can talk and go out again."

"See you around, weirdo!" said Monica smilingly as she walked away, still shaking her head and smiling at the silliness of Roy's conversation.

Hilton pulled in the troops for a happy hour at The Capitol Grille at the corner of Broadway and Pine Street that evening. The upscale restaurant had the most extensive cellar of rare expensive wines in the whole of Manhattan. Servings of calamari, lamb chops and truffle fries floated through the private section reserved for Da Vinci Capital. The atmosphere was abuzz and sounded like a million bees humming together, for to make any conversation, one really needed to shout directly in the others' ears.

Same anecdotes which were really funny the first time were being repeated by the same set of people for the hundredth time, and for the hundredth time everyone was laughing at the same stale joke. There could only be two reasons – either everyone had a memento kind of memory, or this was that potion of hypocrisy that we have all been so consumed with, that it had now become a part of us.

Hilton raised a toast for the eighth time that evening. The Italian Prosecco sparkling wine collided in the thin champagne flutes in the midst of chants of "To the Wall Street...to the Wall Street." Hilton got a call on his phone, which he ignored. The phone rang again. "This may be business, folks. You'll have to excuse me, and someone watch out for my black card." Hilton answered the phone. After exchanging the introductory pleasantries, the conversation on the phone soon got serious. Hilton stepped out of the restaurant. Monica's hawk eyes followed Hilton through the glass window overlooking the street-side parking. Hilton was still talking on the phone when he quickly jumped on the back seat of his Cadillac.

Roy tapped Monica on the shoulders. Monica turned around with a smile. "So, you are the hotshot trader now!"

"Hardly," Roy said humbly. "I still have to learn from your highness who has never lost a trade. Ever!"

Monica smiled. "You are very...different," she said with a mysterious undertone.

"Being different is also karma. I may not be what I am and..." said Roy.

"Well you are different and weird and...," Monica paused, "...crazy too," Monica spoke up in her teasing tone.

"Okay! So what do you think karma is?" asked Roy.

"You seriously want me to answer that?"

"Yup."

"When I work for something really hard and I get it, I call it results. Not karma. Karma is something people use to give as a logical yet fictional conclusion to their actions or their reactions. To me, it's like religion, but just more modern. If religion is ancient myth, then karma is modern myth."

"Well, be careful what you say about karma. Someone said karma is a bitch, when you are!"

"I am a tigress, not a bitch. But it looks like karma is for bitches," Monica said smilingly.

The conversation was interrupted by a buzzing text message tone on Monica's phone.

"Interesting conversation, bitch. Let's continue this later," said Monica.

Srini chipped in, "Yo! Breaking Bad. Bitch," just as Monica walked out of the restaurant.

"What a view," said Roy as he watched Monica walking outside on the sidewalk before disappearing into Hilton's Cadillac.

Roy turned around, finished his summer fresh Blue Moon in one shot, banged his empty mug on the table and steered towards the rest of the merry, drunk crowd.

The dimly-lit parking lot of Ricochet College was apparently dubbed as the 'Making-out lot', for as soon as the smiling sun set its charm for the darkness of night, it would be swarming with lovers with burning desires to devour their better halves.

A fully-bathed, clean shaven Shammi casually strolled towards a parked car, opened the door and led himself in the car. He was cognizant of his surroundings. *I wish there was a better place I could have picked Sona from.* He put the single stem of white rose on the back seat, lay around on the reclined driver's seat and looked around the car with an unsatisfactory smile, thinking of the conversation he had had with Thakursaab.

Thakursaab's words, "And listen, Makhmal will give you your new car keys," echoed in his ears. Excitedly, he had walked out and tried the new keys on the swanky new Maserati.

"It won't work on this car, Baba," Makhmal said. "It's *that* car," Makhmal raised his arms to a little dusty Maruti Zen parked far away on the driveway.

Earlier that day, Shammi had rushed to the carwash and made sure that it had been sanitized in and out. The whole deal cost him a fortune considering his limited allowance, but it was his royal blood perhaps. No way he would let his date sit in that dump of a car. Deep in his thoughts, Shammi was interrupted with a light thud noise. He looked through the foggy windshield; there was nothing. He slowly pulled over the front seat of the car and smudged the fog away with his hands. Still, there was nothing but the tall brick wall. The thumping- grew louder and faster. Shammi closed his eyes and with alert ears, focused on the sound. He turned to the driver-side window and there it was – a fine booty impression and lovers leaning against his car. Shammi wasn't surprised, but that didn't mean he wasn't pissed, especially when he had just dropped five grand to get his date car waxed up. He pulled the lever and slowly opened the car door.

"Oh! You have super powers baby. I love whatever it is that you are doing with my booty," said the lover girl.

"Really, thanks!" said the lover guy. "You don't need me for your beauty. You are already beautiful."

"Learn English baby...I said booty," replied the lover girl, pointing to her booty.

"Oh...But my hands are up here baby. I think there is someone else who is playing...," lover boy said casually without realizing the meaning of his own words.

"What?" the girl jumped away from the car.

"It's the horny car who is doing that, honey," said Shammi. "The car is saying that if you want to make out, don't fuckin' spoil my wax," Shammi said in a not too happy tone, while also emulating a car horn like sound.

The lovers sped at lightning speed. Shammi could hear the voice of the girl as they walked away. "Get a car or we are off. I can't deal with your parking lots and bandstands anymore."

"My papa is an understanding man. I'll tell him you don't like making out in the parking lot. He'll understand," the lover boy said in an ambiguous context that could have been sarcasm or pure bliss of dumbness.

Shammi was still bewildered at the lover-chase scene, when the passenger door of the car opened and Sona stepped in. His eyes froze looking at the magnificent, breathtaking beauty of the gorgeous damsel.

Sona dazzled in the light lemon *chudidar* with narrow mystical silver *zardosi kadhai* along the border of her *kameez*. A mellow melon-lime perfume aroma had begun to mix in the air, enough to run adrenaline even in the dead. Sona fixed her earrings as she turned around and spoke to Shammi, cutting the air with her sensuous light pink lips, "Nice car!"

Shammi was frozen in the moment. A thousand thoughts were running through his mind, hiding under the cloak of his poker face, impairing him with the hopelessness of his heart throbbing under the spell of Sona's beauty.

A faint echo in the background grew louder. "What happened?" Sona gently nuzzled Shammi's cheeks, slowly undoing the spell of her own beauty.

Shammi tried to recompose himself but struggled to make any of it work. His one-liners were not working and he just couldn't steer himself away from Sona's innocent yet dazzling beauty. He was in a space he had never felt before.

"You look amazing," said Shammi, rather seriously.

"Thank you," said a smiling Sona.

Shammi couldn't gather the courage to look into Sona's eyes; he turned his head straight to the wheel and turned on the ignition.

"What happened to your chatter box?" quipped Sona. "You didn't turn into that alien, did you?" Sona asked jokingly.

"Naah," said Shammi while shying away from Sona. "Just..." Shammi was still at a loss of words when his car disappeared in the Mumbai traffic.

The coffee shop of the Oberoi Hotel in Downtown was a big lofty place but it did have some cozy sea facing spots, reserved for its exclusive guests. Shammi obviously was more than just an exclusive guest.

The wine had kicked in; Shammi was back in his element. "Movie after this?" Shammi asked as he sipped the Moscato.

"You don't give up, do you? All you want is a nice dark cozy spot," Sona said teasingly.

"There are better or worse 'cozy dark spots'. Trust me, you haven't seen what I just saw in the parking lot," Shammi said with vivid excitement and full throttle body expression of all the lovers he had seen pressed against one another in the dingy parking space.

Sona laughed so much she had tears in her eyes.

Shammi gasped and threw his hands on the table. Their fingers gently collided; the warmth had already begun to make Shammi heady.

Sona cleared her throat as she sluggishly pulled her hand away.

"Tell me what you think of me," Shammi tried to change the topic.

"Well, you are witty, very different than me, and, I don't think we can ever be together," Sona said mischievously. "You know, romantically."

"Don't say that," Shammi interrupted, softly putting his finger on his lips, gesturing her to seal her lips.

"*Kahin dil se mat bol dena...har din mein dil se nikli ek baat sach zaroor ho jaati hai...*"

"I am speaking from my mouth, not from my heart," Sona came back with a clever reply.

"*Feeki syahi se bana naa silvet*
Waqt ka dhoka bana de naa kahin sarhad
Bani sarhad to thanedar bana chahat mayoosiat mein ro dega
Khoonkaar baarish hogi us din
Shikan kho baitha aasman, bulandi se koodega
Aur teri meri kahani ki hichkiyon se sara jahan goonjega,"
Shammi replied hypnotically.

What the fuck? Did I just spit out poetry? What am I now, Gulzar? For Shammi, a date meant getting a girl in bed. His three-step process had always worked, and it was working so far on Sona too. But tonight, it wasn't happening.

On the other hand, Sona pulled back. She had never imagined this romantic avatar of Shammi. *What is wrong with this guy? Is he really a romantic or this is his set of elaborate tricks to get a girl weak in her knees? I can't look at those eyes. I know I'll get caught in them. This is too soon.*

They both sat in the car and didn't speak a word to each other.

"Alright, let's just hit reset," Shammi tried to salvage his date before it ended with a very foreseeable 'The End'.

Sona looked at him, shying away from looking straight into the eyes still. She raised her face, "We can hang out ...as friends."

Shammi looked at Sona and smiled.

"By the way, did you write that yourself?" Sona asked with a naughty smile.

"No," replied Shammi with a straight face.

"I thought so," replied Sona.

"I didn't write it. I just composed it on the fly," said Shammi as he turned to look straight into her eyes.

"Were you trying to impress me?"

Shammi shrugged it off sportingly. "Nope. Not you. I was trying to impress the chicken that looked so sexy pole-dancing on that kebab stick."

"You are mad."

Shammi looked at her and smiled as he peddled the car through the suburban streets of Mumbai. The rest of the drive was drowned in a pleasant silence, invoking invigorating thoughts in both of them.

It was already past 1.00 a.m. when Shammi got back to the hostel after dropping Sona off. He quickly parked the car in the 'making-out lot'. He strolled through the side lanes to reach the hostel. The hostel's main gate was bolted and locked, not to be opened till the crack of dawn. Shammi had nowhere to go, and even if he did, he was too stubborn to go anywhere. The stubbornness ran in the family, it seemed. But there was one other way he could get to his hostel room. He put some sand on his hands, rubbed them and like Spiderman steep climbed up the perforated wall leading straight up to the sixth floor window and then quietly descended down to the fourth floor.

"I'll keep this here. Keep it safe." Sona kept the white rose in her diary and finished the page with her happy thoughts. "Ever since this guy has come in my *kundali*, things have been...let's just say different. I don't know what he wants, but I like this new feeling. I am happier. Not that he is funny all the time; he definitely knows how to get on your nerves. But that's okay. Not all was ever gold."

The black dropping on the Uber app displayed five minutes wait time. Roy sighed as he opened Twitter and browsed through the top news on his feed.

"Trying to find another Dabble?" A voice came from behind him.

Roy turned around and was pleasantly surprised to find Monica.

Several days had passed since his glorious win and the after party. Roy had all but forgotten about Monica; she was scarcely on the trading floor.

"Hey...Houdini," said Roy.

"Haha, Touché," started off Monica. "It's been crazy for the last few weeks. Anyway, see you around," said Monica while looking for a cab.

A black car with a grey Uber sign on the passenger side window pulled in. Roy hopped in, rolled the windows down and offered her a lift. She looked around and then jumped in.

"Where would you like to go?" asked Roy trying to make sure that they dropped Monica first.

"Park and 45th," said Monica.

"Oh well! You are a neighbour then."

"I know. Remember our first Dabble encounter?"

"How can I forget that? That encounter changed me in so many ways," said Roy jokingly.

"Fuck off," Monica said lightly. "Do you ever give up?"

"You are right," Roy could sense that something was bothering Monica. "So, what's cookin'? Where have you been travelling to?" He tried to steer the conversation to something light.

"All over," said Monica as she sagged on the seat. "West coast, Ireland, Amsterdam, Switzerland..." Monica paused. "It's really a round-the-world fare that I am trying to get the value out of." She said in a hushed tone, closing her tired eyes.

"So, what are your plans for the evening?" asked Monica.

"Nothing. I'll walk a couple blocks, it helps me clear my head and then I have to take my vitamins too," said Roy. *Why the hell did I say that? Who says I'll spend my beautiful night taking vitamins.*

"You are lucky. A walk can do that for you." Monica paused. "And that vitamin...." She recomposed her thoughts. "I need to get piss drunk to clear my head."

The taxi stopped at her address. Monica opened the door to get off and said before stepping out, "Do you care for a drink?"

Monica and Roy entered a neighbourhood Italian bar next to Grand Central. Roy was ready to place an order for a draft beer when Monica banged the bar counter, "Patron please. Beer is for Pansies."

Several rounds of Patron had been served. Roy hadn't been a heavy drinker ever since he had vowed to abstain from alcohol – at least on most occasions. He liked the feeling, the state he was in – the inebriated heady feeling of Tequila had washed away his reticence.

Within a couple of hours, the tequila shooting pair headed out of Park Avenue and on to the old cobblestone streets of the Meatpacking district; the abyss of red hot nightclubs stacked on both sides of the streets. Roy and Monica hopped from one club to another like frogs hopping in rain.

The grinding dance, the blurriness of alcohol and the adrenaline of dancing to foot tapping hip-hop music had become this exotic cocktail that only got wilder with each passing hour.

Roy sprung out of bed and inhaled a sharp breath. He had another one of those nightmares. He looked around; things looked different. Even in the darkness, the soft light of a night lamp illuminated the impeccable bedroom. *This ain't my bedroom.* He glanced around in surprise, eyeing every object that came in his sight.

He moved his gaze away from the room and to his hands, and to his body. *I am naked!* He slowly turned to the other side of the bed. Monica turned over to reveal her calm soothing face. *Oh well, I believe I just had break-up sex. Alright, so now is the time for me to walk away. I am not ready to take anything beyond a night. It's not good for me. It's not good for her. It's not good for anyone.* Quietly, Roy tried to get off the bed when Monica gently threw her hand on his, softly holding on to his fingers. He stopped, leaned against the headboard, lost in the maze of his mind; he just sat there, looking at Monica's soft hand holding his fingers.

The dagger of bright sunlight lit up Roy's eyelids. His shallow breath was entangled in the soreness of his neck. He had slept sitting up with his head half rested on the headboard.

"This was a drunken mistake. I am sure you agree that this was our first and also our last mistake," Monica said as she skinned up a black dress on top of her black lacy lingerie.

Roy just nodded as he walked towards the bathroom.

"C'mon, don't tell me you will cry now," continued Monica.

Roy hummed negatively. Monica seemed irritated with his sparse responses and walked up to the bathroom where Roy stood looking for something.

"What are you lookin' for?"

Roy signalled for a toothbrush. She took a brush out of her linen closet and handed it over to him.

"Sorry…I don't talk unless I have brushed my teeth," said Roy.

"Good boy," said Monica in an innocent sarcastic tone. "You got the first and last time part though, right?" She had become serious.

"Yup. Got it. First mistake... Last mistake... Together that is," said Roy.

Monica opened the main door when Roy stopped her. "Wait for me. I'll come to the office too."

Monica smiled again. "Really! You want us to go to work together? What else do you want us to do together?"

Roy shrugged his shoulders apologetically as Monica waved and whispered good-bye.

As night fell in the sky, the sheets of Monica's bed rolled again with Roy and her.

The first and last mistake bit had gone for a toss.

Monica and Roy lay on the bed: Monica sleeping like a baby and Roy awake like an owl.

Monica woke up to the aroma of an exotic breakfast. The freshly-squeezed orange juice sparkled in the crystal jug. She was impressed at the tidiness of the apartment and just how neatly the breakfast had been laid out on the modern glass kitchen table. The white bone china plates were placed right in the centre of the placemats, and the silverware positioned with a guided-missile like precision neatly lay next to the plate. The grand breakfast feast filled up the plate with a skinny toast, oatmeal pancake with honey syrup, a well done fried egg with spinach, and a light spread of Italian pesto well complimented by a side of grilled mango with balsamic glaze.

Monica hopped on to the tall chair carved with an s-like seat. Her thin silky white see-through pajamas were like a veil to her sexy hips in the nude. Covering everything but covering nothing and showing nothing but showing everything. Roy came in from behind and gently wrapped his arms around hers, softly burying his face in her silky hair, nuzzling her neck with kisses; his hands covered hers as she took the steely knives and cut through the soft toasty layer of pancakes.

Roy slightly turned his head up, sprinkling warm air around her earlobe, gently pursing his lips on her helix. Monica's skin was beginning to firm up, her mind had grown numb; she had become reluctant to the noise of the outside world. Blurred by the ecstasy, she wanted the feeling to last forever. Their appetite of the moment had drifted away from the Cadillac breakfast.

He swivelled the chair around, and she jumped right into his arms. Clasped in his bare muscular arms, Monica's entire body quivered. The aesthetic of her feelings was unimaginable. She loved to feel weak, it was the gentle rough touch that danced her feelings into the naughty arena. "Talk dirty to me!" she whispered.

Enchanted with the devouring urge to make love, he rushed her to the bedroom. Moving his lips closer to hers, gently rubbing his nose to hers, with a thrust he pushed her on the bed and hopped on top of her.

An aroused Monica lay flat on the bed, as he wildly pulled her dress out with his teeth, bringing to bare her goosy pink nipples. Her hands reached the back of his head as he dabbed his mouth in her soft breasts, then her belly, before slowly drifting down below. Like a symphony, his tongue dove in and out, alternating a soft touch and a firm rhythmic tapping. The desire, the temptation was scaling new heights of longing to immerse her defenseless body into the pleasure beyond the realm, in a world of fantasy where only the ecstasy of her orgasm could take her, embrace her, cuddle her, pleasure her...over and over again. The spell reached its height as screams of pleasure resonated, infusing life in barren portraits hung on the wall, bringing them to life with the echo of the indulgent euphoria of the timeless moment.

Monica felt like she had been to paradise and back. Within seconds, she was ready to go again.

The newly-found friendship between Shammi and Sona was blossoming like a maple tree coming out of brutal winter and into the warm arms of spring. Back-slapping buddies would be going too far, but they had become the boy and girl that everyone was envious of, that everyone suspected to be a couple.

A few silent lovers had accelerated their obsession. The frequency of fruit baskets, bouquets and letters drawn in blood had ramped up significantly for Sona.

"I think he was a mute," Sona said as the old Maruti Zen zipped through.

"Nah, I think he can talk," said Shammi. "I heard him say, that wasn't my blood on the letter, it was my dead goat's," Shammi chuckled.

Sona brushed off the remark with a smile. "Okay, there is something you should know. I have never missed the trailers at the beginning of the movie," said Sona putting on her cute pout.

Shammi drove in a whiff, and with a skid and a skad, parked the car in the parking lot.

Sona and Shammi rushed to the movie auditorium. The doors of the auditorium were just opening up. Shammi secured Sona under the ring of his arms as they hastily tried to squish through the half-open French door. But as if the world had conspired for many lives to make this moment happen, Sona and Shammi got stuck in the door passage along with a heavy-set big girl. The three of them moved together like a tangled string puppet. "People are so big that they can't wait to enter the auditorium," said the heavy-set girl whose only fault was perhaps using the word "big" out of context.

Shammi and Sona made very dignified attempts to contain their laughter.

"Madam, you go first. At least there will be some breathing space," said Shammi in his completely made-up serious avatar.

The heavy-set girl wiggled out, puffing and fuming. "I don't know what's wrong with people. They should learn how to control everything around them."

Sona and Shammi laughed defiantly. The heavy-set girl turned back, "What now? You can't explore it all in one day," she mercilessly said that, pointing the finger to herself.

They laughed some more before Sona put her arms around his and they walked to Bumpy and the gang eagerly waving to them. Shammi looked at Sona who was cuddled in his arms, smiled and marched ahead with pride.

"So, how many girlfriends you have had in the past?" asked Sona, trying to fend off the boring movie.

"Foreplay or all-the-way?" reluctantly interjected Bumpy.

Shammi looked at Bumpy and pinched his fingers. "Oww," screamed Bumpy.

"Shhh," someone from the back shooed.

Shammi slouched in his chair, and threw his long legs wide apart on the floor as he spoke softly. "The past is history," said Shammi playfully, like he had just invented the light bulb.

Sona smiled, shrugging her shoulder and rolling her eyes.

It was really late after the movie when Shammi's car pulled up outside Sona's house.

"Damn. Keep moving, keep moving," Sona looked at her mother through the living room window. She was pacing back and forth, furiously.

Shammi kept the engine going and took a left turn to park on an adjacent street. Sona's mother peeped outside at the car; her puckering forehead eased up as the car moved past the house.

"Damn! What am I supposed to do now?" Sona blinked owlishly. She quickly took her phone and texted her friend. A few text messages later, she sighed. "Okay. Aarti was smart. My mum called and she said that I am with her. But she also said that I'll be home late."

"So what did you tell her?" asked Shammi.

"I can't face my mom like this. She knows something is wrong," Sona said worriedly.

Shammi was surprisingly supportive. "Wouldn't it be better if you went home than not going at all? I can come with you, if that helps," Shammi offered.

"Right! I don't think you know my mother. She was an army doctor. She will dissect you like a hapless frog," said Sona.

"I knew it," exclaimed Shammi.

"What? That you are like a frog?" Sona replied.

"Huh! Never got that compliment before. Frogs are cute. Actually girls in frocks are cute. Frogs can jump right in," said Shammi.

"Here we go again;" said Sona. "Let's go back to what you were trying to say. Maybe that will bring your one-track mind back."

"Actually I wanted to say…I knew it's the army canteen eggs," said Shammi looking at Sona adoringly. "All the army girls are so hot. I know it's the eggs."

"…and my mother will whip you like one right now," said Sona.

"Dissected like a frog. Whipped like an egg. Nice," said Shammi rolling his raised big eyes. "I think I'll pass."

"We can always go to my apartment," Shammi paused for a second, "Oh Wait. We can't. I forgot. I have been banished from that."

"Banished…by your parents? Why is that not a surprise?"

"Thanks for believing in me," Shammi exhibited his trademark sarcasm. "*But*, I believe the more pressing question right now is, where are you going to park your boo…" Shammi arched a sly brow, looking at Sona's glimmering hour glass figure. Sona looked at Shammi. Her brows knitted in a frown. *Ok. Looks like it's time to recalibrate that raunchy thought.* "…booot-ee-ful thoughts tonight," finished off Shammi wickedly.

Sona winked and a breezy smile covered her face. She had grown very fond of Shammi. It was these small little funny things that she loved about him. She lost all sense of fatigue and boredom, for every moment spent with Shammi was like a revelation about the wackiness of a drifter's mind.

She quickly texted Aarti and then slouched in the seat. "Drop me at Aarti's. I have told her to call mum and say that I have dozed off."

"Do you trust me?" asked Shammi.

"Yes. What kind of question is that?" said Sona.

"Okay," Shammi turned the ignition on. "Tonight, I'll take you on an adventure you have never been on before." Shammi hit the gas, zooming through the streets.

She looked at him and then retreated back into the seat. "Okay. Let's see what your adventure is."

$\mathcal{T}$ime flew by in a jiffy. Roy and Monica had hooked up one too many times. Staying over at each other's place had become part of their lifestyle. Slowly and steadily, Roy was getting to a happy place. At least, he was trying in earnest. He cherished every moment spent with her, and was lost in thoughts of her as he commuted to work.

Roy's poker face broke into a big grin as flashes from what had happened a few days ago assaulted his mind, perhaps triggered by the song he was listening to – *Somebody I used to know*. It was the same song he was humming when he and Monica had snuck in to the server room in the office and started making out.

It was a fantasy that Roy had wanted to live out; making out in the office was like a spine-tingling adventure that made him feel like a spy with a sexy damsel by his side. Monica's Irish kinks were at work. She didn't mind this occasional escapade that Roy pulled her into. He had pushed her against a server rack, held her butt in his hand and was about to kiss her when Srini had barged in. "Did someone turn off the main server?"

Roy's hands froze, still holding Monica's butt. A startled Monica had muffled her own scream, and buried her face in Roy's chest, then quickly jostled out of the room, shying away from any eye contact.

"She was upset," Roy had just blabbered, knowing that it made no sense whatsoever.

"And that was counselling?" said Srini with his swinging head and the ever-sleazy smile.

Roy was brought back to the present by the realization that everyone at the traffic stop was watching him like he had lost it. Roy hadn't realized that his burst of laughter had made him look like a lunatic.

Roy looked away and walking past his building, took a left turn on the following street and went inside Monica's building. On the penthouse floor, he opened his Kenneth Cole executive leather office bag, and pulled out a set of keys meticulously marked as 'Monica's apartment keys', unlocked the door and entered the penthouse. He neatly kept his office bag on the kitchen chair and strolled in the open area kitchen. He pulled the bright yellow sticky note off the fridge

"I'll be late. Your favourite food will be delivered by 7.30 p.m."

Roy looked at his black Movado watch. It was a quarter-past-seven. *The food would be here in fifteen minutes, which gives me just enough time to take a shower.* Roy went to the bedroom, undressed himself and slipped in to the fancy Jacuzzi shower stall, turned on the knob, and dozens of nozzles jet sprayed water from all sides. Roy stood in the centre, resting his hands against the glass wall, enjoying the deep threaded hydraulic massage.

After a few minutes, a half-wet Roy wrapped in a towel answered the door. "*Shank* you, *shank* you very much," said the delivery man as he looked at the twenty dollar tip he had just received. Roy smiled back and opened the boxes on the table, settling into his meal.

He had just scarfed down noodles and chicken and was throwing the boxes into the garbage can when his eye caught something, causing him to freeze. He hastily opened the drawer, pulled the disposable gloves on to his hands, and curiously started scavenging through the contents of the garbage can.

He lifted a knotted plastic carry bag and rashly tore it up. The carry bag had a thermometer and an empty box that had been ripped open. Roy lifted the thermometer and at the first clear sight of the instrument, like the unpredictability of London monsoon, his face turned crimson red. His heart was beating as hard as the lofty drumbeats straight out of a heavy rock medley. The instrument in his hand was not a thermometer.

Roy stood motionless, like he had just been stuck by a flash of lightning. He shook his head and looked at the little indicator on the device. The device had two red lines, and to the left of the indicator were the instructions – "2 Red lines: Pregnant".

Oh fuck. What have I done? Oh my god! What should I do now? Roy's mind wasn't functioning anymore. *Breathe. Breathe. Focus. Calm down. I need fresh air.* Roy threw the pregnancy test kit back in the garbage and ran outside the apartment to the staircase leading directly to the terrace. His heavy breathing had intensified. He bent forward, held his knees, and focused on calming his panting. After a while, slightly calmed down, he sat on the four-feet wide railing looking down the twenty-one storey building. In shock due to the discovery of Monica's pregnancy, he was oblivious to the steepness of the ledge he was sitting on or to the knotty tightening of his cremasteric muscles.

Roy sat there for hours, thinking. *I need to be rational. I am twenty-nine years old, and still single. I have money. Why am I scared of commitment? Isn't that what everyone seeks? Am I making my bitter past experiences the cornerstone of all future decisions? Is that it? I had promised myself that I won't dwell in the past... I must not.*

Opportunities are presenting themselves, like a god-sent salvation, like the world wants me to live.

Back to the present. Back to the present.

Let's just for a second think about abortion. Really, am I seriously considering it? It's like perishing a new life. A new life is a new beginning. This child will be mine and hers. I'd have to teach him how to walk, how to talk, how to flirt, how to drink. Oh my gosh! Why am I nervous? It's incredible.

In the midst of these internal battles, his mind digressed towards Monica.

What is she thinking? Is this why she is away? Not able to face me? She has changed a lot in the last couple of months. Couple of months? That's how short our relationship is! Can I even take it to the next level? But, all the arranged marriages really have no relationship before marriage and they survive.

Roy's mind kept pacing back and forth between the *yay* and *nay* of the relationship, but in all of his mind games, there was one fact that was not up for debate – there was a baby on the way and the decision on how to take things forward was something he must make together with Monica.

I must talk to Monica. Perhaps she is excited about the baby too. Is she nervous? Probably both. I think we are in a good place in our lives to take this forward. Nevertheless, I want to make this special for Monica.

Roy went back to the apartment. He was calm by now. Moments of solitude always helped Roy compose himself suitably from a state of panic and frenzy, and now he knew what he had to do.

A knock on the door woke Roy up. He had fallen asleep on the couch. The entire apartment was beautifully decorated with pink and blue helium balloons, raised to the ceiling with colourful strings dangling all over the living room like a picture of rain frozen in the moment. Roy had spent all night decorating her apartment. He knew that he had to be her pillar of support. *She must know that I am ready for this. I must be strong for her and together we can figure it all out.*

The knock on the door grew louder. Roy quickly went to the bathroom, poured mouthwash in his mouth, quickly gargled and ran to the door. The calendar by the door displayed sixth of September.

He excitedly opened the main door but it wasn't Monica; it was the FBI.

The engine of the car grew quieter. Shammi turned off the headlights and slowly brought the car to a complete halt in absolute silence.

He turned to Sona. "Tonight, you will sneak into a boys' hostel."

"Are you mad?" Sona virtually jumped off her seat.

"Don't worry, sweetheart. I am your knight in shining armour. Come, it will be fun. Plus, you get to haunt Bumpy. Isn't that the sweetest revenge?"

"No, no… you are mad!" said Sona.

Shammi was insistent; Sona was nervous, but also excited. A part of her wanted to liberate herself by doing something so daring and spontaneous. "I am not going to do it," she said in a tone that faltered in conviction.

"Trust me," said Shammi holding her hands. "I am called Shammi the rip-Bhai. Like Jack the Ripper, but this is really more desi and dangerous."

Sona giggled. She had grown to trust Shammi completely. Her life was no longer populated by only the nine hundred-page medicine books but spur-of-the-moment decisions to live life to the fullest, to laugh, to have fun, to be happy. *Maybe it's destiny. Like a little girl following in the footsteps of her mother. Oh my god. I love it. Wait! Is this romance?*

She looked at him as they held hands, sneaking her into the campus through the bushy side roads. "Let me see that. Did it hurt?" said Shammi. A branch had barely scraped them.

"I am not a baby," said Sona smilingly. But in her heart, she adored every little gesture he made.

Shammi and Sona now stood below the hostel building. He took her *dupatta*, made two knots, undid the laces from his shoes, and attached the shoe strings to the knots. Just like that, he had designed a contractible harness. Sona stood behind him, and then with the pull of the harness, pulled them together.

Sona's heart was palpating harder than a rock.

"Hold me tight," Shammi turned his neck and looked at Sona's scared face. "I'll keep you safer than my own life.

"Just remember that," he was waiting for her to nod. "Say you are okay, and hold me tight like one of those teddy bears."

Sona clutched her arms around him.

"I'd have told you to scream but that won't be wise, considering we are trying to break-in, you know," said Shammi with a smile.

Sona and Shammi were harnessed to go on a midnight adventure. With a light jump, Shammi had clawed on to the holes in the perforated wall. They had already climbed up two floors when he looked back to check on her.

Sona had her eyes tightly shut.

"C'mon Sona! Open your eyes. Think of this as a preparation for a top secret mission."

Sona's eyes were still shut tight. "I can't do it. I give up."

"Ha. Think that there is no reason to be tensed, because this is just a rehearsal and you cannot fail. Because today you have realized that failure is merely an option, and you have decided to not choose it." His words were beginning to braid a lattice of credence. Sona slowly opened her eyes and leaned backwards; her resolve had begun to stew up. As Shammi galloped up the wall, Sona snuggled in his warmth and he felt a gentle kiss on his cheek.

"I should have realized that taking you to a boys' hostel would do it."

A smile broke the icy patch of anxiety, "You are completely mad."

"Alright, take a deep breath and get razor sharp focus now," whispered Shammi. "Now we are going to make a small jump on to that little hinge to get to the window. Sounds good?"

Sona nodded and then exhaled deeply. Shammi nuzzled her arms that were wrapped around him, and quickly took a leap, locking on to the hinge. The panic-stricken situation was not that frightening anymore. The chill in her abdomen was a feeling that she was beginning to enjoy. The adrenaline was nerve-wrecking. Shammi moved his other arm on the hinge, clasping the hinge with both hands. Like a gymnast, he pulled himself and Sona on to the ledge. With the stealth of a ninja, he untied the harness and squeezed them both inside the hallway of the sixth floor.

The hallway was like a coal mine and the canaries had now arrived. It took a while for the cornea to recalibrate to the darkness. The thick layer of darkness was no match to the zest of Sona's victory dance. "Oh my god…I did it!!" She said and then hugged him again, letting her passion flow through her twinkling eyes.

Shammi wanted to throw in one of his half-ass jokes, but words betrayed him and he stayed mum. Sona's infectious passion had begun to spin away; the darkness wasn't dark anymore. Sona looked at Shammi. "You have a very cute smile," she said, spiking a sensuous feeling through his veins. He slowly leaned forward, nuzzling his nose to her lips.

Just then, a light beam bathed a part of the pitch dark hallway. "Who is there? I can see you," Pasha emerged, wearing a full vest and crushed pajamas. He was definitely not a happy man tonight.

Sona got scared and screamed. Shammi put his hand on Sona's mouth and quickly ducked her behind the adjacent door into the storeroom.

The laser beam light was closing in.

"What should I do now, oh my god," Sona was shivering with fear.

Pasha walked faster than a flying ghost. "You want to know what to do. I'll tell you what to do," Pasha said inching closer.

Shammi quickly jumped out the window and down on the thin eight inches wide slab. He had to think fast before Pasha got to Sona. *I have to distract Pasha.*

Pasha was not too far away from the door. Shammi looked around and realized he was wearing a t-shirt with a scary old-lady face. He quickly put it on his face. "What will you do, *Chudail*? Tonight is daddy's turn. I have waited too long to whip your ass and..." Shammi didn't know what to say, "...eat it too." His tone was cadaverous, ghostly.

Sona started giggling.

Shammi quickly intercepted to digress Pasha. "Ha ha ha. Cry chudail, cry. More crying equals sweeter blood. Sweeeeeeet...I even have the blender," Shammi had reached the height of absurdity.

Pasha stopped just short of opening the door in the midst of all the confusion. "But first you said you will eat. Now you want to drink too? What is this nonsense?" For some reason Pasha had become heavily conjured in the conversation, "And what is a blender doing in all this?"

What the fuck, thought Shammi.

"Hmm. I get it you are not a chudail. You are a *daayan*, and talking like a sleazy pimp now." Only Shammi knew how hard it was for him to not burst out laughing.

"I am not a daayan," Pasha said earnestly.

"Okay. Just a sleazy pimp then," replied Shammi in the same retarded ghost tone.

Pasha for some reason was oblivious to what was going on or perhaps it was his decades of experience as a warden in which he had practically seen all the pranks there could have been.

Pasha walked away from the storeroom door, towards the window. He reached the window and normally snooped outside. Shammi sprung out, moving his head around like the horny ghost from the movie *Evil Dead*, while consistently throwing in the cliché of the screeching sound and the mocked up ghost giggle. Pasha stood still and looked Shammi straight in the eyes.

Shammi was like a stage artist in the moment, improvising on the go, customizing based on audience reaction. He quickly pulled the serpent tongue stunt pulling his tongue in and out through the hole in the t-shirt. Pasha looked at it closely, lifted his arm and was slowly readying his fingers to feel the slimy tongue stunt.

What the fuck is this guy doing? Shammi quickly thought out his last act and was all set to get on with it. *If this fails, then Sona will be left alone. Alone in a hostel full of vultures. Let's get to it sunny boy.*

Shammi ducked past Pasha's fingers, kneeled down and used his flexible body to jump downwards to grab the metal rods sticking out below the slab. That made him disappear from Pasha's sight.

Pasha was confused, startled and perhaps even a bit terrified. His primal instincts nudged him to look outside the window. In the midst of an occasional gust of wind, all Pasha could see was the emptiness of the dark night. There was nobody outside.

The confusion had melted away and the terrifying thought that he was not alone had begun to slither out of his furtive squints. He had lost his voice in what was appearing to be a permanent slack-mouthed face. He was screaming, at least in his mind, but the screams failed to go through his vocal band. He pulled his head back in the corridor, turned around and ran like there was no tomorrow – stumbling and slamming through the dormitory door, sprinting across the corridor. Some students had heard the knock on their door and turned the lights of the corridor on. Pasha was oblivious to all this and kept running with his mouth open, as if in a mute scream.

"I think this is an emotional epilepsy attack," said one of the students.

"I don't think there is anything called emotional epilepsy," replied another.

"There is, and it has a very natural cure – one tight slap," said the first student.

"I can't see Pasha in so much pain," said a third student and while he was saying that, a tall hulk-like student came forward and gave one big tight slap to Pasha running past them.

Pasha swivelled and fell on the floor. His big eyes were wide open, just like his mouth.

"See, I told you," said the student smilingly.

In the meantime, Shammi quickly climbed back up and took Sona's hand to scurry down the staircase, rushing into his room. In the midst of panting, there was a moment of deep silence, only to be annihilated by fits of uncontrollable laughter.

Sona caressed Shammi's cheeks, ruffled his head and gave him a tight hug. Shammi embraced her cautiously, hesitantly.

The pages in Sona's diary were filling up fast.

"What happened today? I have no clue! All I can say is that it was no ordinary moment. I felt like a good girl...I felt like a bad girl...I felt like a wild girl... and, I felt something about him. Oh my god, I felt something special about him! Don't know if the masquerade of friendship can hide it anymore. It seems like a dream, but this is happening for real."

Roy was dumbfounded. He was face to face with the FBI, and he had no idea why.

"How can I help you, officers?" asked Roy.

"I am FBI Special Agent Cooper," said one of the officers and then he pointed to his fellow FBI Officer. "He is my partner, FBI Special Agent Moon," changing the direction of hands to the police officers, "And these are officers Newman and Reese from the Sheriff's office. May we come in?" Special Agent Cooper stood a step ahead of the rest of the team, standing out as the leader.

The two uniformed cops stood there with a straight face, evoking intimidation with their posture and build.

"Who are you looking for? Are you sure you have the right address?" Roy said to a cold stare from the officers.

Roy cleared his throat, "I don't know why you would want to talk to Monica..." said Roy in a calm tone.

"It's not Monica we are interested in," said Special Agent Cooper. "It's you, Mr. Roy. We would like you to come with us."

Roy couldn't believe what he had just heard. "I am sorry?" He said questioning the officers.

"You heard us right. It's you, Mr. Roy. We are here to talk to you," repeated Cooper, enunciating in a serious tone.

A frisson of chill pierced through his heart and Roy reached for the wall as his knees went numb, causing him to stumble against the door. "I am a bit confused as to how you knew who I was and that I was here. I don't even live here," Roy said leaning against the door, hiding his quivering fingers.

Roy had been in serious situations many times before, but this was gravely serious. All kinds of thoughts were running through his mind – *What could it be? Is this a case of mistaken identity? Even if I am innocent they have the power to put me in a hole that no one would ever know about. How could it be? I don't even have a parking ticket. This has to be a mistake.*

Special Agent Moon stepped forward, "Sir, it'd be best if we talk at the station."

Roy had realized that his efforts to manage the situation would be futile without proof and documents. *Documents, yes!*

"In that case, I'd like to see a warrant, officer," said Roy.

One of the uniformed officers took out two warrants and handed it over to Roy. "The first one is a search warrant. We are conducting a search on your apartment as we speak. And the second one is your arrest warrant, sir."

Roy was glued to the sheet of paper that held his destiny for now. "Now, I'd have to ask you to slowly turn around and put your hands on the wall," one of the officers said.

"I'd like to extend you the courtesy of letting you change into professional clothes if you'd like to," interrupted Special Agent Cooper.

Roy was grateful to the agent and quickly traded his shorts and t-shirt with his charcoal suit, pink shirt and maroon tie.

It was clear by now that there was no easy way to resolve the situation and whatever lay underneath all this was far more serious and threatening. "I'd like to make a call to my lawyer," said Roy as he turned around, raised his hands and placed them on the wall.

"Sure, you can make the call as soon as we are at the station," said the uniformed officer as he put the silver metallic handcuffs on Roy's wrist and pulled the fastener. "You are being placed on the charges of insider trading at Da Vinci Capital. You have the right to remain silent. Anything you say can and will be used against you in the court of law." He tapped on Roy's shoulders, held him by his cuffed arms. The entire entourage turned back and marched towards the elevators.

As soon as Roy stepped out of the building, he was mobbed by a battery of photographers and TV news anchors. A helicopter hovered at a dangerously low attitude broadcasting the aerial arrest view live on news channels.

Reporters were having a field day with catchy headlines like "Millionaire banker arrested at his girlfriend's apartment" being spat live. The rapid commotion that had gathered in a whiff of a moment was swelling with every step the entourage took towards the parked SUV.

It started to make sense. Why Cooper had offered him the courtesy of changing clothes, if it wasn't for this. *The bastard actually wanted me to dress up like a coiffed hedge fund manager.*

Roy knew exactly what the federal prosecutors were trying to accomplish with this perp-walk. They were setting the stage for a guilty verdict, violating the constitutional right of "presumed innocent until proven guilty".

Roy kept his head lowered, ignoring the whirl of questions being thrown at him. He just wanted it all to be over. He was smart enough to realize that the prep-walk had been pre-planned and the agents escorting him were in no hurry to rush to the car. *All I can do is pretend I am not even here.* Roy tried to divert his mind but his will power succumbed to the loud screams of the media.

After a long and treacherous walk, the officers finally reached the SUV. They pushed Roy in the back seat, hopped on and zoomed through the streets of New York City. Roy was humiliated and hurt. *This has to be a mistake. This has to be a mistake.*

The SUV pulled into the underground garage of the FBI building in Downtown NYC, and Roy was escorted inside. Roy sat in the interrogation room staring at the big mirror wall. Behind the mirror wall, Cooper and Moon stood watching Roy. Cooper stepped out of the observation room and entered the interrogation room.

His dark grey suit and bright white shirt fitted well with his wheatish complexion. "Let me re-introduce myself. I am Cooper, and I'll tell you this, son. I have handled hundreds of cases in my career," he pulled the chair and sat opposite Roy. "And this one, I tell ya, is open and shut.

"Now, as I know you value time, as you guys on the Wall Street say – what is that?" Cooper scratched his bald head, trying to remember, "Oh yeh, time is money. So why don't we get this done?" After a smirky pause, he was ready to savage Roy again. "This will be mutually beneficial to both of us.

"I tell you what – if you confess right now, I'll write a recommendation that you be jailed closer to the city, and I get to go home and have dinner with my wife." He paused, waiting for Roy to start talking, confessing, or something.

Roy was quiet. Cooper looked at him and smiled. "You don't realize the kind of shit you are in, do you? Now I would rather go catch murderers, but the new District Attorney hates people who make money. See, he thinks because guys like you cheat other people of their hard-earned money, they become poor and have no food to put on the table. When they have no food, they either get high, or commit crimes or do what we are seeing these days – get high and commit crimes." Cooper paused. "So now, you see, it all comes back to guys like you. If we take criminals like you out, we automatically reduce violent crimes. Isn't that just amazing?"

Roy looked up to Cooper. "But I have not done anything wrong. I have never broken the law," Roy paused. "Insider trading is a serious offence and I have never even broken parking rules!" said Roy, bewildered.

Cooper looked straight at Roy. "See, I think you are a very convincing man, but I have what we call evidence, and for some reason, it just doesn't support all the gibberish you just said."

Roy just looked straight at Cooper. "Let me show ya, son. I mean you did a great job at hiding it, but we got some great computer men. They can dig corpses – electronic corpses – no matter where they are," Cooper said proudly.

Cooper in his twenty-year-long career had been a traditional detective and relied on real evidence. However, DNA and then computer evidence had now taken an important role in all investigations. Even though he had his Jurassic methods, he was amazed by the use of technology and his 'Computer Men'.

Cooper pulled out a folder from his leather briefcase and dumped it on the table. He placed a sheet of paper before Roy. "See, this is what we call a trace route; it tells us that you were in touch with a firm called Piso Capital."

The confusion was just piling on. "What is this Piso Capital?" asked Roy.

Cooper smiled. "Like a genie, I knew that a genius like you will ask this very question. So let me present your highness with another paper, discovered by the same Computer Men."

Cooper pushed multiple sheets of trade records. Roy looked at the sheet and his eyes popped out. "This is a set up. I placed those trades with a broker. I had no idea who the other party was," Roy blasted.

"Genie coming to life again." Cooper smiled as he pulled a little disc out of the folder. He bent down and pulled a laptop from his bag, inserting the disc into it. The voice graph started flickering on the laptop. "Hmm, this is supposed to be the Lady Gaga CD. I don't know what is wrong with her," Cooper put on his reading glasses and started looking at the laptop.

"You don't have the volume turned on," said Roy.

Cooper looked up at him as his glasses had slipped to the lower anchor of the nose. "Volume, volume…Ah. Found it," smiled Cooper. "See, now *you* are the genie."

Roy's voice echoed in the room, "Sorry about that. Hey. 4.95 cents is my offer. The price is firm. There has to be at least one firm out there. Look harder man." The voice was undoubtedly his. He slowly leaned back on his chair. *This does not look good.*

"See I told ya, son. My Computer Men are good. So, now, confession time?" quipped Cooper.

The door slammed open and Monica and a lawyer barged in. "I'd like you to leave, right now. I need to talk to my client," the lawyer said.

Cooper turned back and looked at the lawyer standing tall at over six feet and dressed in a black pristine suit. The lawyer stared right in Cooper's eyes with brimming confidence. Cooper nodded and walked out of the room.

"And I need video and audio feed turned off," demanded the lawyer.

Monica ran and hugged Roy. She was in tears. Roy tried very hard to control himself but a drop of tear slipped through the shackles of his mental restraint.

"I'll take care of you, Roy. My name is Neil Werline and I am a partner at Werline, Cooper Law firm," said Neil.

"What happened to Joyce?" asked Roy.

"Joyce is on sabbatical," said Monica.

Roy shook hands with Neil and discussed in detail what had happened today and the day that the trade was placed. Neil listened carefully, feverishly noting down all the details on his leather binder notebook.

"Well, luckily today is Thursday, so we can apply for bail tomorrow. Bond for charges like these is generally on the higher side of around one to two million dollars." Neil looked at Roy and Monica. "Is that gonna be OK with you?" Roy answered affirmatively. "Good then. See you tomorrow morning. Not to mention, I am deeply sorry for tonight. It's past the court timing and tonight you will have to remain in holding. The good news is that you are at the white collar crime holding unit, so no drug dealers and addicts." Neil smiled.

Roy quenched his lips and looked at Monica. "It's going to be okay. Don't worry about me. Just take care of yourself." Monica was still teary-eyed. He hugged her again. "Don't stress out. This is a big misconception and I'll sort it out." Roy stopped short of talking about pregnancy. He didn't want to have the first conversation about their baby in an FBI holding room. *This is not how I want to remember my baby.*

An officer knocked on the door.

"It's time to leave now," Neil said softly.

Monica slowly moved away, and then their arms drifted away too. The balmy comfort of her touch was being snatched from him, breaking Roy's heart into a million pieces. *What did I do to deserve this?*

The soft sound of giggles reverberated in the college library. "I am sorry...just a weird...never mind, forget about it," Sona said to a bewildered Raju. Sona had totally lost her focus. The bookworm had transformed into a beautiful fluttery butterfly.

It had begun to unsettle Raju's buried feelings. He wanted her to stop...to study with him. That was the only thing he was good at. The only thing he could talk about for hours with her. There wasn't any awkwardness for whacked attempts to start a fun conversation only to realize that Sona almost always failed to get the humour in them. *I don't have the adventures or the tales of Shammi.* Self-pity was the only constant feeling Raju had felt for as long as he could remember, but now was the time when the genesis of revolt within was peeling out of morph. *But I have my genius, my intelligence, my selfless love.*

"We have our semester exams in four months," said Raju in an eerily serious tone.

"You know what Shammi would say to that?" Sona curiously questioned him back.

Raju shrugged his shoulders.

"He would say, have fun for three and slog it out for one. It's like buy one, get three free," said Sona with a smile.

"This is not a washing powder offer," murmured Raju.

Sona laughed out. "Comeback and all, nice!" said she as she threw her bag on her shoulders and waved Raju goodbye.

Raju watched her walk out of the library. His eyes were fixated on Sona and even though the intensity of his stare would gross out any girl, in his heart he had the cleanest and most innocent thoughts.

Sona hopped down the staircase to the campus area and rolled into the gang comprising Shammi, Bumpy and their friends.

As night reigned in, music blared from a giant speaker at the night club. The entire gang was jumping to the peppy hip hop tunes or as Biggy Smalls would have called it - 'toones'. Sona danced with the group for a bit but then found a spot away from the speakers and stood there resting against the solid circular beam.

"They call me stone-hearted too," a stud tried to start off a conversation with Sona.

"I'm not interested," said Sona.

The flagrant stud wouldn't give up. "Me too. I act..."

"Really?" Shammi stepped in looking straight in the eyes of the stud.

"Hey man, I am so sorry," the stud's tone had taken a complete one-eighty degree turn.

"I really am. Ahh..." he looked up to Sona with a shit scared expression. "...ma'am. And," he turned to Shammi, "I didn't know she is your girlfriend."

The stud sped off the spot, disappearing into the smoggy club as Sona slowly snuggled to Shammi.

"You are a *pakka gunda*," said Sona mischievously.

"Arey, not at all. We have mutual respect," said Shammi trying to steer away from the topic. "That's all."

She looked at Shammi in the eyes and nodded her head with a sarcastic smile.

"Do you want to get some fresh air?" she was feeling suffocated in the packed club.

Shammi held her in front of him, joined his arms around her making a ring of protection and steered her through the packed club, exiting out in the moonlit windy night.

"Maybe we crossed paths, sometime, somewhere, not even aware of each other, until destiny brought us together," Sona spoke from her heart.

Shammi stretched back on the street paver they were sitting on. "You believe in destiny? That you, me, sitting here, is all destiny?"

Sona looked at Shammi. "They teach us in medical school that this destiny and all is crap…"

Shammi looked at Sona with a curious expression.

"And maybe in future it will change, but for now, I have blind faith in destiny," Sona said with a bright smile. "And you?"

"I haven't thought about it, per se. But I'll go with you," said Shammi caressing hair streaks away from Sona's eyes. "And if we don't go inside, destiny has rain planned for us." Thunder rumbled in the sky above them, following brief flashes of lightning.

"I don't want to go inside," said Sona innocently. "Can we just walk?"

Shammi stood up and Sona grabbed his hand to pull herself up. Both started to walk on the street, side by side, carefully fighting against the magnetic attraction of the heart. A big raindrop fell on their hands. Hands shrugged the drop off and fingers gently touched each other, moving in the rhythm of a piano, apprehensive at first but then and locked in. A moment of tender truth was beautified by the monsoons of the city subsuming two young souls.

They stopped, took a step back, then two steps forward; body symphony harmonizing with the wet rain. The walls were fast crumbling, and melted away with the tender hug. And how could it stop when the passion was overflowing with the rain. Their lips met warmly, and exploded with passion.

Sona hastily pulled back, her hands slipping out of Shammi's. Her heartbeat was pounding off the chart, her body shuddering in the aftermath of the passionate kiss. Shammi looked at her; his eyes had turned moist. She turned back and started walking away, faster and faster. Shammi ran behind her and closing in, curled his arms around her bare waist, softly tugging her body to his.

Sona's mind was paralyzed by the mystical sensations her heart was dancing to. Shammi pulled her closer, as rain poured down profusely, inspiring the brazenness of elation. All inhibitions drained away, and their warm tongues skirted and rolled, heedless to the incursion of rain. Sona just let it go. The time, the place, the setting, all were seconded and she wrapped herself in the blanket of his strong arms. Shammi cuddled her in his arms, closed his eyes, relishing the moment. The feeling was different. *Maybe I have experienced this before, but I have never felt it before.*

Inside the wet walls of the majestic sculpture, the morning session court was busy with lawyers walking in and out of offices, judges presiding over hearings, witnesses wandering around to find the correct court room and accused being escorted by officers to hearings.

Roy in an orange jumpsuit emerged on the steps of the court. Cooper, Moon and a couple of uniformed officers hastily made their way up the long steep stairs to the courthouse, trying to fight off the light showers. The media outlets were already parked outside the court, impatiently following the entourage.

"Roy, do you think you will have additional charges?" yelled a white female reporter dressed in a yellow raincoat.

"Officer Cooper, we have come to know that Roy worked at Goldman Sachs. Do you think the FBI will look at their books as well," a Latino young lady quizzed, her voice getting muffled by her blue rain poncho.

"No comments," said Cooper as Roy kept walking with his head bowed.

All of a sudden, the paparazzi took a detour and with the same fierce force rushed towards a man, who came to the forefront of the courthouse, moved his arms straight up front and locked his fingers together. An assistant quickly opened an umbrella and pulled it right over the man. A team stood right behind him, covered in an army of colliding umbrellas. The frenzied media halted right in front of the six-feet-one-inch tall man, well-built with short, curly hair that he gelled back, light skin and fizzy green eyes.

"Mr. Karara, you have been a crusader of Wall Street for financial crime. Do you think you will win this case too?" asked a female reporter.

"I want to tell the entire country that these people in suits, who use unfair means to make money, do not make money; they rob your money and I'll continue my crusade as long as these grave crimes are being committed," announced Karara, propaganda style.

"Is this a coincidence that your heritage is Indian and ever since you have joined the office, most of those accused of financial crimes are from South Asia?" another female reporter demanded an answer.

"Shawna, I know you always have a controversial question," Karara looked at the reporter. "But here is my take – I'll take cases as they are discovered. It could be a South Asian, Chinese, White or Latino." Karara put on a smile. "Thank you everyone." Mr. Karara turned around and disappeared inside the court.

"Mr. Karara...is this going to be the poster case for your campaign for the post of Governor?" A reporter shouted.

"We don't comment on rumours." His battery of aides was just getting bulldozed by the reporters.

Roy looked at Karara. He had seen his pictures in the newspapers as the crusader of Wall Street. Roy had always appreciated his effort. In many ways, Karara was like Roy; both shared zero tolerance for anyone who didn't play by the rules. But now it got him thinking - *what if any one or all of the guys sent in by Karara were like me too? Framed?*

The courtroom was packed with people. The security man announced that Judge Harpe was arriving. "Everyone rise." Everyone rose. The judge walked in and took his seat, followed by everyone taking theirs.

Roy sat in the stand and looked at the audience. Monica sat there in the front row in a formal dark black suit. Neil and Karara took their respective stands. The court was in session now.

Karara bulldozed Neil from the get-go with his exemplary lawyer skills abetted by exaggerated theatrics.

Trying to save himself and his client Roy from this bombarding of wickedly designed allegations, Neil jumped in the ring with his own argument. "We can save the theatrics for the trial. This is a bail hearing, your honour."

Karara shot back. "But there will be no trial, if the defendant has left the country," raising laughs across the courtroom. Neil sinking in his boots tried a failed attempt to interrupt Karara, but he continued, "Your honor, in the past year itself, he spent eight months outside the country."

Neil marched forward and argued, "An integral part of Mr. Roy's job is to travel and that can't be held against him."

"But now he is accused of a grave crime," Karara shot back.

"Alright, Mr. Karara and Mr. Werline. The bail is set to ten million dollars," Judge Harpe wrapped up the hearing.

Roy was speechless. Just last night the dapper Neil had assured him that the bail wouldn't be set at more than two million dollars, and now he was looking at the mind-boggling number of ten million dollars on top of the thousands of dollar, he would owe Neil as legal fees.

Monica and Neil rushed to Roy. Neil smiled and congratulated Roy.

"But you said that the bail would be one or two million dollars," Roy was disappointed.

"Roy. Listen to me. This is a victory. I can assure you this is a good deal," Neil shot back.

"What victory? The guy completely shot down my credibility. The jury would already be biased," said Roy. "I would, if I was on the jury."

"Well. Then it's good news that you are not on the jury," Neil said sarcastically, putting on his fake smile.

"But we don't have ten million dollars," Monica tried to come back to the main issue. "What are we going to do now?"

Roy looked at her. "It's okay. I can sell my Goldman Sachs shares from my last job. I never cashed out. I guess I was saving for this one." Monica heaved a sigh of relief and hugged Roy.

"See, all good. I told ya," said Neil to Monica and Roy.

Garbed in his expensive perp-walk suit, Roy stepped outside the police building. His hair was dishevelled and a stubble had appeared on his otherwise clean-shaven face.

Cooper whistled. Roy looked at him. Cooper and his partner were seated in the black SUV parked at the footsteps of the building. Cooper signalled that he would be watching him. Roy stepped out of the shade into the falling rain and climbed down the stairs to the parked SUV. Roy leaned on the car window and looked at Cooper in the eyes.

Cooper was confused. "I didn't do it. You seem like an honest and intelligent person," Roy said.

"That is what Bonnie said," Cooper said sarcastically.

"One day, you will believe me," said Roy and then he turned and walked away. Cooper closely watched as a drenched Roy walked away in the rain.

"Yo, do you think that the whole Karara targeting only South Asians is true?" asked Moon.

"That's bull. He even captured the Gambino family," said Cooper.

"But there was like one guy left in the Gambino family who he caught, and all that Gambino guy did was some check fraud," said Moon.

"Let's go," Cooper told his partner, dismissing his comment as the SUV rolled away from the police building, trudging through the busy streets of Manhattan.

The mellow red gaze of the sun slowly dispersed into the endless body of blithe waves at the curvaceous far end of the boundless ocean. Almost magically, the city of chaos and mayhem was waking up to nature's transcendental realm.

Sona's parent's bungalow was nestled in the placidity of the city. Her dad's mouth was wide open as he slept tucked under the white comforter. Sona's mom slept on her back, her face calm, energizing her cells to run her home for yet another day. She was the cornerstone of the house and a confidante that kept the entire family together. Always ready to lend her shoulder to cry or rest your head on, or a keen ear to patiently hear frustrated souls vent their troubles, and always the fiery tigress ready to do everything to protect her family.

A slight thud dribbled in through the cracks of the otherwise airtight window. Sona's father turned to the other side, slimed his lips and continued to sleep away. Sona's mother woke up; her big eyes were wide open like a hawk. She turned around and moved her arms to wake up Sona's dad, but stopped short. *Maybe it's a cat. Let me check myself.* She alighted from the bed, put on her fluffy night sandals and walked out.

The windowpane of Sona's bedroom opened with a creek. A hand clawed on to the window frame, and Shammi's face emerged, peeking in the room. The room of Sona's door opened and her mom looked around. Sona woke up and sleepily looked at her mom. "What happened mommy?"

"Nothing beta. Just wanted to see if you wanted tea," Sona's mother didn't want Sona to be bothered.

"No mommy. I want to sleep," Sona covered her face with the blanket.

The window was open. Sona's mum pulled and latched it, kissed her daughter's forehead and walked away, carefully closing the door behind her.

A slight knock resonated again. Sona threw her blanket off and sat up on the bed. "What now, mommy?" she said with childlike anger.

But her mother was not in the room.

She carefully traced the slight knocking to the window and right then Shammi peeked up. Sona smiled, rushed to the window and opened it. Shammi quickly jumped in the room and just stood there with a big smile. Hesitantly, he raised his arms.

"You are mad," said Sona smilingly and slid her hands in his arms. "You have a special love for jumping in and out of windows," she said with a giggle. "Tell me right now if you have a past of some *chor* that I need to be aware of."

Shammi merely smiled. "By the way, how did you know that I wished you were the first face I saw today?" said Sona.

"I had a dream," said Shammi, mocking the rhetoric of Martin Luther King.

"Get ready," Shammi's tone was full of energy.

"Get ready for what?" quipped Sona.

"It's a surprise. Trust me. This will be another experience that you will remember forever," replied Shammi.

"But...today..." Sona exhibited signs of discomfort, but Shammi immediately shot it down.

"Okay baba... Now go and wait outside before mom finds out about you," said Sona.

"Not bad if she finds out. I can ask her to come along as well," Shammi said playfully.

"Haaa, right! I don' think you fully realize the repercussions," said Sona and pushed Shammi back towards the window.

"Beta, are you OK?" Sona's mother yelled from outside.

"What happened?" Sona's dad sprung out of the bed.

"Whoopsie…" said Shammi as he quickly ducked and slid out of the window, disappearing just in time before Sona's mother and father both barged in.

"Everything is okay. I need to go to school," said Sona.

"School?" quizzed Sona's dad.

"Yup," said Sona with a straight face.

"Okay, I love you beta," he said as he walked out of the room.

Sona's mother smiled. "Okay. I'll make something for you quickly then."

"Nope, mommy. I am already late. Now go and let me get ready," Sona said with a pout.

Sona's mother smiled and started walking away, but not without noticing the window that was no longer locked and the dusty boot print right next to the window. However, she quickly looked away and walked out.

The classic red Maruti Zen zoomed through the eastern express highway to the exotic Alibaug. Sona was still sleepy but her face looked fresh as a melon, infected by Shammi's cheerfulness. Her love for him was spreading fast in her veins. For now, Shammi wasn't just a guy she was infatuated with; she had begun to care for him, and wanted to be with him. Nothing was mundane when they were together; even the silence between them was a treat to her throbbing heart. Today, however, was different. She was with him, but there was something that was keeping a part of her away.

Almost two hours later, Shammi and Sona stood on the Alibaug fort wall overlooking the ocean. A swanky car pulled in, followed by a couple of trucks. On the docking stand, men undocked the sleek and shining Yacht fitted with Volvo Penta engines. They carefully pushed the Yacht down the docking stand on to the water. The other truck rolled down two jet skis on to the water. "Whose boats are these?" asked Sona.

"My dad's," replied Shammi.

"But I thought you were banished?" quizzed Sona.

"Technically, yes. But I didn't want you to miss this. The moon will be fabulous to watch from over the water. I wanted you to experience this in a way you have never experienced before. And for that, my love, I can take the risk of irking anyone, even my father," said Shammi boastfully.

"I don't think it's a good idea to irk your parents," said Sona rather seriously.

Like any other time Shammi's wrongful boasting was going against him and he had to quickly salvage the situation. "Besides, we haven't used these boats for years. He doesn't even know that we have these."

Sona continued to look at Shammi.

"There is a reason Bumpy got these. He is my *bakra* on standby in case anything went south," said Shammi with a wide grin.

Sona smiled but still shook her head in disagreement with her classic comfort line.

Bumpy and gang approached closer to Shammi and Sona.

"Are you ready for the ultimate thrill?" Shammi turned to Sona.

Sona looked up at him. "Maybe, but what are we doing?" She could figure out why the Jet Ski was there, but she was clueless as to what ultimate thrill the yacht would bring. She decided to play along. She put on her smile and inquisitively asked, "Jet Ski?"

Shammi smiled. "Yup. And more…much more…" He held her hand and ran down the fort to the water. The entire gang excitedly descended down to the boat. The boat sped away holding the Jet Skis aboard the deck.

The swanky yacht sped away and stopped in the middle of the water.

Ropes were pulled out and the set up was ready for parasailing. Shammi got Sona in the gear and together they scaled the dizzying height while tied to the yacht. The experience was so liberating and thrilling that Sona was no longer just dipping her toes in the water, she was completely at ease with it. Especially with Shammi's warm company.

The clock seemed to have ticked faster than usual. A bright day followed by a mellow evening, and now the night was setting in. The Captain and marine support team were folding back the equipment on to the yacht.

Shammi looked at Sona sitting on the upper deck, oblivious to anything around her. He hopped on to the upper deck and slowly held Sona from behind, wrapping his arms around her.

"Look at the moon. It's so pretty... and look at these tides, getting all roiled up looking at the beauty of the moon," said Shammi.

"Like they want to hold the moon, love it... but, they are tied by the force of nature, tied to the ground," said Sona hypnotized.

Shammi looked at Sona. "What's wrong? You look tired. Not feeling well? Shall I get you something to eat?"

Sona looked at him and smiled. "Feeling much better now. With all the daring stunts you made me do, do you think I'll have any appetite," she patted his cheeks.

"Can you do me a favour?" she asked Shammi. "Can you get me a bottle of water?"

"I am disappointed," said Shammi in his usual prank-laden tone. "I thought you would say a bottle of beer. Right away, my love," Shammi hopped on to the lower deck and fetched a bottle of water.

Sona tried to open the bottle but her fingers slipped away. "Even the bottle loves you. Doesn't want to let go of you," said Shammi. Sona looked up to him.

Shammi opened the bottle in one go. The weather was changing, and there was a nip in the air now. Sona put her scarf on her head and wrapped it around her neck. She looked beautiful. "Indulge me..." whispered Sona. "Feed me today."

Shammi smiled and slowly poured a bit of water in her mouth. The water fell on her mouth and snaked out through her neck disappearing under her poncho. Shammi couldn't help but watch.

The wind blew in. Sona tried to hold her dupatta but it fell over, hanging on the deck surface. She quickly kneeled down and got her dupatta back. She stood back up and looked at Shammi. "Can we go home?"

"Of course," said Shammi. "But first let's eat something. I promise no more daring stunts that will make you throw up."

Shammi called out to the Captain. "Captain Singh. Let's get to the shore. Do we have dinner?"

"Yes sir. It will be another fifteen minutes to the shore. Dinner is ready to be served," said Captain Singh.

Sona and Shammi went down to the living room cabin. The table was set with five-star dinner. The entire gang and crew gorged on the dinner as the boat turned and made its way to the dock.

Sleepy Sona was visibly worn out. Shammi lifted her and carried her to the car. Sona smiled and cuddled up to him. The car whisked from the deserted roads to the bustle of the city. "Relax. Go back to sleep. When you sleep, the beauty of your face is breathtaking." Shammi meant every word of it.

Sona was trying to fight off the sleep; she closed her eyes and smiled. "Talk to me."

"Ok. So tell me. What is the one thing that you want to do, when you grow up?"

"I want to provide care to the needy. To the homeless, to the soldiers in war, to children..." Sona's tone was slowing down as she slipped into sleep.

"Why?" asked Shammi

"Because...that is rewarding...." Sona's voice was barely audible. He looked at her, not wanting to disturb the serenity of her sound sleep, the aura surrounding her innocent face. Shammi looked outside. Women all decked up with *thalis* in their hands were walking down the street. And like a thunderous lightning it struck Shammi. Sona's reluctance to come for the trip today was for a reason. Something that his juvenile mind couldn't fathom even after her skilful act to stay away from food all day, that was, until the moon had set in and she had tricked him into feeding her water right after she had pretended to hold her flying dupatta and also in the process looked at his face through it and then at the moon.

His teary eyes looked at the innocuous face of Sona and he fell in love with her, all over again. He had now become complete... But it wasn't to last forever. The dark etching lines of worry had invaded the mushy dreams. A duel between his heart and his objectivity had begun.

For heart is for fools and genius is no fool, Thakursaab's words drummed in his thoughts. Shammi had been taught to be a man. He had been raised like one; always forced to deal with challenges – in the form of sports, martial arts, debates. A deliberate design to condition his conscience into staying off the foolhardy path of emotions and following the heart.

He was fast getting sucked in the sinkhole within. It felt like his soul was cut in half. The dark side of his objective mind ruthless to any incursion of mushiness; and the vulnerable heart, violently gravitating to the tune of love.

A glimpse of her and the innocence of Sona was like a soft beam of light, steering his foggy mind away from the battleground to placidity. The soothing sight was one Shammi wished never went away, for this kept him away from the chaos of his own mind.

The sound of his watch beeping at midnight nudged him. *Is it midnight already? How will she go back home?* He drove towards his Bandra apartment instead.

The car came to a halt. The watchman hurriedly opened the main gate and greeted Shammi with a smile loaded with overtones of dilemma.

"Lift is out of order, sir," said the guard with a hesitant tone.

Shammi looked up at him. "Who told you to say that? Was it my Dad or that idiot Makhmal?" Shammi's expression was not the one to mess with.

"No sir, nothing like that. All lifts are down, even the ones going to other floors," the guard was visibly scared.

Shammi's gaze hadn't gone off. After a few moments, Shammi got off the car. "Okay. You will go before me to open the apartment. I'll follow you," he again looked at the guard. "We'll take the stairs." Shammi said it firmly, enunciating every word very clearly.

The guard tried his best to not look at Shammi and rushed away through the staircase.

Shammi followed the guard up the stairs, carefully carrying Sona in his arms. Like a dutiful army man, he climbed up thirty floors carrying Sona in his arms, sate to the brim even at the slightest glimpse of Sona's peaceful face hiding behind her unfurled hair.

In his apartment, he put Sona on the bed and threw himself on the chair next to it. The apartment had been restored to its original beauty. The smudge on the 'Reclining Odalisque' had been erased. Everything was neatly in place and all of Shammi's junk was trashed away. Shammi, however, was oblivious to anything around him, for his focus was just the beautiful sight of Sona, cuddled in the cosy comforter.

The fight between his mind and his heart hadn't given up either. The forbidden state of cruel objectivity was stewing up; striking a match, lighting up the incubation of anxiety. *It was never like this before. Why? Why? Why did I have to fall in love?*

$\mathcal{A}$ yellow cab stopped to wavering soaked hands of Roy. He slumped in the back seat, pulled his head back, traversing the maze of deep thoughts as splashes of rain sprayed all around the cab, humming through the eastern expressway.

"Everyone must wonder, why is it that the most catastrophic hurricane to hit US cities have always been named after women, even since 1979, whereas the National Oceanic and Atmospheric Administration equally alternates between men and women names?" the faded radio voice echoed in the background.

Roy opened his eyes, "Could you please turn up the volume a notch?" he softly asked the cab driver.

"Hurricane Lucy is expected to make a landfall in the late evening along the east coast with possible torrential rains to the entire tri-state region," announced the weatherman on the radio.

It was fate's addiction to irony that on the day the second hurricane of the season was to hit east coast, Roy was dealing with the aftermath of his trade betting on the first hurricane Kay that had hit east coast barely a couple of months ago. Back then, he was tucked away in the cosy company of Monica. Monsoons notoriously rip open the deepest emotions within humans, and Roy was currently sucked into the dark tunnels within.

The train of thoughts was taking Roy through a dreamy path. Nothing made sense, yet everything seemed connected. The pregnancy, the arrest, the accusations, and the media frenzy. It was like a puzzle that he had to solve. *Why is this happening, and, why to me? But I need to first make sure that Monica is okay. She is pregnant and the stress of my arrest couldn't have come at a worst time. I need to make sure that she is shielded from anything that happens from here onwards. I need to persuade her to go someplace...someplace far.*

He took his phone out and sent a message to Monica. "Babe, where are you? I need to talk to you. I am out." Roy clicked send and was waiting for the screen to pop with her reply. But instead, the phone buzzed with an alarm saying: less than 2% battery left. *Oh man. Really? Even the phone is gonna fuck me up?* And within seconds, the phone went dark. *Great. Fuck me, now.* He threw his head back on the headrest and closed his eyes.

The cab slowed down and stopped at a curbside. Roy got off the cab and walked up to his building. "Hello, Mr. Roy. Good afternoon," said Willis very sympathetically, yet very professionally.

The elevator bell rang and Roy squished in the busy elevator. Everyone around him was trying to look the other way, yet trying to look from the corner of their eyes to see if this was the man whose face had been splashed all over the media.

He was beginning to live with the fact that the embarrassment of being the infamous money swindler was here to stay...at least, till he cleared his name. *I gotta get used to this look, people staring like I have just been set free from a zoo. Like I am some serial offender. Whatever happened to the whole "presumed innocent" right? Oh well, those bastards snatched that away with their sleazy media and PR tactic.* Till the previous night he had been an anonymous New Yorker who could roam freely anywhere. But the last eighteen hours had changed everything, everywhere.

Roy got off the elevators and went straight to his apartment. He searched his pockets for the keys. *Ah, it's in my bag at Monica's. Damn.* Roy chose the stairs this time, sure he wouldn't be able to endure being stared at and watched uncomfortably anymore.

Roy emerged in the drizzly streets and fast hopped his way to Monica's building a couple of blocks away. He didn't have keys to her apartment either, but he knew where Monica kept her emergency-spare-key. He moved the stone pebbles around the terracotta flower pot at the entrance door, located a black key holder in the shape of a rock, opened it and took the key out.

The celebration balloons had retraced back from the ceiling, the Archimedes' principle of helium was like an apt reflection of Roy's own inner feelings. He set his phone to charge and set coffee to brew in the machine. As he waited for the coffee, he sat on the kitchen table staring at the trash can. *It was in this trash that I got to know about the pregnancy.* Roy stared away into infinity, with the worldly illusion that he was looking at the trash can. He noticed a few pieces of torn paper scattered around the trash can. The bits of paper bore a peculiar inscription that caught Roy's attention.

He hastily dug out the remaining torn pieces, and placed them on to the kitchen table. Roy gazed at the torn pieces that he had assembled and dashed back to the trash looking for more pieces, but there was nothing in it. *Where is the rest of the trash? Did the FBI take it? Think...Think...No...the search warrant was only for my apartment, so they could not have searched Monica's. Okay... Chute...the trash must still be in the chute.*

Bright sunlight pierced through the balcony glass door lighting up the grand bedroom. The soft touch of Sona's hand caressed Shammi's face from his forehead to his lips. He lazily opened his eyes with a smile; quite contrary to the multi-faceted dilemma that was still pacing back and forth in his mind.

"Surprisingly, my mom didn't call me even once," said Sona, sparkling with innocence and mischief.

Shammi yawned. "I actually texted her last night, saying that you were with me and that you wanted to have sex real bad," he said while casually stretching his body.

For a second she was startled, but then a smile from Shammi gave away his joke. She quickly scrolled through her cell phone and looked at the text Shammi had sent. "Mom, just got done with work and didn't realize it's past midnight. I'll sleep over at Aarti's and get home tomorrow. Sleep tight."

"Nice...Genius...! Do you think my mom will believe this?" said Sona in true amazement. "Never in my nineteen years have I once told her to sleep tight!"

"Well, she didn't call you," said Shammi while brushing his teeth. "That makes me believe she likes being told to sleep tight." He smiled showing off his toothpaste lathered teeth.

"*Achha baba,* your plan was pure genius," Sona said teasingly.

Shammi stepped out of the bathroom to a delicious breakfast that Sona had cooked.

"Finish it up and I'll see you later," Sona kissed Shammi on his forehead and scooted to the door.

"We just established that your mom is okay. So why the rush?" quipped Shammi walking behind her.

"I know. I know. But...," Sona turned back. "Just like I know you more than you do, I know my mother. It would be better for me to go home now." Sona smiled, and pressed the button of the elevator in the living room.

"Oh, the elevator is not working," said Shammi, and right then, the elevator button glowed up the down arrow sign as the French elevator doors slid open. Sona waved from inside the elevator as Shammi ranted, "Do you know I carried you up thirty floors' worth of stairs last night?"

Her lips moved ambiguously to the rhyme of "I love you" as the elevator doors finally closed shut.

Shammi ruffled his hair and smiled. He stood there looking at the lovely breakfast Sona had prepared for him. But today he didn't care for food either. His mind was juggling dozens of thoughts of what had happened the previous night. *Was it real?* He was happy with her, very happy indeed. He looked forward to his time with Sona; he would count every passing second until he could meet her. But now he also felt nervous, confused, riddled. *Is this what it means to fall in love?*

The lift sound chimed again. Shammi was oblivious to any noise around him. A sound resonated louder. "Baba...Baba...."

Shammi's spell was broken by a hand on his shoulder. He slowly turned back. Makhmal was standing behind him. "Thakursaab will see you at the kothi."

The words fell on Shammi's ears like a faint echo after waking up from a coma. He calmly turned his head back and stared away at the dining table.

Thakursaab sat by the pool on the plush wicker chair, his shades reflecting the sun drowning in the blue pool.

"I don't know what to say," Thakursaab took his shades out. "Makhmal said you went back to the apartment, and that too with a girl," his tone was full of pity.

Shammi stood with his head partially lowered, not listening and still deep in thought about his relationship with Sona. *This is the first girl that I have not slept with. Still I don't feel the need for that victorious feeling. It is not about sex.* "Damn! Fuck!" exclaimed Shammi.

"Oh...I didn't mean to. My deepest apologies Dad," Shammi tried to diffuse the awkwardness.

"I don't know how much you care about me. But your old fragile grandma is here," Thakursaab frowned at Shammi while turning towards Mataji.

Mataji, wrapped in a crisp white sari, had dozed off on the plush wicker chaise by the pool. Her mouth was half open. Her hand hung off the chaise, dangling like a hanging pole in the middle of an army of empty scattered bloody Martini glasses, all drained of every drop of alcohol out of it.

Shammi was expressionless. Thakursaab was still looking at Mataji. He then turned back at him. Shammi quickly gathered his wits, "I apologize for my behaviour, but the truth is I wanted you to catch me at the apartment."

Thakursaab was attentive, silent. He knew Shammi had more to say.

Sona stepped off the turtle shaped auto-rickshaw. She took a deep breath and waited a few minutes to calm herself. *It's okay. Remember the last time you were at Aarti's. Just remember that night and repeat all the details. No chances of error. No chances*

of being caught. Chanting her thoughts repeatedly, Sona slowly entered her home.

She closed the door behind her as she walked across the foyer on to the living room. The living room was dark. *Thank god...Looks like they are in the hospital.* She was relieved; her stiff shoulders loosened up as she threw her handbag on the couch. Walking past the living room, she went straight to her room and turned the light on. Her mother and father were sitting on her bed, and now, looking straight into her eyes. Her face turned crimson red. Her vocal cords weren't too kind either. Whatever she spoke came out lathered with stuttering.

"Hi beta. Were you able to finish off your assignment?" Sona's mom asked succinctly.

"Mom, Dad, why are you sitting in my room like this?" Sona said in one go, devoid of any stutter. She had taken total control of her vocal set, even though she was still a bundle of nerves.

"Beta, we are here because this room was empty last night and we were missing you." It was clear Sona's mom didn't want to waste any time dangling around and was ready to get to the point.

"C'mon Mom, it's not like this was the first time I went to Aarti's," Sona was trying her best to diffuse the tension.

"Right beta. But the thing is..." Sona's mom stopped. She was still staring at Sona.

"You called Aarti?!" Sona murmured.

Sona's mom walked up to her. "We need to talk."

Sona followed her mom and sat on the bed. Sona's dad was still sitting on the rocking chair next to the bed.

The soothing sound of water flowing down the stone-carved trinity fall softly echoed the words coming out of Shammi's mouth, "I have a problem," Shammi paused momentarily.

Thakursaab was calm, and his attention undivided.

Shammi looked up and straight in his father's eyes. "I think I have fallen in love." He stopped. "Actually she has fallen in love with me and I think I may have fallen in love too...but, I don't know...Maybe not...But then again...May be," Shammi mumbled away his inner thoughts out loud. He had no idea why he was opening up to his Dad now, of all times.

Thakursaab was still quiet, sitting stoically, listening to every word coming out of his son's mouth with sincere dedication. He was a seasoned man who had handled very complex problems in his life. But this problem was far bigger than any other, perhaps not from the monetary standpoint, but this was his son, his heir and even the smallest detail mattered. He had to let his son vent all that he had in his head and in his heart.

"I have never felt like this about anyone in my life, ever," Shammi continued after a pause. "She brings the best out of me and I bring the best out of her. But is this love? What is love, anyway?" Shammi ranted away.

There was a long silence.

Thakursaab took a deep breath and said, "Love is an imaginary state for people who are confused or have nothing to do in their lives." Thakursaab had a flat tone, minus any emotion or sensitivity. "But, to answer your question directly, I think what you are experiencing is normal. You are questioning your feelings, not because you want reassurance but because you realize that your feelings are incorrect, out of place, irrelevant, unnecessary; at least at this point in your life."

Shammi was listening attentively. "But what if she feels the same?"

"In all likelihood, she would feel the same," said Thakursaab patting on Shammi's shoulders. "But as a responsible man, it is your responsibility to talk to her and make sure she realizes that these are immature thoughts propelled by a make-believe atmosphere stemming from your fondness for each other."

"But it's not make-believe, dad," Shammi was sure.

"What is make-believe?" Thakursaab quipped rhetorically. "I'll tell you."

Sona's dad sat sternly on the rocking chair, rocking back and forth. He hadn't uttered a single word yet. Sona looked at him with her pitiful, innocent eyes, trying to pull the sympathy card. She was hoping it would work because if it didn't, she was in a lot of trouble. Her dad was her saviour, saving his little girl from the tyranny of her mother, saving her when she would throw vegetables under the table, or sneak out to a rock concert. But today, he was quiet, grim, disappointed.

"I'll tell you a story," Sona's mom started off. "There once was a dusty print. A dusty print of size ten shoes." She paused. "Size ten men's shoes, that mysteriously appeared in the princess's bedroom. The evil mother of the princess was doing her routine evil ritual of protecting her daughter when she spotted the dusty print."

Sona was beginning to get teary-eyed.

"The evil mother didn't think much about the print. After all, she trusted her princess. But then that night a strange thing happened – She got a message 'Sleep tight'. That made the evil mother come out of the spell that her own princess daughter had put on her. A spell that made her evil mother dumb and stupid, fuelled by her blind trust in her daughter."

Sona rushed to her father. "Daddy...Mom is being very mean," and she started sobbing.

"Enough now... don't...," Sona's dad broke his rigid look and gestured at her mother to stop.

"Please don't protect her. She needs to face this," Sona's mom was blatant.

"Beta," Sona's Dad looked at her. "We love you and you know that. And we are worried about you because we love you more than anything else in the world."

"But what did I do?" asked Sona still cuddled to her dad.

"Where were you last night?" asked Sona's mother. "And you know that we don't have a problem with your sleepovers. You and Aarti have had sleepovers many times. This conversation is about our trust in you. And the shaky grounds it is now on."

Sona's dad turned to her. "Who is this boy?" He was visibly worried.

Shammi's ears were glued to Thakursaab's words. "Encounters are real. But the situations are make-believe." Thakursaab paused and watched Shammi; he was listening. "The fondness between you and the girl is real, but if for either of you it has reached a point where you think that this relationship is love and possibly marriage after that, then I'll tell you son...that is make-believe. You have to experience so much in life. Bring so much to this world, to the community – like a leader. And, in your role as a leader, you must start by fixing the situation you have at hand – right now!"

Shammi was surprisingly quiet. He was still torn. Shammi loved every second spent with Sona and cared too much about her to hurt her. But the truth was also that the previous night's events had spooked Shammi in a way that he had never felt before. Life thus far had been filled with flings with like-minded girls. Even if some girl got serious about him, he didn't care. But now, it mattered.

"A leader is like a king. He has to make decisions. Now some would be great decisions while others would not be that great; but, a leader must face the situation at hand and must make a decision looking at the long-term impact, even if it brings some disappointments in the short-term," Thakursaab didn't want to hand out a decision to his son, but rather wanted him to take ownership of his life, make his own decisions – nevertheless, the one that he wanted.

"What about you, Dad? Have you ever come across this situation in your life?" asked Shammi in a sombre tone.

Thakursaab smiled. "Why are you standing here today?"

"Because I went to the apartment even though I was banished from it," replied Shammi softly.

"And that, my son, was a decision I had to make for you – my own son. Do you think it made me happy to do that to you? To send you to a hostel? To ask no questions when you decided not to go to Wharton? No.

"But, I wanted you to understand that actions have consequences. And that it is our job to direct the ones we care about in a direction that will make them a better person." Thakursaab ruffled Shammi's hair.

Shammi's tender age was no match to Thakursaab's experience. But that also meant that his mind's processing power wasn't sharp enough to digest everything that he had just heard. His innocent heart rhymed to the tunes of sona's charm and love. *What the hell! Does it even matter? I am overthinking all of this. Love isn't an appointment that you can schedule at your convenience. I am lucky that it has come in my life. In a way that is so beautiful and innocent.*

"Take your time. Sleep over it. Don't make hasty decisions," Thakursaab said.

Sona was beginning to realize that there was no point in hiding the truth anymore. Her mom was right. Their trust in her was on shaky grounds. Aarti had come to her rescue even when she had been out with Shammi, sneaking into his hostel. But for better or worse, it was about time she came clean with her parents.

"I was with Shammi," Sona whispered. "He is doing his engineering," said Sona.

"Which college?" came the prompt question from her Dad.

Sona had slowly crawled away from her dad as she sat on the rug, holding her hands together around her folded legs. "Same, Ricochet."

"Why would you hide it from us? We..." Sona's mom was disappointed.

Sona's dad quietly signalled her to be quiet. "Beta, we are not ancient people. We understand that you will have friends, even though I personally don't want you to be friends with this boy – any boy for that matter. But, that is beside the point." He turned to her and held her hands. "We as your parents are worried. We want to have visibility in your life. We are scared too, that you might end up in a situation that we could have protected you from. And..."

Sona laid her face on his hands and started crying.

"That's why we would like to meet this boy Shammi." The clog of anxiety was quickly draining out as a faint smile grew across her rosy pink cheeks. She looked up.

"Is that fair?" asked her Dad.

Sona nodded her head in agreement.

"And why would you Google Karwa Chauth? You are nineteen years old, for god's sake," Sona's mom was still very distressed.

"It's okay. She is a kid," Sona's father tried to move away from that topic. His soft spot for their daughter had taken over his wife's feelings of anxiety and anger. He had one and only one goal in mind – to meet the boy she was hanging out with. If he found out that the boy was a jerk, he was more than capable of handling the boy in ways that would not be very good for Shammi. His mission was to protect Sona.

"Okay, Daddy," Sona said with a smile. "I'll call Shammi," Sona's excitement was beginning to seep out of the concealed persona she had put on for her parents. All she wanted to do at this moment was to go in a quiet corner, blast out loud music, throw her hands in the air and scream out loud, really loud, telling everyone in the world that this is what love feels like...like an ecstasy cloud around her, transforming every bit of her into something magical, something beautiful, something special; like a princess in the spell of a wizard.

"Why don't you try now?" asked Sona's dad.

"Is there any particular, ahem, day?" A smiling Sona whispered.

"Within seven days," her Dad replied promptly. "I hope that's fine?"

Sona smiled and nodded. Her parents stood up and slowly walked out of the room, as she got busy texting her special friend. She carefully closed the door, kept the phone on her dressing table and hopped on to her bed, turned on the music system, put her wireless headphones on and threw her hands in the air as her feet started jumping feverishly on the bed. She was on cloud nine. Everything around her was surreal. Like a fairy tale things were falling in place for her first love, her first and only love. Her face glimmered with exuberance even as her eyes flooded with tears of joy. The paradoxical symphony of mankind – tears and happiness had foregone their rivalry, synthesizing away with the tenderness, the euphoria and everything else that was Sona.

Shammi clenched his lips and smiled, a smile hopelessly projecting the confusion of his mind, failing to hide it. He reached out to his pocket and took his phone out.

"12 New Messages" flashed in the centre of the phone screen.

Shammi calmly unlocked his phone. A battery of messages from Sona started flowing through the screen as he scrolled through. He took a deep breath and dialled Sona's number. He turned around to look at his reflection in the mirror – grinning artificially, and still confused.

Roy scurried down the stairs to the garbage area where the chutes open up. He jumped in the smelly puddle of trash bags, crazily opening any and all of them. Finally he found the one he had been searching for, took it over to one side, and dumped its contents on to the ground. When he had assembled the pieces together, the writing was absolutely clear. His worst fear was becoming a reality. He couldn't believe what he was looking at. *This is not possible. How could this be?*

A jittery Roy had tears dripping down his cheeks. Still standing in the smelly trash area, his legs stumbled backwards, colliding to the wall before gravitating his entire body to the dirty floor.

He sat there, still, crying, as he looked at the assembled document in front of him. It was Monica's abortion report, carefully shredded and thrown away, never meant to be found by anybody.

Roy slammed his eyes shut as he lay in the pool of trash in his inert state. A little mouse crawled up to his boots, nibbling on the dirt on his shoe sole. He had plunged so deep into the rationalization of the 'Why?' that he had lost his logical and cognitive ability to sense anything around him.

In his mind, battle lines had clearly been drawn. *Focus, think! There must be a plausible reason, another explanation.* On the other side, the emotional sponge of the brain was squeezing guilt-ridden, self-ridiculing explanation leading to one and only one conclusion – *it's entirely your fault, Roy.* His outside demeanour had stripped him naked of all layers of camouflage; his frantic mind was now out in the open, growling at the pitiable muddle. He wanted to stand up, but he felt powerless and incapacitated.

In the depth of his melancholy, somewhere the fire in his heart told him: *nothing can come out of grief, for one must turn grief into a weapon, to fight against grief. If I let this feeling control me, then I'll become what I was back then, and that is not what I want. I must fight it. But how? Clear your head and open your eyes... open your eyes...*

The voice grew louder in his head and slowly he opened his eyes, held his palms against the dirty floor, hammered his feet on the ground and with a sudden thrust, pushed his torso up and stood firm on the floor. He climbed his way back to Monica's apartment, cleaned himself up and looked at his phone. There were no new messages.

Roy mulled for a few seconds and then decided to send one. "Where are you?"

An hour had passed and still there had been no response from Monica. Roy jumped to type the message again but pulled his fingers back. Still in a state of confusion, he clicked on the 'Monica' Contact name and hit the 'Track my contact' feature on an app.

Roy thought back to the lovely evening when he had gifted this new iPhone to Monica. He had bought two identical handsets.

The transponder like signal beeped and appeared with a grey dot on screen. Roy lifted the phone up and looked at the dot transponder on the map. She wasn't at the office. In fact, she wasn't even in Manhattan. She was at some remote location, at the far tail end of long island. Roy's eyes gushed with the dwindling thought. *Monica is in danger.*

The last twenty-four hours had not been easy on Roy. The only solace in his life was slipping out of his hands. The tighter he wanted to hold on to her, the faster she was slipping away. In his mind, he knew that something wasn't right, but his heart was beating to a different rhythm, believing that there will be a miracle that will sweep out all the turmoil away from his life;

and his life would be back to where it was – smooth, happy and blissful. *That is fantasy. Reality must be dealt with; escapists are losers.* Roy covered his ears in a futile attempt to stop the loud familiar voice echoing in his head.

Roy stormed out of the apartment and ducked into the elevator.

The old lady in the elevator looked at Roy sheepishly.

He turned back to her, looked her in the eyes and said, "What?" The old lady pulled herself back in the corner, avoiding any eye contact.

The phone lit up on the dressing table and Sona jumped out of the bed to hurriedly reach for it.

"Hello," said Sona excitedly.

"Hello to you too," Shammi replied. "Everything okay?"

"Well. You take a pretty young girl to your apartment for a whole night." Sona giggled. "And what do you expect?"

"I expected fireworks in the night," said Shammi. "But thanks to your beauty sleep..."

"Shut up. One track mind..." Sona said playfully. "Guess what happened when I got home?"

"Let me guess," said Shammi. "Your mother said that Shammi is a rockstar, and that next time you can hang out with him not just for one day but perhaps for an entire week and..."

"Uff!" Sona exclaimed. "Alright, my five-year-old...Focus now!"

Shammi laughed. It was these conversations, the comfort that he had grown accustomed to when he was around her. It gave him a sense of security, a blanket of warmth that he could cuddle in for all his life.

"Okay, so I walked in and the first thing I saw was a dark room..." Sona vividly retold the entire episode from earlier in the day. Shammi had forgotten all about the confusion in his mind. The echoes of his conversation with Thakursaab had been shoved away to a dark corner in some dormant part of his brain. He was lit up and happy, like he always was in Sona's company.

"So?" said Sona

"So…what?" asked Shammi hesitantly.

"When can you meet Mom and Dad?" Sona repeated her question. "Were you even listening to what I was saying?"

"You voice is as intoxicating as aged scotch. It's hard to comprehend the words when the voice is so beautiful," even though his words were cheeky, Shammi meant every word of it.

Sona laughed it off. "You are a little baby."

"Whenever you want, I can come over," said Shammi.

"I love you," Sona said.

Shammi froze. The words fell on his ears but dropped right out of there, like he could not handle the weight of her words.

"Sorry…" Sona was embarrassed. "I don't know why I said that."

"I love you too," Shammi said, his voice heavy with emotion. "It's the first time I have felt this way."

"Me too," said Sona, sighing with relief.

Sona and Shammi knew in their hearts that they have found each other. It was fate that they were fortunate enough to have felt, touched, and experienced true love; a longing that many souls die searching for.

But that also meant that Sona had to make extra sure that everything was right when Shammi met her parents.

"Not now…silly. In a week," said Sona. "We need to go through a few things and have rehearsals….a lot of rehearsals. So, we start our drill for D-day tomorrow."

"Let's do it right now," Shammi said. "Why wait? I am a natural. I've impressed all the parents I have met till date."

"Stop it!" Sona whispered on the phone.

Shammi laughed.

"Tomorrow. 9.00 a.m. then," Sona confirmed and hung up, jumping back on her bed, cuddling the giant teddy bear.

They met in the library the next morning.

"I am so nervous," said Sona.

"Don't be. Someone needs to be the man in the relationship," Shammi joked.

Sona looked straight into his eyes, holding him by his cheeks. "Are you sure?"

"Yes," said Shammi managing a deadpan expression. "But, it may help if we try to add a little context here."

"...about you and me," Sona was happy, but had nervous excitement.

"That is set, babe. I think it was etched in stone many lives ago and we, here, are just reacting to a destiny that is always to be," Shammi said in a sombre tone.

Sona sighed. "Thank you. I wanted to make sure that I am not pressuring you into this. It will do no good to us, to our relationship, if we were not happy and didn't want this from deep in our hearts."

Shammi held her by the waist, slowly caressing her bare skin from under her white tank top. His hands ran over her stomach all the way to her neck, causing goosebumps over her smooth skin.

He pulled her and gently seated her on his lap. Sona was excited and nervous. Her hands trembled, lips quivered, and eyes closed, as she felt his warm breath on her face. Shammi slowly moved his lips towards her, nuzzling her nose, gently colliding his lips with hers. Magnetized by passion and longing, they kissed deeply and hungrily, their tongues fondling one another.

A couple of days had already passed. The clock was ticking; she only had a few days before the seven day deadline and she couldn't risk it going wrong. Shammi as usual rolled in a bit late to a fuming Sona. "Where have you been?"

"Relax. I am just fifteen minutes late," said Shammi calmly. "Is this a new you I am seeing every day or what?"

Sona clinched her lips. "You know how nervous I am. Anyway, I think you are good and we just need to work on four or five things," Sona paused. "Actually five to be precise..."

"Ok, then let's call this a five-pronged approach that we will go through," Shammi said, calmly playing with a tennis ball.

"Nice. I really like it. It's like a framework, like guiding principles," said Sona. "I see you are getting smarter."

"What is that supposed to mean?" said Shammi as his eyebrows rose up a cliff. "You really think I am not smart?"

"Nah, baba. I wanted to give you a compliment," said Sona putting on her delicious smile.

"Let's start now. Let's pretend that I am my dad and you have come to see me," Sona stiffened her posture on the chair, put on a frown and sat stoically. Shammi couldn't control his laughter but Sona looked like she meant business.

"Hello uncle..." He said while sleazily caressing Sona's thighs.

"*Uh ho.* Please. Serious!! You don't know... this is the only chance we have."

"Okay, okay." Shammi got in order.

"Hello uncle. How are you?" he said with a professional smile.

"Hmm," said Sona imitating her father. An awkward silence followed.

Shammi cleared his throat, "How is your health?"

"Actually I have been feeling stuffy," Sona said in a deep-throated voice.

"Where?" asked Shammi.

"Excuse me?" Sona didn't get the question.

"Where are you feeling stuffy?" Shammi repeated his question.

Sona gave him a cold stare.

"You know stuffy in nose could mean you have a cold, whereas stuffy in the gut could mean it's constipation," Shammi said slowly, like a student answering a question he wasn't sure he knew the answer to.

"I am glad we are doing a rehearsal. So, the first prong is – no bad jokes." Sona paused. "In fact, no jokes at all."

Shammi raised his eyebrows in perplexity. Sona continued. "Great. Now, on to prong number two."

"Have you ever watched a pornographic movie?" Sona asked, causing Shammi to stir with excitement.

"Who is asking this? Is it you or the frowning daddy?"

"It's the frowning badass daddy," replied Sona.

"Thanks for the clarification. And ask again. I need to sync in that different point of view...ahem...I need to make sure I don't get too excited. You know. Sensitive topic, Porno...," Shammi had his serious act back on.

Sona ignored the joke and repeated the question putting on a serious frown.

"Not that much. I don't like ménage. And a lot of these sites are international and categories such as interracial, fat chick, etc., are not that applicable to us," Shammi replied.

Sona said nothing and just stared in stony silence.

"No sex talk is the prong number two. And, by the way, how did you know about all that?"

"This is basic biology," Shammi was trying to pull himself out of the hole he had just dug. "Standard tenth."

"You boys..." Sona sighed. Just then, Shammi's phone rang. A few moments later he came back with a truly surprised expression look on his face.

"What happened? Did you win a lottery?" asked Sona.

"No. Maybe," Shammi said. "My dad called me. He wants to have lunch with me. Now."

"That is amazing. But, why are you so shocked?"

"You don't know. This is huge. Up until now every time he has called for me, I have been reprimanded. I gotta go. I would have asked you to come but..." Shammi paused.

"No, no! We are not meeting your dad till we sort out the situation with *my* dad," Sona said.

"Cool," said Shammi as he gave a kiss on her forehead, grabbed his bag and walked away.

The fancy five-star restaurant was bustling with business executives dining to the finely-catered menu of exotic dishes from across the world.

Shammi walked in, casually dressed in his college attire, causing the hotel staff's heads to turn. But before anyone could say anything, a battery of security guards greeted him and escorted him to a private dining room. There was only one person in the dining room – Thakursaab.

"Come beta," Thakursaab said looking at Shammi. He walked to the table as the security team pulled out of the room and closed the door behind them.

"This is very cool, Dad." Shammi was amazed looking around the plush room that could fill a crowd of many dozens. "Where are the other guests?"

Thakursaab stood up, walked up to him and gave him a warm hug, dwarfing Shammi in front of his well-built body. "There is no one coming. I wanted to have lunch with my son."

"Wow! You just called like thirty minutes ago and you already have this room reserved." He was getting to know cooler stuff that he never knew his father was capable of.

Thakursaab patted him on his back.

Items from the seven course menu were being brought in, and crowded the table while Shammi ate quietly.

"So, how is your relationship with the girl?" Thakursaab broke the ice.

"Good. So far…" Shammi replied back. "I am sorry about all the confusion before. I shouldn't have bothered you with my trivial matters."

"Look here, beta," Thakursaab looked at Shammi straight in his eyes. "Nothing about you or for that matter any member in our family is trivial. Remember…family is the only thing we have. Everything else is acquired."

Shammi eased up a bit. "Thanks Dad," Shammi said while gorging on the Chicken liver ravioli cooked in a golden brown creamy peanut sauce.

"So tell me now. How are things?"

"Quite frankly dad, nothing has changed since we last spoke...I love her... I know that. I still want to be with her, but with each passing day we are getting closer to meet her dad, I have this...." Shammi stopped eating and looked away, falling short of putting words to his feelings.

"Feelings sometimes are notorious. They overpower words. I understand," Thakursaab paused. "So, you said you want to meet her dad?"

"No." Shammi replied sharply. "I mean yes. I don't mind but that is not my idea and I don't know if it is the right time, right now."

Thakursaab smirked. "Well, remember – There are situations, and then, there are solutions. There is nothing..." Thakursaab paused, "...nothing that cannot be solved."

Shammi looked up. "So Dad, how would I solve this? If I don't meet her dad, she will think that I am not serious and she will never talk to me. And, if I do meet her dad, then I don't know, what if there would be expectation that we get married?" Shammi sighed. "I have no clue what to do, so I am just gonna have to go with the flow."

Thakursaab continued the conversation as the main course was served; Shammi and Thakursaab took their steely knives and dug into the lamb chops. "Why don't you go to Wharton?"

"Wharton? In the middle of the term?" asked Shammi.

"Don't worry about that. I know the Dean very well and we have been donating there since you were born. They would be more than happy to accommodate you even if it was the end of semester."

Shammi looked up at his dad. "But then, I have a life here, Dad."

"That is exactly what you would be testing," Thakursaab put his silverware down. "When you are at Wharton, you will have time to ponder and think about whether this relationship is really what you want. If after three months you still think that it is, then you would have solved your dilemma."

Shammi was quiet, listening, thinking.

"I am just trying to help you as your father. Sleep over it. You don't have to take any decisions right now. In fact, take that as a lesson son. Never make any decisions without deliberation."

Shammi was ecstatic. He now had something that he could talk to his dad about.

The door opened, a man walked up straight to Thakursaab and whispered something in his ears.

Thakursaab took his napkin and put it back on the table. "I am sorry, beta. There is something urgent that I must attend to. But think over it and let me know."

Shammi nodded in agreement and stood up. Thakursaab clapped his shoulders. "No, no. you continue. You have lost a lot of weight as it is. You need to eat more."

Shammi smiled. Thakursaab waved him goodbye and the entire entourage outside the room left with him. Shammi sat down on the table and called for a waiter. "Get me some butter chicken and naan also, please."

The coffee shop in the middle of the campus contrasted sharply with the five-star lunch Shammi had relished a couple of days ago. Sona and Shammi sat on a chair in the far end of the open area. The hours passed in a jiffy as Sona and Shammi traversed through the five-pronged approach.

Raju stood by the hostel window, spying on them. He was suddenly disinterested in the only passion he had in his life – books. He lay by the window all day watching Sona slip out of his hands. In despair, he would lay on the floor, curled into a ball, crying endlessly due to his failure.

In the coffee shop Sona had already covered the easy third prong – love for food. She was all smiles to find that this was one thing that was common between her dad and Shammi. They both loved food and as long as Shammi could manage to steer any conversation towards food, she was confident that the meeting would be successful. She still had two more prongs to go.

"Okay so tell me this," Sona said, "What will you do if there are four guys teasing a girl?"

Shammi looked up stretching his body even as his long legs bambooed on the wooden bench. "Am I one of the four guys?"

Sona held her head in despair. "No. You are just passing by."

"Oh, okay!"

"I am still waiting for a response," Sona broke the silence induced by the relaxing Shammi.

"What do you want me to do? Baby…" Shammi said in a tone dripping with sleaziness.

"Can we be serious? Please?" Sona was pleading with him.

"See, this is confusing. I think you should put on a moustache when we do this act thing."

Sona didn't smile and just waited.

"Okay, okay." Shammi sighed. "I'll knock those bastards down. I'll draw them to a place where I have cover from three sides. Then I'll incite the strongest member first. I'll observe his hand and feet coordination. It will give me an insight into whether he is left-handed or right. Once I know that and if I have time, I'll try to tire him out and then punch him in the centre, between his lungs and lower torso. If he tries…"

Sona put her hands on his mouth. "Bas! That's enough, my Superman. You have passed the fourth prong – ready to protect." She smiled away. "You know, being an army man, he is really passionate about justice, so just keep that in mind."

"Thank you. By the way, I always thought army folks had a sense of humour too."

"They do…but you have to cross this barricade to reach that part of him. So, okay. Now on to the last prong – Are you ready for this?" Sona asked.

"If we go to watch a movie after this, then yes!!" exclaimed Shammi.

"No movie tonight. Tomorrow you have to come to my house," Sona said. "Prepare tonight, okay, especially for this last prong – Career. I know Dad will ask you what your career plan is for the next five, ten, or twenty years."

Shammi heard Sona but it took a while to register the relevance of the question. But when it did, Shammi understood where his own father was coming from, when he asked him to reconsider Wharton. *May be it's not my dad's fault that he asked me to get serious about my future. Perhaps it's what every dad thinks and perhaps it's the right thing to do.*

"I know we are young and we may not know what we will do in future, but…" Sona was trying to navigate the topic reasonably.

"You know though," Shammi interrupted. "You know what you want to be in future. You will be a doctor. It's just me who still needs to figure it out."

"You are into engineering. That's something to start with… Think about it. I'll let you dwell on this on your own and I am sure whatever you come up with will be great." Sona held his hand. "For me, all that matters is that we are together."

Shammi pulled his feet off the bench and hugged Sona.

Raju closed his window and threw himself on the bed, sobbing profusely and murmuring. "What was wrong with me? I am smart, intelligent. What was wrong? What was wrong?"

As Sona walked out of the coffee shop, a distraught Raju wiped his tears, stood up and hurriedly climbed down the stairs. He went out of the hostel burying his face away from the eyes of everyone and marched right into the college building. Engulfed by mixed feelings, Raju entered into the college infirmary and carefully snuck into the medicine dispensary. In the darkness of the room, he took a little flashlight out and haphazardly beamed through the medicine cabinet from the top shelf to the bottom, until his eyes stopped at a transparent storage container labelled – 'Depression – Controlled substance, by prescription only'.

He hastily pulled a stepper stool, hopped on to it and rummaged through the box. His moving hands stopped at a little medicine box. He lifted the box up, shook it. The box was full of medicines. He emptied several of the pills in his palm. He dumped the pills in his pant pocket, carefully placed the box back to where it was, put the stepper stool away and secretly walked out of the dispensary.

In the meanwhile at the coffee shop, Shammi was gazing through the skies asking himself. *What am I? What do I want to do? Do I even know that?* He took his phone out and like in a trance, dialled Thakursaab's number.

Thakursaab instantly picked up the phone.

"Dad, I just dialled your number by accident. Sorry I..." said Shammi.

"No worries. Now that you have called, why don't you join me for dinner?" Thakursaab said to a relieved Shammi.

Sona woke up to the sound of thunder, and peeked out of the window. Mumbai was getting ready for another day of piercing rain, and Sona embraced the thunder like it was drum-rolls commemorating the biggest and grandest day of her life.

She quickly got dressed. Her glowing face was further magnified by the light pink salwar kameez she had put on. The little black bindi on her forehead was like a riveting companion of the black mole that sat right above her lips. Slight drizzle of Burberry Weekend around her ears and wrist were enough to make even the air around her fall in love with her.

She quickly got out of the house and hopped into an auto-rickshaw. She didn't want to be late to the common rendezvous point. Her confidence was still shaky.

As the little wheels of the rickshaw rolled blazingly fast, racing like a trinity of rats running through the puddled road, her mind was pacing back and forth with the minutest detail, to check every answer; every possible scenario to be worked out before Shammi came face to face with her dad.

The rat wheels stopped outside the Bandra station in front of a coffee shop. Sona opened her pink umbrella and quickly ran towards the coffee shop trying to dodge the stubborn rain hell-bent on providing dramatic background to her frenzied state of mind. Her mind was reeling as she agonized, mentally playing out every possible conversation or situation that could come up between Shammi and her father. She was restless. Her feet were tapping to a tune that only her mind could listen to; her arms had developed a fatal attraction to the watch, looking at the watch every two minutes. An occasional smile driven by the nostalgia of happy funny times with Shammi was the only saving grace, helping deride the delirium of passion.

Shammi was always late and this would have been nothing new, but the anxiety going through Sona's mind made her numb, incapacitating her from fully comprehending anything.

An eerie feeling that someone was watching her was beginning to creep. She looked around, but everyone seemed busy in their own worlds. An old man stared into infinity. She smiled at him and focused on her steamy companion, the coffee, and the anticipation of the forthcoming evening. *Must be my anxiety.*

A space grey BMW X3 rolled out of the parking garage. The flickering indicator lights went dark as the car took a turn and whisked into the blurry lights of the city. Dark clouds were gathering in the sky, setting the stage for nature to unleash mayhem on the civilization. As the car sped through the queens' tunnel onto the long island expressway, Roy was redolent of all the times he had spent with Monica. The agony of the startling discovery he had made earlier in the day had dissipated in a jiffy. A skewed view of beautiful moments spent with Monica played in his head like a montage.

Her teary eyes when she came rushing in the interrogation room; her overwhelming hug in court; her naughty expressions when they snuck into the office server room.

A glimmer of smile broke out on his gloomy face. The pathos of the present outweighed the lightness of the montage, and he helplessly plunged back into the anxiety of present danger. *God help me. What kind of trouble could she be in?*

Roy's car got off the highway and raced through rows of multi-million dollar estates shielding the sins of the rich and powerful behind the tall walls and gigantic metallic gates. The husky GPS voice announced that the destination was two-thousand feet away. Roy's heart was racing savagely. Fighting off the receding feeling that his worst fear might come true, Roy hoped that all this would turn out to be a big nothing, led by some stupid reason like a dead phone battery.

As the rolling wheels of the car slowed down, it set in motion an unpredictable and precarious path that Roy was about to tread on. Roy had stopped the car some five hundred feet away from the GPS location. He turned off the ignition and set the headlights to manual switch.

The clock ticked past 3.00 p.m. It had been over two hours. The rain outside had intensified. Sona ditched her seat, walked outside the coffee shop and stood by the entrance, looking at every passer-by. She took her phone out; there was no message from Shammi. She quickly typed another message to him – "Where are you?"

Even after several minutes, there was no response. Sona leaned back against the wall, fighting off the rain under her pink umbrella when a familiar boy jumping in the rainy puddle came rushing to Sona. He had a big smile on. He took a letter out of his pocket and handed it over to Sona. "Bhaiya gave this love letter for you," he said excitedly.

Sona was curious. She slapdashed her finger through the envelope and ripped it open. The boy still stood there staring at Sona, giving an intensely expectant smile. "Oh, I am sorry," said Sona as she pulled some money out of her purse and gave it to him. The boy was ecstatic. "Thank you, didi. When you meet Raj, tell him he is bad."

Sona brushed his comment off. "His name is not Raj."

The boy turned away in the rain, splashing his way through puddles, muttering, "And don't tell me your name is not Simran."

Sona took that as a compliment. *It must be the Indian dress,* she thought.

The storm was turning violent; the gale was beginning to rip apart the canopy off the spokes of Sona's pink umbrella. Sona tilted her head to the left, clinching her umbrella, as she hastily crunchily unfolded the letter. The empty envelope fluttered away with the wind.

Sona's excitement was paramount. She knew Shammi liked to surprise her, but even she hadn't anticipated the old-fashioned love letter or perhaps the letter with all the answers for tonight. Taking a few deep breaths, she slowed down the racy palpitations before setting her eyes on the letter.

Sona,

Let me start with this – you are the only person I have loved till date and the only person I will love, ever. Our love has the splendour of Shakespeare and the tenderness of Cinderella. I know ours is the greatest, most cushy love story, and I feel so happy, so free, when I am around you. I'll do anything to make sure that you are happy and successful.

I know you must be wondering, what the hell is wrong with this guy? But there is a reason why I have chosen the most romantic medium to express that we are right for each other.

But maybe, the timing is our nemesis…

The words on the paper started to swim before Sona's eyes. An eerie silence tunnelled through her brain. Disoriented thoughts flurried to the surface. *I probably didn't read it right. Let me start over.* She gasped, slowly reading word by word until she had reached the sentence again.

But maybe, the timing is our nemesis...

The contagious smile slowly broke strings and flung open the conduit to the evil darkness. Word by word the letter was snatching away her soul. Her heart was sinking in the numbness of darkness. The rest of the letter felt like pelting of stones to Sona's crumbling heart.

If we take this forward right now, I'll get into my family business and that would mean that I'd have to kill my entrepreneurial aspirations. And you, you would be a great lover, a better wife and the world's best mother to our children. But what about the doctor who wants to go to shelters and help the needy, the war-torn people, and the homeless? Would you be able to do that? I won't be able to let myself be the reason for you to not be able to do that.

I know I won't be able to say this to your face, but I know if I am near you, I could be a hindrance. So I am making a hard choice – I am going away, far away. Perhaps then we will realize that this was just attraction, an infatuation that we will always treasure. And if not...

Her shaky fingers dropped the letter, which fluttered away with the wind.

The five-foot brick wall was covered with creepers opening up on the inside to tall thick bushes that lent a view of the French Chateau, hidden behind the manicured botanical landscaping luminescent in the soft yellow garden lights.

Roy stopped short of the main entrance gate and rapidly stepped back. *What the fuck am I doing? I am not the fuckin' police; I am breaking in. Where is the fuckin' back door?* Jammed in adrenaline rush, the eluding fear of arrest came striking back to him. Roy stealthily walked along the boundary wall to the back of the Chateau and briskly leapt over the five-foot wall, carefully making his way under the cover of small trees lined along the boundary towards the house.

A deluge of rain had begun to pour from the thunderous dark clouds. Soaked to his bone, Roy continued to stride ahead, ducking below the windows until he reached the only open window in the chateau, and saw bright light streaming out of it. Roy pivoted his knees, cutting his tall erect posture in half, well below the hearthstone of the window. He exhaled quietly, trying to focus on the murmurs coming out of the room, and as his breathing calmed, the murmurs started to morph into more audible sentences.

Roy slowly lifted his head to get a quick glimpse of who was inside. Neil sat on the couch sipping his vodka screwdriver. "Hey, I did what I had to do. In my own little rank sheet, I'd tag that as a success," said Neil.

"Really?" Came a distant voice.

"Sorry." A familiar voice erupted. "I didn't know he would have some kind of hidden cash," Monica emerged from the back of the room. "And don't you talk to me like that. You didn't have to babysit him in bed while your sweet process of fraud detection took months to finish."

Roy speedily arched down to the floor on his toes, lost his balance and fell in the puddle next to the paver.

Neil got startled. "Did you hear that?" he said.

"Yeah Neil, it started pouring real hard and guess what, it's fuckin' noisy," said Hilton.

A despairing Roy raced and ducked to the little space right under the window panes.

"And you," Hilton turned to Monica. "Are things in control on your side?" the distant voice had become louder as Hilton roosted on the loveseat and took a sip of Oban single malt out of the impeccable crystal glass.

In the meanwhile, Neil peeked out of the window and, still perplexed, closed it and walked away.

"You know me better, Hilton," said Monica as she went and sat next to Hilton.

"Remember folks, if the firm goes under, so does your partnership and all your unvested fortune," said Hilton while rubbing Monica's thighs over her knee length flowery silky white dress.

"I know that Hilton. I know. Anyway, I need to go. We still need him to consent to a guilty plea," said Monica.

With window panes closed, the conversation was barely audible from the outside. Roy had his ears plugged to the wall, trying to pull his focus away from his sunken heart.

"We have to end this quick. I have a major investor who has threatened to pull his funds. I want to curtail this at the earliest," Hilton said in an authoritative tone and then gulped down the scotch. His hands softly landed on Monica's thighs. Hilton closed his eyes, enhancing his touch sense aroused by Monica's soft fragrant body.

"I've got to tell you Monica, you are the best I have ever had."

"And you old loser. You need to wear latex," Monica's mood had changed and she pulled out. "Or next time, explain the baby to your wife."

Hilton haphazardly tried to salvage the situation but Monica walked out.

"Okay," said Neil with great emphasis, "is this a problem I can solve?"

Roy swathed his mouth under both hands, not trusting his own senses that had been knocked off with the second shocking revelation in the last twenty minutes. *She would know my car; it's parked right outside.* Roy wriggled out of the bushes and sprinted to the boundary, jumped over it and quickly ran back to the parked car. He hastily opened the door, turned the ignition on and hit the gas, scuttling through the muddy side road. The car made a screeching turn on the main road and disappeared in the murky drenching night.

The brave Sona was trying to pave off the fatigue of the heartbreaking betrayal but she caved in, and with a loud thump she collapsed on the side-walk. The black tears dripping out of her eyes blended with the splatter of rain that fell on her face.

A swarm of sympathizers quickly started gathering around her. A guy quickly cut through the crowd, screaming "I am a doctor; move away." He lifted her in his arms and carried her inside the coffee shop. He cleared a table and gently laid Sona on top of it. He quickly took his windcheater out and wrapped it around her, wiping her face with a handkerchief. A girl in the coffee shop started rubbing her hands to warm up her drenched body.

Sona slowly opened her eyes after about a minute.

"Welcome back," the guy said hiding his face. "Feel better?" He shied away, taking a couple of steps backwards, opening up the space for Sona to not feel claustrophobic.

"What happened?" Sona was oblivious to what had happened.

"Nothing, you slipped," said the guy as he revealed his grim face.

Sona slowly got off the table and said in a voice laden with melancholy, "Thank you, Raju." She slowly walked out of the coffee shop.

She stepped in the rain and pensively walked towards her umbrella that had flown off when she fell and was now caught in the spokes of a bicycle wheel. A sudden gust of wind blew the umbrella towards the road.

In her distracted state, Sona followed the umbrella on to the road when suddenly a flash of light shone through the misty rain and the echo of blaring honk blasted through.

The auto-sensor wipers were working tirelessly, swishing away the profuse splashes of rain. The visibility had deteriorated severely, and even the all-wheel drive SUV was cruising like a surfer board, fighting the body of water stagnating along the road.

Roy's quivering hands tried to control the steering wheels as his right leg kept alternating between the brake and gas pedals, but his eyes were gaping wide open.

The radio channel was broadcasting non-stop commentary from the weatherman when suddenly some words nudged Roy to laughter. The weatherman had said, "When it rains, it pours."

For Roy, nothing could have been more befitting than those words. Covered with the blanket of hopelessness, he had become the laughing stock of his own subconscious. He had neither the courage nor the desire for anything else in his life. *Everything, everything that I had ever thought of as the cornerstone of my life has drifted away from me. Love that I thought was mine...wasn't. Baby that I thought was mine...wasn't. Life that I thought was mine...wasn't. What do I need to do to redeem myself? Is that it? Is it because I am not tagged as redeemable in your books?* He looked up at the sky.

Just then, his BMW hit something and bumped. Roy's gaping eyes glanced through the rear-view mirror, fearing he had hit someone and hurt him. His eyes were batting fast; his emotional limbic system was alert. He was still trying to comprehend what that was, when suddenly he saw a full human figure barely a few yards away. He hit the brakes hard, rampantly turned the steering wheel to save hitting him, but to no avail. The car swivelled out of control, skidding dangerously along the slippery road before hitting the tree with a bang. Roy tried to put on the seat belt but it was too late. The warning light of "Airbags off" started blinking rapidly as his body jolted with the impact, flew and banged against the windshield. Glass shards were everywhere. A thin trail of blood grew thicker. Within seconds, there was blood everywhere and Roy slipped into unconsciousness.

A red light started blinking by the side-view mirror. Slight white noise echo cleared in the car. "Mr. Roy. This is your BMW monitor support. Hang in there. Help is on its way."

Outside the car, rain was falling hard on the broken windshield washing away the blood. There was nobody in the vicinity – no shadow, no sign of a human, not even an animal.

The visibility was worsening with every passing moment. The heavy downpour didn't look like it would back down, ferociously hitting down on the foggy naked roads.

The barriers sprung open at the special entrance of Winthrop Hospital as the blazing sirens grew louder. An ambulance pulled into the emergency ward, and with Olympic grade precision, halted right on the spot. Under the makeshift hood of rain ponchos, a bloodied Roy tied to a portable bed was carefully lifted out by the paramedics.

"On the count of three," said the paramedic.

"Three, two, one, go!" and paramedics cautiously lifted Roy and put him on the waiting stretcher trolley. The temporary bandages around his head had lost the glory of white and were now red, as blood profusely gushed out of the smashed head. The hospital staff quickly put him on the stretcher and pushed through the hallway straight into the operation theatre. A battery of nurses gathered around the stretcher. One nurse held the drip attached to Roy, while the other took out sterilized cloth, wiping away blood that was snaking out of the bandages.

Roy's face was pale as he lay on the stretcher, lifeless. His inner demons had finally won and his will had surrendered to them, relinquishing all desire for life.

"We are losing him," yelled a nurse. "We need the doctor here."

"He is coming," gasped another nurse.

Running footsteps grew louder. "Prepare for Defibrillation."

"Yes, doctor," replied the nurse.

The nurse took the Defibrillator, positioned it and replied, "Ready, doctor."

The doctor's hands took over the Defibrillator. "Ok. Let's save this life." And on the count of three, she applied the electric charge straight to the chest.

Roy still lay lifeless.

"One more time," said the doctor. "On the count of three. Three...Two...One..."

Roy remained motionless. "C'mon, don't die on me! Give me a chance to save you."

The electrodes of the shock polarized Roy's body and with a whimper he took a loud breath.

"Thank god...Rush! C'mon, to the operation room," said the doctor.

The doctor was pacing alongside the stretcher when Roy's hands touched the doctor's hands.

The operation room door opened. The nurse at the operation room door eyed the feverishly moving stretcher. In his semi-conscious state, Roy's mumbling grew louder – *"Feeki syahi se bana na silvat..."*

The doctor shuddered. Roy's eyes opened for a split second. Like a shutterbag, the quick glimpse induced goose bumps even on his swollen hands as his tired brain inside his ravaged head electrified for a second and he saw the beautiful Sona pacing alongside him.

The rush of emergency drifted away, as the words of the poem decimated Sona's feelings, crushing her confidence. Her gaze was fixated on Roy. Her eyes filled with intrigue and confusion were still as beautiful as ever, unfazed by time, agony and perhaps a lot more. She was no longer the teeny girl. Like a rare wine, she had grown up to be a beautiful young woman.

Sona gasped.

God must have been in some mood. Roy's soft words were humming to the clairvoyance of nature, for as soon as he said "... *khoonkhar baarish hogi us din...*" the barrage of rain spluttered on the glass roof of the hospital, enchanting the corridor.

Startled and shocked, Sona tried to slip her hands away, but the slow spate of words had cast a spell on her. She had become impassive as the words mumbled out of Roy's subconscious.

"Teri meri kahani ki hichkiyon se saara jahan goonjega..."

She couldn't move. She was frozen in place and time as the stretcher paced past her and her hands slowly drifted away from Roy's. The nurse looked back. "Doctor?" but her words fell onto deaf ears as Sona collapsed in the hallway.

"What happened? What happened to Dr Gill?"

"We have Dr Bhat on standby," the nurse at the operation theatre yelled.

The stretcher zoomed into the operation theatre. Raju barged in and the door slammed shut while another nurse rushed to Sona.

The nurse patted on Sona's cheeks, took some water and haphazardly sprinkled it on Sona's face. Sona's starry eyes opened to drops of water.

Her gaze through the drops of water transformed into an invisible force triggering her tucked-away memory of that rainy evening some ten years ago – the moment of provenance that had changed everything.

A young Sona stood in the middle of the road, drenched in heavy rain when a flash of light pierced through the rain and the echo of blaring honk blasted through.

Arms of compassion stretched out and pulled Sona to the side.

Young Raju had confidently come forward. "Hi Sona! Today seems to be my day to save you, over and over again." He pulled her in a cab to her home.

"What are you doing?" Sona's voice was fainting away. "Where are you taking me?"

"Let me put the phone on speaker," Raju pressed the speaker button on the black and white screen of his bulky Nokia cell phone.

"Hello beta." It was Sona's dad on the other side.

A flurry of emotions had begun to swell up rapidly in her heart. Her many attempts to speak up had been betrayed by the wounded words, that seemed to have lost its way in the hammering sound of the rain, drumming up the taxi roof with its hounding force.

Hiding away her tears, she had looked away, glancing through the bleary curtain of rain, bringing with it thousands of gullible dew drops colliding with the window, only to scatter away in stupor. Her racing heart was locked in a battle of its own, pacing through an infestation of remorse and despair, jumbling through a montage of countless memories of her time with Shammi, desperately trying to find something, anything, that could console her, rationalize, bring sanity to the chaos that had spread like a wildfire, consuming every bit of her.

The faint voice of the radio announcer said, "The next song I have for you all is from the lovely movie *Khamoshi*. Music is by Ismail Darbar in the voice of Hariharan and Chitra...."

The cab driver turned up the volume a couple notches. Soft stream of words "*Bahon ke darmiyaan...*" fell on Sona's ears, slowly carving way out of the chaos, and steered her in a zone of thoughtlessness.

In the corridor of Winthrop Hospital, Sona slowly got up and sluggishly dawdled down to the operation theatre. The nurse walked behind, shadowing her, ensuring a safeguard in case Sona collapsed again. Sona politely told the nurse that she was fine.

"Are you sure? Dr Bhat asked me to be with you. Do not get her out of your site. Period. That's what he said." The nurse was genuinely concerned.

Sona laughed it off. "Raju is too protective. You can go Rachel. I'll deal with him."

Sona walked closer to the operation room.

The intricate and complex round of surgery was in full swing. Half a dozen assistants and nurses were gathered around Roy, monitoring endotracheal intubation and blood pressure to providing surgical assistance as the calm-faced Raju steadily stitched patches of skin, one at a time.

A glimpse of Roy with a tube in his mouth caught Sona's sight. Sona wanted to know all the answers. *How come a man who looked nothing like Shammi could say something that was so personal and a secret just between her and Shammi? But was it? It has been a long time. He could have gotten the poem from anyplace. Facebook, Twitter, Instagram? Nothing is personal anymore.*

$\mathcal{T}$*en years ago.*

A young Shammi looked outside the plane window, fighting between freedom and love, between his mind and his heart. *It will be the first time that my mind will win over my heart. Even in a metaphor, that doesn't make sense. But then what makes sense? Nothing. Focus in the moment. The light feeling, like a truck load of worry had been taken off your back. Now you are a free bird. Ready to get back in the groove.* Trying to see the world in a new light, and to scribble away the past, Shammi tore down a piece of magazine paper, took his pen out of the deluxe airline kit and started scribbling on the white space margins around the pages, writing in small letters –

"I feel light because I am still me. Single. Free. But, why do I feel that there's a shadow that lingers on. There is a knot that I can't untie. Do I even want to do that? Maybe. Maybe not. Maybe this is my destiny. Maybe this will go away...who knows...but I have heard somewhere that time heals every wound. But what if time makes it chronic? I'll deal with it...Man up...like dad always says...decisions are important...good or bad...they all shape what we are ....and what we become. But if we didn't take any, then we have no identity..."

Slowly Shammi dozed off. The pen was still in his hand. The grip around the pen had loosened and with a small turbulence shake up, the pen fell to the floor, falling straight down, hitting the floor and breaking away the ball of ink, opening a deluge of black tears.

At the same time in Mumbai, Raju got off the taxi and rushed to open the door for Sona. She slowly stepped out of the car, looking away, for she knew that her heart would crumble even at the thought of empathy. Dodging off the rain, Raju pulled the umbrella over Sona and dutifully walked behind her, himself drenched from head to toe. It was his time to be the anchor to ensure that she was safe, and his own state didn't matter to him

"Oh my god, look at you, kids! You are soaked. Let me get a towel," Sona's mother rushed Raju and Sona into the house. She could sense what Sona must be going through; her maternal instinct had kicked in, but she had to be strong for her baby.

She quickly rushed to get towels. Sona buried herself in her arms, safe in her mother's safety net, in just a bat of an eye her heart gave in as she started crying a river of her love, her passion, her life, but still dwarfed by the sea of chaos engulfing her mind, her heart, her soul.

Sona's mother wrapped her tight in her arms, battling her own tears of sadness, rage and hopelessness, for her baby was heartbroken and she couldn't do a thing to fix that.

Sona's dad quietly came out of the living room. Calm on the surface, but his eyes were turning crimson with rage. His fist was tight and indentation carved out of his own nails was beginning to rip open the skin. The paradoxical state of a tough man, caught between his anger and his vulnerability to his daughter. The fury of what Raju had told over the phone was raging. A persona defying every reason to cross the forbidden lines to the emotional landscape was broken as he saw the devastation his daughter was going through. But today was the litmus test – The years of conditioning to bury emotions deep that he received in the army was failing, as he stood hopeless, unable to do anything to help her delicate girl.

He quickly turned his eyes away from Sona and turned the other way.

Raju still stood at the doorway, drenched to the core.

"Oh, I am so sorry. Let me get you a towel," he was embarrassed that no one had paid attention to Raju.

He handed over a towel to Raju and patted him on the back.

"Thank you, beta. Thank you very much." He said with a tone so pure that it had to come straight from his soul.

It was almost three hours since Roy had gone in for surgery. Sona was getting impatient waiting outside the operation room. Today had been a weird day for her. She wanted to forget about it all; like it never happened. But could she? For every reason she could find convincing her to look the other way, there were two to debauch the sanctitude, pulling her in the intrigue of the man Roy was. At the moment, however, there was a more pressing matter – Will the man live?

The door opened and a tired Raju stepped out, taking his surgical mask off. Sona's wandering eyes stopped at him. Her eyes lit up.

Raju smiled. The chubbiness of young Raju had been gutted, extinct as the mighty T. Rex. With his finely chiselled face and lean body, his past was like a case of mistaken identity.

"How are you feeling baby? Why are you still here?" He asked Sona compassionately.

"I am okay. How is the patient?" Sona replied.

"He is going to be fine, hopefully. But I am more worried about you. We need to get a full blood work done." Raju gently held her hands.

Sona smiled. "Don't worry about all that. I know what it was. It was just weakness. I hadn't had sugar since morning and I skipped lunch."

"As your doctor, I am ordering you to get a full blood work done," Raju was genuinely worried.

"Trust me, Raju. There is nothing like that. Okay, now tell me how is that patient? I am feeling really guilty for not being able to help him," asked Sona with a dash of jitter in her words.

"He should be fine but this guy is really careless and I don't think this is his first Rodeo. We removed all the clogs and were able to stop the bleeding. I don't think he is going anywhere for the next few weeks. His recovery should be normal though," said Raju.

Sona was relieved.

"Okay. I have to go scrub. Are you sure you are okay?" He asked again.

"I am fine. Really. Now go." Sona said with a sprinkle of laughter. Raju kissed her goodbye and walked away.

Nurses prepared Roy to be transported to the ICU. "It was a tough call tonight. This guy must have some lady luck..." said the nurse.

"Yup, you would think." Sona replied still looking closely at Roy, trying to find a clue that could rid her mind of the dubiety. But, there was nothing similar between the man who lay on the bed and Shammi. Roy and Shammi were as different as chalk and cheese. "Thank you Jen," said Sona as she smiled and walked out of the OT. She had brushed it off as a trick of her heart; a devious attempt to resurrect the scourge of her life...the part of her that she remembered and forgot every day.

As an unconscious Roy was being transported to the ICU, a soft smile snuck out on his insentient face, only to fizzle out into the wilderness of his past ten years ago.

An Eminem song had been blasting through the gigantic subwoofers in an upscale Philly club. The diverse young and beautiful crowd was hypnotically grooving away in the smoggy setting. Shammi took two steps forward, one to the side and glided forward hitting up the cute Shaina; grinding her to the tunes of *Guilty Conscience*. The loud beats were beginning to fade away as he squeezed her closer to him. In the warmth of her skin, Shammi was trying to drown away the lingering memory of Sona. Shaina turned around and threw her hands around his neck. Shammi's drunken eyes were interlocked with her naughty eyes, trying to decipher the clues of seduction exhuming out of her subtle lip bites and spell-inducing provocative boobs. The sexy smell of her Burberry Weekend rubbed on his Kenneth Cole Black. The erotic blend was the perfect precursor to the scourging night that lay ahead, but instead it threw him back and he instantly pulled away with a paralytic sense of shock as countless memories of Sona blasted through the roof. "Are you wearing Burberry Weekend?" A confused Shammi asked Shaina.

"Don't you like it baby?" Her wicked tone was weighing down under the desire of sex.

Shammi smiled darkly. "Of course."

"Let's go to the car." Shaina whispered.

The motionless Silver BMW X3 strung sideways trailing way behind the super charged acrobatic spring motion of a moaning Shaina jumping on the naked Shammi who laid there staring away through the moon roof.

Sounds of "Yeh baby... Ain't you my boy toy..." struck on Shammi's ears and crashed to the floor without much ado. The wrestling between his inner angel and demon was like a guilt-inducing pathogen. His inner demon was fighting to tuck away Sona's impressions in a place so far away that no good deed could ever get to. But could it be?

A few months had passed by but a part of Shammi was still living with Sona. An anomaly, more so for him. His brazen attitude to recover from any relationship had been on a rocky path and he still hadn't figured out why.

A shivering hand reached out to a thermostat. The display read Eighty Degrees Fahrenheit. Shammi pressed the button and moved up the setting to Ninety Degrees Fahrenheit. *Damn this flu.* His face was pale. Three days of fever had drained him. Carefully, he walked back to his bedroom and snuggled in a thick comforter.

He could still feel the chill running through his bones, shredding through his veins, chilling every molecule in his body. His arms began to curl, his legs folded up. Trying to ward off the hastened thoughts, his shivering fingers lit up the phone under the covers. There were no messages. No missed calls. Slowly, he browsed to Shaina and thumbed the call button.

"Baby, you sound sick," Shaina said on the phone.

"It's just flu," Shammi said with a tone to draw mercy.

"Oh really! Thank god we didn't have sex today." Shaina paused. "You would have taken me down too. And then I'd have been mad at you. Now wish me luck for my business trip. I leave tomorrow and will be back in six days."

"Good luck," Shammi said softly.

"Thank you. And by the time I am back, get rid of your entire virus otherwise no action for you," Shaina spoke in her own sense of humour.

Shammi was quiet.

"Okay, my boy toy?" she said.

"Yup. You got it. Bye." Shammi hung up the phone; cuddled away in the comforter with his eyes wide open in reminiscence of his tender blithe past.

The last time he had fallen sick, a black hooded Sona had stealthily entered his hostel room.

"What? What are you doing here? And how did you get in? It's late in the night," a pleasantly surprised Shammi asked.

"You said you were sick. So I came to see you," Sona said with loads of innocence. "And you were the one who showed me all the mission impossible tricks to climb up and down a boys' hostel."

"You are mad. You should stay away from me. This cough and all is very contagious." Shammi's smile refused to get off his face.

"I am a doctor. Remember? Now keep quiet and lie down."

Shammi lay on the bed. She took her little kit out and looked at his throat, ears and checked his fever.

"You will live," she said with a smile. She then took a medicine out and popped it in his mouth, chasing it with a bottle of water to his lips. "Rest now!"

"Really, and let you climb up and down boys' hostel on your own?"

"Who said I am climbing down?" Sona smiled. "Squish over."

"Okay. I'll go to a different room, or stairs, or roof, or bathroom," Bumpy walked out like a zombie, closing the door behind him.

"Don't try anything." Sona said as she put Shammi's head on her lap, caressing his hair, softly pressing his forehead, rubbing away the thinking lines of tension.

The phone was still lit up from the call Shammi just had with Shaina. He turned off the phone, put it on the side table, turned off the light and tucked himself back in the comforter. His owlish stare was still as steady as the snowy range of Andes.

A tired lonely gasp broke the dull patch that Shammi's face had become. But it wasn't enough to infuse life, either in his dreary eyes sunk in the isle of unfurling dark swamp, or in his slight body, unfit to even muster the power to rail out of the bed. Even the faintest bid to do so and his frailty staggered him back.

The memory was fading away. It wasn't clear how many days or weeks or months had passed. Many shades of white powder, crystals burning up the tube, had fogged Shammi's mind. Clarity had become a myth. *What the hell am I doing...have been doing?*

The voicemail numbers were counting down, like a loop repeating the same anxious messages from his family. *"Beta... where are you...please call us...we are all worried..."*

Flashes of intermittent past skid past his eyes. His mind wasn't clever enough to keep on with the cloak of his dark self. Spatter of images from past tore through the cloak; one after another, they flew in front of his eyes, stacking up across the lines of his destiny. "What the fuck do you want? Why can't you leave me alone?!" Shammi screamed in a miserable attempt to muffle his own demons, the mocking voices within laughing at him, the tyranny of his own guilt had cheated him of the one thing he craved – silence.

"What is wrong with me? What is wrong?" Shammi began sobbing. "That's it," he groaned frailty out of his blood, stood up and scampered out of the apartment. He stumbled and fell across the filthy floor checkered with mouldy Chinese paper pails, rancid pizza boxes, empty booze bottles and a crushed paper stub of an international boarding pass dated only a couple months back. That one momentous secret trip back home that had transmuted everything. Now only the flesh remained; the soft hums of his soul had forsaken the roost.

The Nor'easter wind cut through Shammi's thin cotton shirt. He gasped. The warmth of the Scotch wasn't kickin' it, at least not yet. *It's time to double down* and he took the concealed Macallan Twelve Years out of the brown bag. As the freckled frost strewed up the bottle, his parched lips siphoned down the golden tan whiskey, fuming a singular solace, for in this moment, the barking of his demons had stopped, the tyranny of his guilt had gone back to the shelter, and the battleground had become placid. The savoury moment of oblivion had arrived.

A gust of ruthless chilling wind slapped through his face, catapulting him back into the tiger jaws of his inner demons. *No… no…no…no…* The agonized screaming swirled away in the bluster of the gusty wind. Snow bites were swarming rapidly on to the exposed parts of his body. Shammi didn't care. He didn't want to care. He aimlessly sped through the sidewalk when a girl behind a glass wall caught his attention.

The girl waved to him with excitement. Shammi looked around. There was no one around him. The girl pointed her finger straight at him, signalling him to come inside the bar. Hesitantly, he walked inside the bar.

The girl rushed and excitedly jumped on him. "Do you remember me?"

"No," Shammi gave a baffled look. "But I want to…Hell, maybe that will help."

"Haa," said the girl. "I am Annie and we fucked many times last month."

"Wow," Shammi quickly shot back. "Let's get on with it then."

"Sorry. Not today. My Husband is planning to drop by here," she was apologetic.

"Then why did you invite me?" Shammi said monotonously, his voice void of any emotion.

"Because I want my piece of shit husband to know what it feels like to fuck someone else." She took a long drag of the Pall Mall and rolled her vengeful eyes.

"So you fucked me to fuck with your husband?"

"Well, why do you think you were fucking? To forget… whatever that name is… Sauna or something."

"It's Sona…bitch," Shammi fumed. "And do not say that name with that little slutty mouth of yours."

The glasses on the table rolled down; Shammi skid flat on the table and dropped in a whiff along with the million shards of glass falling all around him. Bloodied on his face and hands, he casually stood up. A tall, well-built white cowboy stood in front of him. "She doesn't have a slutty mouth." He said with a strong southern drawl. "Please say sorry to Annie."

"Who the fuck is Annie?" Shammi said calmly. The blood was beginning to drip fast.

"She is your mama," said the cowboy.

A crowd had gathered around quickly. Everyone laughed.

"I knew I shouldn't have fucked her on a horse…Your mama, you know. Should have realized that she would end up spitting you out of her pussy," Shammi's reply was succinct. His moderate tone was scary.

The cowboy took a swing at him again. Shammi stumbled a few steps back but managed to hold his ground.

"By the way, I fucked your mama and your wife." Shammi smiled. "How fuckin' sick is that! For you, of course, it should be a bit traumatic unless you are like your daddy," Shammi smirked while pointing to him.

The cowboy was furious. He threw a solid punch at Shammi, bloodying his nose.

Shammi swung back, missing the man. The smile was still intact on his face. The cowboy was furiously instigated and came running at him. Shammi's drunken eyes rolled, he ducked, turned around and gave a flying kick. The cowboy flew past and fell several yards away.

"What? Are you a girl too?" Shammi said mockingly.

There was dead silence in the bar. The music had stopped. The crowd around the fight had swelled up. Slowly and methodically, half a dozen skin-headed giant white men stepped out of the crowd and slowly formed a ring around Shammi. The way the gang was forming a ring around him, it wasn't an intimidating tactic; it meant serious business. The skin-headed neo-Nazi bar was not the place to meddle.

Shammi looked up and around. "Did I fuck your wife too?" he smirked, mocking against the gravity of tension brewing up.

The ring of gang was closing in.

"Ahh...I get it...It was all your mamas too," Shammi taunted away.

The claustrophobic ring of doom closed in as darkness spread across. Shammi had no space to move. One gang member raised his head and looked at someone far away, then nodded. The man at the bar went inside the kitchen door and within seconds, the lights of the club went out. It was pitch dark, illuminated only by the light coming through the glass walls. The ring of demons unleashed mayhem on the soulless Shammi as he smilingly lay there even as the sharp hunting knives stabbed through every inch of his face, his body; his bones cracked to the resounding force of ruthless kicks and punches. He had let his defences down. Even though he was a black belt trained to take on a dozen men at a time, today, the path to self-destruction was the chosen path to end the atrocity of his inner demons; to end the haunting memory of Sona that like a fatal infection had spread all throughout his mind and soul. Today was to be the end of it, all of it, all of him. Shammi lay buried in the wrath of the skin-headed. His eyes slowly fluttered down and he slipped into unconsciousness. His body was still, devoid of any movement.

"I think he is dead," a panic voice echoed in the club.

"Get him out of here," another voice said.

The snowstorm had intensified. Two of the skinheads dragged Shammi out of the front door, mercilessly threw him to die and sped away. The bloodied body of Shammi lay like a discard, a trash of humanity, getting buried under the snow, inch by inch, feet by feet. Suddenly a bright headlight glimmered in the snow. A patrol car stopped on the street and a police officer stepped out; trying to focus on the thick trail of blood dripping out of the snow pile, he carefully took his gun and flashlight out and inched closer until the beam struck on the smeared gory face hidden behind the cemetery of snow.

The heart monitor squawked out of the dimly-lit special care unit at University of Pennsylvania Hospital. Shammi opened his bleak eyes, feeling hideous like he had been run over by an eighteen wheeler. *Am I dead?* His weary eyes slowly circled around, glancing through the drab paintings hung on the dark blue walls; and then gazed down at his own body wrapped in a hospital apron and hooked to as many machines as there were stars in the sky. How could he ensure if he was dead, he wondered. His body showed first sign of his being alive – he had managed to move his fingers.

A nurse came rushing in. "Mr. Thakur, you have regained consciousness!" She was rapturous.

"I...ah... want to...get up," Shammi was bewildered by his own voice – it was different.

The nurse rotated a knob at the base of the bed, which made the bed prop up slowly.

Shammi was confused why his voice had sounded so different. "What happened to my voice?"

The nurse sighed. "You have been through a lot, Mr. Thakur. One of the wounds had damaged your larynx…"

Shammi raised his eyebrows, unable to comprehend the medicinal terminology.

"…larynx is where your true and false vocal folds sit. It took a lot to get your voice back, but it will be just a bit coarse now… that's all," said the nurse as she helped Shammi sit up.

She called the doctors and specialists who had all been waiting to see this boy beat his destiny. The reports were better, his blood pressure and heartbeats were stabilising – all in all, he was on the path of recovery. But since he was very weak, he was administered some liquids for energy –through the mouth this time.

A few hours later, Shammi signalled to the nurse to take him to the attached bathroom. He took small difficult steps on alighting from the bed when his eyes fell on the mirror. He walked closer. A chill ran down his spine as the reflection in the mirror turned lucid. His mouth jarred as he turned around to the nurse, hoping she could turn the key and pull some sanity back. Something had gone gravely wrong.

"Mr. Thakur. You shouldn't let this excite you; you have barely gained consciousness." A doctor had also walked in by now, to monitor Shammi's psychological state.

"You have been in coma for the last three months," the doctor said with warm compassion. "Before that, you went through multiple major surgeries." She paused. "Including many face reconstruction surgeries.…It is a miracle that you are alive. You had no heartbeat for almost fifteen minutes. It was the snow you were covered in that saved your life. If you ask me, it wasn't the snow…it was god himself who saved you, or someone's prayers perhaps."

Shammi braved his sinking heart and looked into the mirror again. The face was different, quite different.

It was the face of Roy.

He looked at the stranger in the mirror; a stranger that he had become to his own being, like a mask that would never go off. Echo of "Devil wears a mask… Devil wears a mask…" had begun to march off the seismic charts. *I know that voice. Who is that? Who is that?*

A young Shammi spurted along the verandah, humming "Devil wears a mask….Devil wears a mask…"

Mataji sat by the verandah. "Come here; let me finish the story…"

Young Shammi slowly hopped back and jumped into Mataji's lap. "From the beginning Dadi…pleaseeeee…."

Mataji smiled. "Okay. It's the story of devil – The perfect mind of the devil was such that he hid his face inside a red horse mask."

"Devil wears a mask…" young Shammi's murmurs perished away with Mataji's soft touch. "What is devil, Dadi?" His asked in his soft voice.

"Devil is something…like fire. He destroys anything that he touches," Mataji said with animated hand movement.

"And why did he wear a mask?" young Shammi was curious.

"Because if people knew he was the devil, then they would run away from him. He could only hurt people, if they didn't know who he really was but…"

"But…what?"

"But he had to see his real scary face before he could go to sleep or else he would never be able to take the mask off and would never remember who he really was.

"So every day the devil would put on the mask in the day, take it off at night and put it back on in the morning, never forgetting that he was the devil."

Young Shammi was totally hooked. He squished closer to Mataji.

Mataji wrapped him in her arms and continued, "One day, he came back flustered. He felt horrible, for something had gone wrong. Deep in his maze of thoughts, he forgot to take his mask off and slept with it.

Next morning he woke up and he didn't remember his real face or who he really was! That day onwards he vowed to search for the man he was. For many years he wandered all around searching for himself, until one day, when he met a poor frail boy. The boy had been hungry for many days. A small loaf of bread from the devil was enough to spark a glimmer of smile on the boy's face. "God bless you," the boy blessed the devil from his heart.

The devil asked, "Who is god?"

The boy looked at him, smiled and said, "For me, it's you."

Back in the hospital Shammi softly swabbed his gummy eyes. An unearthly feeling ran through him as he sketched his fingers on the contours of his chin, his lips, his head. Like he was lost in the dubiety of his own shadow. *What am I? Who am I?*

His mind wandered back to the story with Mataji.

"So the moral of the story is?" Mataji asked young Shammi.

"Hmm," Young Shammi was thinking. "That we should give food to the poor?"

Mataji smiled. "That is very important. But if the devil could pay the penance of his sin and become god – even if for one person – then anyone can."

Shammi was still looking at his reflection in the mirror. The new him was like his chance to come out of his shadow of darkness; an opportunity to rid him of his past and to stride into a path of redemption. *But, like the devil, I must repent, not just for myself but to free the ones I love of the sorrows galvanizing around my sins. For my sins are mine, the penance must also be mine. Everything in the past must be wiped out. The one thing that reminded me of my past deeds, my own face, is now gone. It's time for other things to go too. It is time.*

"Can I..." Shammi looked at the urinal and then the door, politely signalling the nurse to walk away.

"Of course," she said and walked out of the room.

Shammi waited for her to leave. Then as an afterthought, exhaustively limped towards the window.

His room overlooked a garden, and the hospital corridor was visible on one side. He could see Thakursaab marching towards the room, his mood upbeat, his spirit electrified with fervour.

Shammi's brain was freezing up at the thought of what he was about to do. *I have to do this. There is no other option. Sorry Dad. You have done all you can. But you can't save me. No one can. No one, but me.*

He carefully opened the bathroom window and stumbled out, falling on the shrubs.

He looked back at the hospital, and a faint smile appeared on his frail face. He raised his arms and bid farewell to his own past, limping away in the cold dark night.

$\mathcal{A}$t Winthrop Hospital, Roy woke up with a jolt. His eyes were half shut, his body trembling.

The incoherent mumbling died down and then like a spiritless object, he collapsed back on the bed. Doctors rushed in to the ICU. Sona came rushing back and held Roy's hands. The monitors stabilized. Roy had slipped back into unconsciousness. She looked at the glimmer of innocence coming out of the resting eyes, those dry lips, lost in the fabric of bandage wrapped all around the face. A thoughtful smile appeared on her face.

"The patient seems normal now. Please continue monitoring." She hung the chart next to the bed and walked out of the room.

A few weeks had already passed. The bright sunny day outside was a welcome change, away from the havoc of storm that had ravaged the tri-state area.

Inside the Winthrop Hospital, Roy lay flat on his bed, uninterestedly flipping through the channels on television. The bandages had narrowed down; his wounds were healing.

Raju smartly walked in to the ICU unit. "How are you feeling now, Roy?"

"Much better. Thank you, doctor." Roy looked at Raju straight in the eyes, wondering why he looked somewhat familiar, trying to dig out an old reference lurking underneath Raju's new flamboyance.

"You look familiar," said Raju.

"Funny. I was thinking the same," Roy said rolling his light brown eyes. His black lenses were gone. The cloak of disguise stripped away from his eyes. It was a blessing perhaps that larynx damage repair had altered his phonetic voice, for that cloak still remained.

"Oh well. Don't all Indians look the same?" Raju brushed it off.

"You have a pretty stubborn spirit to live – and I mean it in a good way. It helped us save your life," Raju said as he flared a soft beam on Roy's iris, carefully checking the eyes for any sign of trauma.

Roy chuckled. *Spirit to live?* That was a first for him.

Raju pulled back and looked at Roy in amazement "Why? What happened?"

Roy shrugged it away. "Nothing doctor…just…nothing."

"Well, trauma is receding. We will shift you to the normal ward. But I think we should go for another round of MRIs and Ultrasound." Raju was calm, confident. "You know, just to err on the side of caution. I and Dr. Gill will alternate as your primary doctors, just managing and saving as many lives as we can." Raju gave that small-talk smile. "Is that okay with you?" he paused to hear Roy's feedback.

"Yup. As long as one of you doesn't kill me."

Raju snickered. "Don't worry, we haven't killed anything since those lab rats in school."

"That's good news," Roy gave a toothy smile.

Raju said, "Good luck" and he signed off the patient sheet.

The day passed and night dawned and passed away. The bright sunlight sparked to life in Roy's hospital room. The door creaked open. "How are you feeling now?" Sona asked graciously.

A cavalry of a thousand horses stomped through his heart as Sona's mystical beauty murderously lunged through his reverie.

"Much better," Roy said with a face as calm as the sea.

"Let's look at you…." Sona started her thorough patient check-up. "Looks like you are healing well. I need to consult with Dr. Bhat, but you may be able to go home in a couple of weeks."

"Did you say weeks?" Roy asked.

"Yes sir." Sona looked at him in the eyes, "it's nothing short of a miracle that you are alive. You were in a pretty bad spot."

"And now I am so much better. I have this *pagdi* on my head." It was like time had stopped. His subconscious spewed the warmth back into life. The laws of attraction danced out of the horde of anxiety he was chained to.

"If you could please arrange for some music, I could at least start my *bhangra*."

Sona burst into laughter.

Roy gave a smothering laugh only to scale it back. The pain breaking out of the head wound only got worse with laughter.

"Yeah, about those jokes…You've got to keep a leash on them until you get better," Sona said. "Unfortunately, laughter ain't the best medicine, not for you."

"Yup. I have been getting to realize that, perhaps the hard way." Roy said while holding his bandage-wrapped head.

"Are you sure I don't know you from somewhere?" Sona daggered straight into Roy's dreamy light brown eyes.

"I have been told I look like SpongeBob." Roy delivered like a stand-up comedian.

A moment of silence was followed by a fresh wave of her laughter. Roy smiled and slowly blended in the rhythm with Sona, laughing while holding his head.

"You don't have the freedom to laugh yet," Sona said laughingly and held his head, briefly caressing his forehead. "Good day funny man. I'll see you in the evening."

The nurse tending to Roy looked at him. "I have always seen Dr. Gill smiling, but never happy. You are the first person to cross that bridge."

"Very observant, you are…very thoughtful…Like a psychic," Roy said sarcastically.

The nurse laughed it off.

Roy lay on the bed, helpless, mocking the travesty of his own destiny. For every bone-chilling fear that Sona would know who he really was, there was this fresh knotty butterfly in his stomach, exhilarated beyond comprehension. *God no...what is this? What should I do? How can I face her?* And his mind dived down the momentous secret trip he had taken to meet Sona ten years ago.

The alcohol wasn't helping much. Even a passing thought of Shaina repelled his wits. The school wasn't interesting anymore. Sitting in lectures felt like sitting in a wake. That's it. My few months of separation are over and I have realized that I love her. Thanks dad for your great advice. But, no thanks.

Shammi was exuberant as he hastily boarded a flight back to Mumbai to be with Sona. How would she react? Would she be angry? She must be. I should have never listened to my dad. All I need to do is to tell you how much I love you. You complete me and whether you accept me today or not, I'll always be there waiting for you.

Shammi spurted off to Sona's house directly from the airport. His cab stopped right outside her house. Here we go! Shammi dragged a long breath of anxiety. Armed with a single long-stemmed rose, he stealthily tiptoed to Sona's bedroom window, split it open with a stray stick, and rolled inside her bedroom. But it wasn't Sona in her room. It was her father, dressed in all white. His temper flared like a balloon of smoke off a meteor crater crash. He pounced on Shammi with his ironclad fists and railed him against the wall. "What did you do to her?"

Raju barged in. "Shammi, what are you doing here?" *He was shocked to find Shammi there.*

He quickly intercepted, "Uncle, let me handle this. Leave him... please."

Sona's father loosened his grip. "Take him away." *His eyes were flushed with tears.* "Don't ever come back," *he said as he trudged out of the room.*

"Why did he say what did I do to her?" *Shammi was hopelessly guilty, perplexed.* "What's going on here? Is Sona..."

"Quiet, there are other people outside." Raju put his finger on his lips.

Young Raju gasped. "Sona is not okay, but this...it's her mother." Raju tried to control his emotions. "She passed away."

Shammi's face paled as the words echoed in his ears. The ground below him sunk down the whirlpool of his own thoughts – thoughts of guilt, thoughts of fear, thoughts of remorse, thoughts of despair. "When...How..." his soft words tumbled.

"You are asking me how? Like you don't know...you...you are the reason."

Somewhere deep inside, the conjecture of Shammi's guilt was no longer the paranormal, for now he knew what his actions had caused.

"You have devastated a perfect family. Why are you here now? To kill the others too?" Raju said in a disgusted tone. "Go away... destroy someone else now."

Roy gasped as he sprung out of bed. He drank some water and then lay back; his eyes still gushing from rivers of tears for the past.

As days passed, he wished he was in any place but here. But with no other choice to avail, he had to do what he had learned to do best – hide the turmoil lurking within him behind the pretentious façade of a complacent joker. But any moment alone was like fuel to fire, making him slip in the haunting dark alley of the treacherous past.

Roy's deep thoughts were interrupted by a knock on the door. The door opened and Special Agent Cooper and Agent Moon walked in.

"Hello Mr. Roy," Cooper said with a wide artificial grin.

Roy looked at him and his whole world crashed down to the reality of today. The shit-storm he was in the middle of.

"Don't you die on me trooper," Cooper looked at Roy. "You know I need you to go P-L-A-C-E-S," emphasizing every letter.

The sarcastic comment was something Roy felt was best ignored. "I am not going anywhere, Officer," he said pointing to himself.

"Oh, yeah. You are not. Not because you are lying on this bed. I know you are, but also, because I got eyes on you, son." Cooper smiled. "Oh well, let me get you back to your beauty sleep. You need to get used to alone time." Cooper chuckled.

"Let's go Moon," Cooper signalled and he and Moon stood up. Moon looked at Roy and gave him a sympathetic smile. "Get well soon, man," Moon said softly.

Cooper looked at Moon and snickered. "Let's go Moon."

Strangely for Roy, it didn't matter much. He wasn't as tense as he was just before the accident. *In fact, I am not tense at all. Why? What the heck? Why am I even thinking about this. It's all nonsense.* And Roy delved back in the life he once had ten years ago, which seemed to him like a lifetime.

The sky was clear and scattered stars were visible to the naked eyes. Roy gazed away in the sky through the skylight in his room.

Sona stood in her balcony overseeing the downtown Manhattan, looking at the stars. The stubborn past was catching up with her. A past that still hung in her closet, hidden behind the façade of her present day life as a successful doctor. Her 'Doctors Without Borders' volunteer work was saving mankind, one life at a time... but what about her own life? The ghost of Shammi still haunted her. And now for the last few days, since Roy, the buried pages of the past had been ripped open.

"Everything alright Sona?" A voice came from behind her.

Sona's father slowly walked to the balcony. He jerked his head up, gazing through the stars. "I am sure the brightest one is your...," he stopped short.

"I miss Mommy." An emotional Sona said. "Why does it always happen with me? Anything I hold close to my heart is snatched away. Like my heart is cursed."

"There is nothing like that," Sona's dad interrupted. "Look at me. You love me, right?"

Sona nodded affectionately.

"And see, I am here with you, in flesh. We are doctors, beta. We don't believe in myths of the world."

Sona hugged him, wiping away her tears. "We have a new patient. Remember, the one that Raju operated on. He is a weird guy. Stupid jokes even after going through so much in his life."

And then Sona went on to relive anecdotes. The stories of Roy had swept her away from the sorrows of her life; the forged smile was no longer to be, ditched for the splotch of a smile that was knitting through the fabric of Roy's stories.

"He sounds like a fun guy. Optimistic and positive. You should hang out with him. He is giving you back what none of us could... your laughter."

Sona smiled and looked at her dad, trying to say something but falling short of words.

Sona couldn't sleep a wink the entire night. The love of the past had come back to the forefront, more alive, like she had just fallen in love, all over again. She opened the drawer and took a brand new diary out.

"It's stupid. I feel like I am nineteen again. I thought I was all grown up. I don't even know this guy. But those words...and those dreamy eyes. Why did he have to say that? And so what if he did? Why the hell is my educated mature mind stuck on that? My mind feel likes a bunny running down a tunnel cage. Uhhh.

"Mommy used to say when there is a feeling inside you, there is almost always at least an iota of truth behind it. Don't ignore any feelings. Face it. Clear the facts. It's not that hard. We make things harder than they are by hiding them in layers of presumptions that we weave out of our own logical minds.

"That's it. That's what I am going to do. I am going to ask Roy upfront."

The unsettling silence in the room was causing tension to build. The Hamptons beach house had become the clandestine fort.

"Where the hell is Roy? And why hasn't he pleaded guilty yet?" Hilton's heavy voice was as rigid as a block of stone in the Grand Canyon.

"I can't find him. His phone is off. His car is missing." Monica was tense.

"You guys can't do shit. Can you?" Fox leaned forward. "Hilton, this is your last chance, man. We'd have to come after you if you can't find Roy." The short but snobby DA Fox was ready to exact his pound of flesh from Hilton.

"If we can't find Roy, I can get you another one...There is Jeremy," Hilton was frustrated to be in the situation he was in.

"We will finish what we started, or..." Fox paused. "You gotta pay up for your sins...and then it won't be an isolated fraud... you can kiss bye bye to your life, your IPO and your entire fuckin' fortune."

"Okay, okay. Let's settle down Fox. It's a misunderstanding... that's all." Hilton was in damage control mode. "We are on the same side. I am funding the entire governor campaign for Karara..."

"I didn't hear what you said," Fox pounced over Hilton's words before he had a chance to finish. "And don't you forget that it's your ass on the line."

Neil Werline walked in the room. "Hey guys..." He was a bit taken aback by the sheer gravity of the tension, all set to crater a sinkhole. "A guy matching Roy's description was in an accident a few weeks ago." He said rather softly.

"How the hell do you know?" Fox jumped.

"Someone owed me a favour, okay," Neil said. "You guys should pay me extra for this." His tone was suddenly full of greed.

"Did he fuckin' die?" Hilton jumped up the chair.

"No, no." Neil paused. "He is in Winthrop Hospital."

Hilton looked at Monica.

"I'll get to it." Monica stood up and briskly walked out of the room.

Fox stood up. "The court date is coming up. Let's seal the fate, guys. How hard is it to nail the coffin on this one? Neil?"

"I am all ready," Neil Werline did the thumbs up.

"Don't you do that! If he hadn't gotten bail, this would have been over." Fox then moved to Hilton. "And you, you pray that he pleads guilty."

A swanky black Mercedes E63 zoomed into the hospital parking lot. A well-dressed Sona and dapper looking Raju stepped out of the car and leisurely walked through the two-floor-high skyway towards the hospital entrance.

"How is the new patient?" Raju asked Sona.

"Good. Quite a miracle that he is alive," she replied, pulling her shades on to her head.

"I am freeing up so I can take him now," Raju said.

"Okay," Sona said tremulously. "Or I can continue...I think it may expedite the recovery."

There were several moments of silence.

"You remember what Dr. Dhoort used to say – Medicine is ninety percent art and ten percent science," Sona said.

"Yup, and after that he would rub your hands." Raju smiled. "What a character he was."

Sona chuckled. Raju looked at her surprised. "I see that the spark on your face is back; like it was in our college days."

Sona shied away from Raju, smiling.

"Maybe helping this patient is helping you too. Go for it, babe," Raju replied back.

Sona smiled as Raju kissed her goodbye, and both went different ways into their respective locker rooms.

Roy sat on the wheelchair in his bathroom. The spankin' new blue scrub glittered on his clean-shaven face.

"And now, let's put this deodorant and the flowery fragrance." A nurse put the fragrance on him.

"Alright, young man. You are ready for your date," the nurse said.

"That's right. I got my blue suit," Roy said raising soft chuckles as the nurse helped Roy lay back on the bed.

Sona walked into Roy's room. "Hello there. Gosh! That smells good."

Roy smiled. Sona checked all the charts and got on to do the routine check-up. "So did you get a good night sleep?"

"Don't know. The stars were beautiful last night," Roy said.

"I know... there were so many." Sona said just as her eyes flirted with his. She did manage to break off the alluring spell when she quickly reached for the patient chart.

"So Doctor, how many more days before I am fed to the wild habitat of New York City?" Roy asked.

"Not too long. You are recovering fast. And why...are you tired of us?" Sona wondered why the hell was she canalling all topics away from the professional line and dragging it towards her personal feelings. It was out of place, erratic and it was bothering the hell out of her. *That's it. I am going to ask him.*

"If you don't mind, can I ask you something?"

Roy nodded.

"Do you write poems? You know *shayari*, etc."

Roy looked visibly amused. "Hmm...maybe. Would you like me to write something for you, Doc?"

"No. That's not why I asked smarty pants," Sona spoke after a pause. "Actually when you were brought in to the hospital, I was supposed to be the doctor to operate on you. But then, I don't remember exactly what happened, but in unconsciousness, you murmured a poem."

"Really? That would be a first," Roy had a blank face. In many years of running away from everyone he loved, Roy had adapted well to the surroundings. And one of the primal skills he had acquired was to draw a blank expression, to not let the other person know how he felt. That way, they couldn't hurt him or he couldn't hurt them.

"What was it?" Roy asked. "What was the poem?"

"Forget about it," Sona felt silly about the entire conversation.

"Are you sure it wasn't from a Shah Rukh Khan movie?" Roy tried to diffuse the situation.

"Feeki syahi se bana naa silvat

Waqt ka dhoka, bana de naa kahin sarhad

Bani sarhad to thanedar bana chahat mayoosiat mein ro dega

Khoonkaar baarish hogi us din

Shikan kho baitha aasman bulandi se koodega

Aur teri meri kahani ki hichkiyon se sara jahan goonjega," Sona recited as if hypnotized, pausing after every line and like an orator placing right emphasis on the right words dispelling the beauty of the poem.

Roy smiled, his bland face fighting off the plethora of sentiments brewing within him. "Doc…"

Sona politely interrupted Roy. "You can call me Sona. That is, if you like."

"Okay, Sona – that was beautiful. Did you write it?" Roy was scrambling ideas to break away from the direction of the current conversation while at the same time he was dying to know how she felt about him, when he had so ruthlessly left her, and now – after so many years."

"No. Someone else wrote it," Sona said.

"Well, if the guy left you, it's clearly his loss. There is a saying – Thou shall hurt no kindred soul, for the curse will destroy the kingdom of god."

Sona looked up at him. "Did you just make that up?"

Roy was at a loss of words, desperately trying to ham his way out of the situation.

Sona smiled. "But I hear you, and thanks. Thank you very much. But, now, tell me about you – The man with a mysterious past behind those dreamy eyes," she said animatedly.

Flooded by nostalgia, Roy was beginning to get a bit heady. He wanted to let go of all inhibitions and scream at the top of his voice: *I am your Shammi. And we are destined to be together. Why else would we meet thousands of miles apart, decades later? But how could I? After what I did?*

"I thought I had tucked all my dark thoughts in a deep maze inside my heart," Roy said softly.

Sona smiled. "Liar!" She continued, "Was I right?"

"You are right about many things. But you know, it always helps to add a little context," Roy's mischievous smirk was back.

"Hmm, so we are doing that now," she said.

"What was your favourite game? Jeopardy?" he said.

Sona wasn't buying any of that but she had the patience of a lifetime.

Roy continued. "Okay, okay. How about this? Let's make a deal. You will let me in your past and I'll let you in my present? And trust me, my present is like a bizarre batman movie. Weird villains keep popping up, but what they don't realize is," Roy changed his tone to the husky whisper tone, "...that I am not the batman. I am the Sadman."

"Counter!" Sona shot back. "Let's stick to the present. Past is always skewed – to the good or the bad; the present is pure as fire."

"Deal!" Roy said.

"So, I see a big Tiffany on your finger," Roy said.

"How did you know it's a Tiffany?" Sona's face perked up.

"Because it looks like one." An awkward silence followed.

Roy rolled his eyes. "Isn't Tiffany just another name for diamond?"

"What?!" Sona laughed. "You didn't say that to your girlfriend, did you? She will kick you out." As she laughed, the tension in Sona's eyes seemed to melt away.

Just then, Monica walked into Roy's room.

"What happened baby?" she said

Roy altered his beam to Monica. "Hi Monica!" He pushed himself up and adjusted his pillow along the headboard even as his body cringed at the thought of talking to her.

"Alright, Mr. Roy," Sona was suddenly professional and courteous as she turned to Monica. "Hello."

"Hello, doctor. Thank you for saving Roy's life." Monica's tone was so humble that it would have made even a dead man spring back to life.

"I am glad we could help." Sona looked at both of them, and smiled.

Sona looked back at Roy. Roy smiled and slowly raised his arms, waving a gentle bye with his fingers moving slowly akin to a piano symphony.

Sona waved goodbye and walked away.

"You know, I came here last week too. You remember, right?" Monica asked.

"I think I do. Maybe. It's all a bit fuzzy here. You know with the head injury," Roy pointed to his bandaged head.

"Don't worry baby. We'll be fine." She took his hands and pressed them softly.

The plastic persona of Monica was the least of things Roy hated at the moment. The thought of her pre-meditated planning to throw him like a piece of meat to the ferocious wolf Karara sent waves of nausea through Roy's body. *How do I get past this moment?* The monitors attached to Roy started going flat as the loud beep sound resonated in the room. The nurse came running down. "Ma'am, I'd have to ask you to leave now."

"Oh baby. Get better soon. I need to talk about the deal with the lawyer," Monica's tone sped up like a bullet train, trying to spit through all that she wanted at a lightening pace.

"Ma'am, you would have to leave now." The nurse yelled at Monica as Sona barged into the room.

Monica paced out like a little bunny taking small swift steps.

Roy lay on the bed and put on a smile as the nurses hastily hooked up all the monitors on to him.

Sona looked at Roy's smiling face and knew what he was up to. "Stop nurses," she commanded the nurses. "I think the blood pressure, EKG and oxygen test for the patient are normal. Let's check the wires and give the patient a little more rest."

"What!?" exclaimed Roy. "How can you be such a stone-hearted doctor?" Roy said with his full scale teasing tone.

"Hmm, I didn't kick my girlfriend out," Sona had a witty comeback.

"Ah! Are you jealous, doctor?" Roy said with a glimmer.

"Nope. But you will get a good beating," Sona giggled.

The nurses had left the room. Sona walked back up to the doors when Roy called back. "By the way, she is…" Roy ate his words and stopped short of saying anything further.

Sona stared at Roy. Her eyebrows were squashed. Thinking, deciding, what Roy would say next? But, Roy stayed mum.

The past is always skewed – to the good or the bad. Sona's words echoed in his mind. *Why hasn't she let go yet? Ten years of her life. She has wasted ten years of her life on me. Even after what I did to her? To her family? Is that even pardonable?*

Roy's inner voice, his conscience, was becoming persistent. *Everything that could happen will happen and everything that must have happened had happened. There is nothing you could do to change the past, but there is a lot you could do to fix the future.*

That's it. That is what I need to do, that is why I was left alive – I need to give Sona her life back.

The camaraderie between Roy and Sona was growing dangerously fast. Roy for the first time in the last ten years had found a purpose for his life. Skilfully using his masterful oratory, he had planted the right idea in Sona's mind. She had begun to warm up to the idea that the past wasn't worthy of the agony it bestowed upon the present. She was beginning to delve onto the path forward – devoid of any strings of the past. *All the strings must be cut, and the bird shall fly.*

Roy's words echoed in her heart randomly. This was something new that Sona was growing increasingly fond of, looking forward to it, like a mad girl, talking to herself, laughing out of turn, and the stares of people didn't bother her anymore. Her mind and her heart were in a good place, or at least were getting to a good place, fading away her haunting past.

187

Sona stood behind a wheelchair right by Roy's bed. "Today, my friend, you will go out," Sona said with a smile.

Roy looked at her and smiled. "Don't you think you took the whole darkness thing quite literally?"

"Alright, Mr. Smartass. Let me help you get on this." Roy gently wrapped his right arm around her neck. His arms touched the bare skin around her neck, just enough to electrify the lethargy out of Roy's body, letting a fresh warmth permeate his bones.

Sona pushed the wheelchair through the corridor. Roy was still frozen in the moment, smiling, as he jerked his head backwards and opened his eyes. Sona looked down and smiled. "Try to control. You are trying to hit on a doctor, that too, the one who is trying to fix you."

"You think you are fixing me? You have no idea in how many ways you are breaking me." Roy smiled.

"*Waah* w*aah*! What are you? Shakespeare meets Gulzar?" Sona chuckled.

Sona's cell phone vibrated and she took the call.

"Hi Raju," Sona said on the phone. "No, I know. There is a lot of time. I am not going to Libya for another month."

Sona pushed the wheelchair even as she continued the conversation on phone.

"Nope, just helping Roy get ready for Physio...Okay, okay. Bye...Me too." And she hung up the phone.

"Was it your boyfriend?" Roy quipped.

"Yes, it was," Sona said as she steered the wheelchair through the landscaped walkway opening up in the huge park.

"Are you going to Libya?" asked Roy.

"Yeah! I am part of 'Doctors without Borders'."

"So, you treat patients in Africa...Ebola patients?"

"Yup. Guilty as charged."

Sona stopped the wheelchair. She raised Roy's arm to wrap around her and helped him sit on the bench.

Roy was embarrassingly hesitant. His energy to get back to his feet was racking up. His zeal for life was back in full fervour.

This is like an organic experience, built on its own. Not like the past ten Zen years of trying to live life, because god wasn't ready to take my life yet. Now I know why. I need to salvage what I damaged. This is my redemption...the last of my penance...to unshackle her from her past – my past.

"How about we go an extra step? You help me with your hand and let me see if the old man can walk again."

Sona was proud of Roy. "Very good. I love your spirit. I wish I had that spirit."

"Really...are you going to embarrass me now? You have the courage like no man I know to do the work you do in Africa." He said raising a thoughtful smile on Sona' face.

Roy held her hands and started walking limply. A few short steps and he took a deep breath and then looked at Sona. "Listen. I need to tell you something."

Sona looked at him. "Okay. Just FYI, I don't like open sentences. I like a sentence that has reason in it."

"Understood, Mademoiselle." Roy did the virtual bow.

"I wanted to tell you this. It doesn't take a rocket scientist to figure out that you have had a bitter past and that someone has broken your heart."

Sona listened to Roy, looking straight in his eyes. Roy blinked and shied away.

His legs were beginning to tremble. Sona helped him sit on the bench and sat next to him.

Roy went on. "Let me tell you this. Life is happening right now. When you think about the past, it's like you are ridiculing the spirit of life. The only memory you would have of your life is that of thinking about one thing or one person that shouldn't have been in your life to begin with."

"He wasn't a bad person, you know." Sona asked softly. "I think he just didn't know how to deal with me, us. We were so young."

"Well, but it's not just you, right? What about your family? I mean everyone gets affected in some way....or another." Roy had mustered the courage to let the cancerous riddle out.

"Yeah." Sona paused. "Yeah... But I forgive him."

"You do?"

"He didn't know. He couldn't."

The flood gates of his darkly repressed guilt had been released; a stigma he carried for ten years had been washed away. This was the let go moment. Today his heart wasn't drowning in demonic sin; for today his heart had learned to swim to the shore.

Sona's aura was more magnificent than ever. A kindred soul he fell in love with was still as pure as ever. And he couldn't – wouldn't – do anything to ruin it for her. His resolute was clear as crystal; he must savage any good memory she had of him, for that was the only way she could move forward.

"And anyway, any idiot that could break your heart is the biggest loser on this planet. And losers only get second chance in a Shah Rukh Khan movie, not in real life."

Sona dragged a smile. "It's not about him. It's about me. It was the only real thing, real relationship I have ever felt."

"It isn't real. If it was, he would be with you, right now," Roy said softly.

"If it wasn't real, then why do I still remember it, like it happened yesterday?" Sona paused.

She slowly stood up, raised her hand and asked Roy to hop on. "Round two?"

Roy slowly stood up, held her arms and jumped on to the walkway. With every stumble that Sona rescued Roy from, a gush of the past came running down, melting his heart away.

$\mathcal{J}$t was nine in the morning. The piercing sun rays fell straight on Roy's eyes. But even that wasn't enough to wake him up as he snored through his open mouth.

Sona stood by him, watching, smiling. She stood there for some time; then wrote a note, tucked it in under the pillow and walked away.

Raju hid outside the room. He had followed Sona's path like a child following bread crumbs, leading him straight to Roy's room. As soon as Sona left the room, Raju slipped inside.

Roy lay flat on his back, deep in the company of sweet dreams, even as an occasional smile flickered on his innocent face.

Raju carefully took the note out and started reading it.

His face fell immediately, and he felt like the strength in his legs was failing him. He folded the note and put it back to where it was, lowered his head and snuck out of the room, walking straight to the elevator, and down to his office.

He hastily drew the blinds, dimmed the lights, and jumped to a corner, crumbling his legs under his stooped torso, wrapped in his shivering arms. The desolate state of his mind had robbed the confidence from him. Vestiges of the old Raju were creeping out as he tried to muffle his screams of helplessness. The cry out of his heart was devoid of many tears, but it was filled to the brim with pain, the insecurity. The déjà vu that he feared all his life was happening. His paranoia was arising out of the shadows. The ten years of dedication and love for Sona were all he had to show for himself.

His mind kept pacing back and forth between the times he had first decided to profess his love to Sona, to the evening when he had taken Sona back to her house.

That fateful evening, wrapped in dry towels, he saw Sona drown herself in the tears of Shammi's betrayal. Strangely, his heart was smiling, a hint of hope that Sona was meant just for him.

Sona had pulled herself into the isolation of her room, never stepping out. Raju sat in Sona's room as he homeschooled her.

The cloud of depression had begun to spread following Sona's mother's death to rare blood cancer.

And then Shammi had arrived. It was Raju who had pushed him away; squarely planting the seed of guilt in Shammi that it was all because of him that Sona's mother had died.

A sinister smile lathered in complacency cracked on Raju's face as his reminiscence of brilliant manipulation coagulated. He didn't lie. He just hid a simple truth. The reason for Sona's mother's death wasn't Shammi. It was her rare illness.

Guilt makes you see weird things...Like a doped out addict. And for Shammi it was topping off the brim. All Raju did was to feed the beast.

He wasn't sad anymore. For it was after this incident that one day Sona's dad had walked up to him and said, "We are moving to the US. That is the only way to salvage my daughter's life; she is the only family I have left."

Raju was ecstatic, for he was going to the US too, to be closer to his parents and now also closer to Sona.

I got rid of you Shammi. All your street smartness was for what? And now you, Roy. I'll find a way to get rid of you too.

Raju consoled himself, stood up and opened his drawers. The prescription drugs lay buried under the sheets of papers. Raju wiped his tears, tousled the sheets of papers in the drawer and pulled out a set of bound report.

The cover read "Benji Roy".

He hastily ruffled through the report, hopelessly trying to find something in the randomness when suddenly his gaze firmed up on a piece of MRI report. He pulled the scan out and clipped it on to the illuminated white board.

These are metal implants. This is a facial reconstruction surgery. What are you hiding Roy? What are you hiding?

He quickly snapped on the phone. "Yes. This is Dr. Bhat. I'd like to order a face reconstruction simulation."

He pushed the report back in the drawer. The subtexts of the report "Please approve to publish in system" skid away in the darkness as the drawer rolled back in the case.

"Good night Mr. Batman." Roy looked at the note and something struck him.

He exclaimed out in surprise. "I slept. I slept," and then he screamed out loud. "I slept!!"

A nurse rushed in. "Everything okay there, sir?"

Roy looked at her and smiled. "Yup. Everything is okay... now."

The haunting shadows of guilt camouflaged in bloody red insomnia had finally pulled off the rafter.

The spirit to live had begun to transform into a fascinating recovery for Roy. Just within a few days, he had beaten all recovery records and now was able to walk on his own with crutches.

With childlike excitement, Roy waited for the clock to tick past 5.00 p.m. His physiotherapy had become a hobby of sorts for Sona. Like clockwork, after work she had begun to spend hours helping Roy walk.

"Let's try something different today. Why don't we ditch the old-fashioned four wheeler?" Roy said pointing towards the wheelchair.

"Alright, Batman." Sona smiled.

Gently Sona held Roy's hands as they both slowly walked towards the elevator.

"This is your tenth day of physio, and you are walking like you fell off a bike, not like you smashed your car into a tree," Sona said proudly.

"Thank you. You look very radiant today. What's up?" Roy asked.

"Just today?" Sona said.

Roy chuckled. "Is it some fancy thought of your dashing Doctor Bhat?"

"How do you know about Raju and me?" Sona quipped.

"I have seen you guys together. Besides, he calls you a lot," Roy paused. "You know, during the physiotherapy time."

"Yeah, I have known him for a very long time. He has been by my side during some not so good times. *But*, we decided we won't talk about the past so let's keep it in the present." Sona gave a half smile.

"You can talk about whatever you want, Sona. I mean I think we should do double date. You and Raju; me and Monica," Roy said.

"Where did that come from?" Sona was confused at the change of topic.

"Nevermind. I seem to be recovering physically, but getting retarded by the second," Roy said.

"Can I ask you something?" Sona quickly changed to a rather sober tone.

"Sure," Roy replied as they both walked slowly around the park.

"What do you think marriage is?" Sona asked.

"Isn't that the holy grail?" Roy replied. "Let me tell you the secret of a successful marriage – Do not marry or even think about marrying the person you love. Always marry the person who loves you."

Sona looked at Roy. "But would that be fair to your own feelings?"

Roy looked sideways, away from Sona and said, "It's better to have no feelings than to have bitter feelings..." He paused and then continued "...for your entire life."

Roy and Sona strolled through the park. Roy's comments had triggered a train of thoughts in both their minds. They quietly strolled around the park in silence, contemplating with their own consciences.

Roy knew the impact his words would have on Sona. He was sowing the seeds for Sona to move on with her life, to forget the past riddled with heartbreak. *This would be my redemption. A normal life for Sona, away from my cursed destiny.*

His design to enable Sona to lead a normal life had overpowered every other emotion running through his veins. It was like what he did ten years ago, with a subtle difference – at that time all he cared about was his feelings; and today, all he cared about was hers.

But is this what Sona wanted too?

As she walked alongside Roy with her head lowered, peddling her way out of the swamp of past skeletons, questions kept assaulting her mind. *Why am I getting attracted to him? Is that even right? He is already committed to someone. I can't sabotage a relationship. I know what it does; the effects linger on for decades. But why can't I stop myself from liking Roy? Is it fair to Raju? He has been by my side all this while, saving me from drifting into darkness.*

"So double date then?" Sona broke the silence.

"I'd like that," Roy replied affectionately.

The morning rush hour commuters were lining up at the security lines at the JFK International Airport. The big glass windows overlooked the giant jets as they landed and took off. A private Boeing 777 made a perfect landing on the tarmac, slowing down after the initial run. Thakursaab alighted down the plush carpeted steps. Makhmal slowly strolled Mataji's wheelchair down the handicapped enabled airstair. A dedicated team of officers finished all the paperwork right at the tarmac.

The waiting limousines pulled up one after another. Bumpy got off the limo and touched Thakursaab's feet. Thakursaab stopped him, held him by his arms and hugged him.

"You haven't changed a bit, Bumpy." Thakursaab smiled at Bumpy proudly.

Bumpy was emotional. He looked at him. Thakursaab's tall stature was stooped under the burden of his vanished son. Threads of guilt and stress were chiselled through his face. "Let's go uncle so that we can beat the traffic. The hospital you mentioned, Winthrop, is only ten miles from here," Bumpy said, opening the door of the car. An entourage member quickly stepped up and held the door from Bumpy.

Mataji's wheelchair rolled into the Hummer limousine as Thakursaab, Bumpy and a battery of lawyers boarded the other limousine.

Ignitions turned on and the limos swiftly rolled, merging speedily on the highway leading up to the Winthrop Hospital.

"Mark, what is the latest you have on Shammi?" Thakursaab took out his reading glasses as he flipped through a thick documentation prepared by Mark.

"It doesn't look good." Mark said to an aroused reaction from Thakursaab. "At least for now," Mark tried to salvage the situation.

"All we know at this point is that Shammi has been living under the name of Benji Roy for the last ten years. It's unfortunate that it took us that long to find him, but I gotta tell ya, it takes a genius to vanish like your son did; hiding from Facebook and other social jazz of the worlds." Mark paused.

Thakursaab looked up and took his reading glasses out. "Tell me about the case."

"Yes, he had been working at the Da Vinci Capital for the last few months only." Mark flipped a few pages and pulled another subfolder. "The trades were made through a shell firm and the accusation is market manipulation through malpractice."

"And the current lawyer?" Thakursaab interrupted.

"Yes. The notice of representation has been sent to all parties," Mark replied. "We are representing Mr. Roy...umm...Shammi."

"And when is the next court date?" Thakursaab like a trained executive knew the right questions to sum up a lengthy conversation into a few bullet points.

"That is next Monday. A week from now," Mark promptly replied.

"Thanks Mark. We need to sort this out." Thakursaab looked straight into Mark's eyes.

"Absolutely, sir."

Thakursaab took a deep breath, leaned back and looked outside. "Bumpy, why did this happen? Why?"

Bumpy was quiet. He didn't know how to respond. "Uncle, he must love us too much to not let us be a part of his pain. So many years and I didn't even know he lived right here...that was until your call." His heart spoke words that touched Thakursaab's heart.

"It was ten years ago when I last saw him." Thakursaab looked outside through the side window. "And that was also in a hospital."

The memory of that brutal night was vivid in Thakursaab's eyes.

He had hurriedly left India when he first heard the news that Shammi was hospitalized. His calm demeanour had defected due to the emotional surge of his love for his son as he paced back and forth outside the ICU unit where Shammi lay in coma.

He had leased an office space in Philly, for he wanted to be close to his son as he peddled through weeks of unconsciousness fighting life and death.

Three months had passed. It was spring time in Philly. Thakursaab was being driven to the hospital after work when he answered a phone call with the surreal news —Shammi was out of coma. He had rushed to the hospital, jumping traffic lights one after another, got off the car as soon as it entered the hospital compound and rushed to the ICU only to find that Shammi had disappeared, jumping out of the window into the cold brutal night. A frantic search lasting many days yielded nothing.

It had been a long ten-year journey. Several million dollars spent, hundreds of false leads, everything culminating into disappointment one after the other. That was until a few days ago when one of the investigative agencies he had hired came across Roy's arrest article.

"And here is the DNA report and voice modulation report as well, sir," Mark nudged Thakursaab out of his deep thoughts. "Shammi has gone to great lengths to hide who he was." Thakursaab took the report in his hands, acknowledged, then put the report to his side, continuing in the gloominess of a long arduous journey that was about to end today.

Sona stood in front of the mirror, smiling, giggling. She checked herself out. Something wasn't right. *Maybe it's the lipstick*, she thought. She wiped the bright red lipstick away and put on the lighter pink one. Sucking her lips in and throwing them out, the pout was extravagant. With a smile so pure, Sona took off to the hospital.

Thakursaab along with his family trooped through the corridor of the hospital.

"I told you. You should have stayed. I'd bring him with me," Thakursaab told Mataji, while pushing her wheelchair.

Mataji looked up to Thakursaab, shook her head softly and smiled.

Bumpy spotted the room. "Uncle, here is the room."

Thakursaab paused for a moment. Bumpy softly opened the door.

A gloomy Roy turned around. His eyes widened, his forehead puckered and his cheeks flushed.

"Dad," he said softly.

Thakursaab just stood at the door, still sinking the feeling of looking at his son in the flesh after ten long years.

Bumpy pushed the wheelchair forward.

Shammi got off the bed, and Bumpy rushed to his support. He hugged Roy on the bed, trying to recalibrate to Roy's new face. A flurry of past memories glimmered. "I thought I was your friend. How could you just…?" The otherwise carefree Bumpy cried like a baby. Controlling his emotions, Bumpy gathered his wits and cautiously helped Roy get off the bed.

Roy slowly walked and touched Mataji's feet, but Mataji just pulled him towards her and hugged him, crying a river. "Beta, what was our fault?" she said.

Roy pulled himself together. "It wasn't you, dadi. It was my own destiny."

Roy slowly walked over to Thakursaab, who moved a step forward. The giant frame was stooped, succumbed to the agony of his lost son. Thakursaab softly hugged Shammi.

The family members swarmed around him as tears of joy flooded out. Makhmal ran and held on to Roy's feet.

"Maalik. It's all my fault. If only I knew what I had done." He began sobbing uncontrollably.

Roy tapped him and slowly pulled him up. "It's not you Makhmal. You were..." Makhmal's loud sobbing made the words incomprehensible.

Solemn moments of emotional reunion pacified.

Bumpy looked outside the window. "Is that Sona?" He asked.

Roy got alerted. "Dad, you would have to leave now. If Sona comes here, she will know who I am and then her life will go back to the hell that I put her in for the last ten years."

Thakursaab said, "You are just like me, determined by your will and driven by your heart. But we will not lose you. Not again. I'll talk to her. I'll get her."

Roy interrupted Thakursaab. "Dad, she doesn't know who I am and I think it is better that way. God has given me a chance to reverse some pain I have caused her. And she is happy after a long time. Ready to move on."

Thakursaab looked at his son with remorse and love in his eyes. "But what about you? I know why you did what you did. We found hundreds of drawings of Sona in your apartment..."

Roy said, "Dad, if you love me, you will do this for me..."

Thakursaab was quiet, helpless.

"If you want me to live happily, you would do this one last thing for me, Dad."

"And you promise that you will never leave us, ever?" An emotional Thakursaab asked with teary eyes.

Roy hugged him shedding all inhibitions, all the sorrows.

Thakursaab softly said, "I am proud of you, beta. I really am."

The entire entourage swiftly walked out of the room, and rushed into the elevators, just as the other elevator opened and Sona got off on the floor.

$\mathcal{A}$ suited man pulled the clothes out of the closet, neatly packing them in chrome bags. Roy looked around. A feeling of pending homesickness was creeping in. The hospital had been his home for several weeks now; it was like he was leaving his home. But it wasn't the hospital that he would miss.

Sona sat by Roy.

"I am feeling much better now." Roy said. "Finally, I am out of your hair."

Sona sat there trying to hide away her heavy heart. "Let's stay in touch. And if anything happens, call me." Sona handed over her card, turned it around and scribbled her personal number.

"I will." Roy took the card and his fingers touched her fingers. The quivering fingers lay still as they touched, the warm blood profusely flowing through the veins, stimulated by each other's touch. Sona pulled her fingers away.

The door opened slowly and Raju walked in. "Heard you are all set," Raju said briskly.

"Yup. Thank you doctor. If it wasn't for you and Sona, I would have been in a grave," Roy said.

Raju nodded and acknowledged. "Stay in touch," Raju looked at the card in Roy's hands "Looks like you already have our contact info, very well then."

"Yup...and good luck with your Libya work," Roy turned to Sona.

"Let me snatch her away before she goes in the wild," Raju said and waved Roy goodbye. Then turning to Sona, he said, "Shall we?"

Sona nodded. Her heart sank with a strange feeling. Roy was leaving. She knew it was wrong. *How could I feel that way?* she thought as she robotically walked with Raju, turned back, smiled at Roy and walked away.

The busy courtroom was in session. Roy sat in the court room, flanked by a battery of lawyers. His head was still bandaged. Roy was oblivious to what was happening around him even as Karara furiously took on the case in the background. Thoughts of Sona gushed through Roy's mind.

"Mr. Roy," Mark's repeated calls failed to nudge Roy out of his thoughts.

"You can clearly see that my client is still in trauma. This could be a trial court, but it's still a human court, My Honor." Mark knew how to take advantage of every situation.

"Alright Mr. Wolfe. The hearing will be adjourned till a later date." The judge adjourned the session, even as Karara threw a fit of fury.

In the hospital, Raju calmly walked back to his office, put the blinds down and this time instead of sulking in a corner, he threw his hands in the air and started dancing hysterically. Weird tune, weirder lyrics dating back to some obsolete song of the sixties, half of which he was making up on the fly.

The exhaustive routine ended and Raju threw himself on the chair, panting heavily, pushed his head back and laughed out loud. Moments later he composed himself, pulled open the drawer, took the prescription pills out and threw it in the garbage. The prescription pills that were bought under a false name. Basking in the good news, he quickly opened his laptop and went straight to the file folder. He opened a file and clicked the publish button. Roy's pending report was about to be published to anyone who had access to the system.

The confirm message box popped on the screen. He was about to push the button, when he heard a knock on the door.

"Yes," Raju replied.

"The door opened and an admin walked in. "This is the face reconstruction analysis you had asked for." The admin lent forward a sheet. "Please sign it here," he said.

Raju signed it and nodded with a smile as the admin walked out of the office.

Raju opened the file. There was a zip drive in it. He quickly plugged the zip drive in the computer. The files started to download automatically into Roy's folder.

A video popped up after the transfer was complete. The skin peeled off Roy's face, the image bared down to the skeleton, rotating three-sixty degrees. The rotating skeleton stopped, metal parts began to fill in the pieces of the skeleton, padding the chin, replacing the jaw, as the skeleton rotated around, adding one piece at a time. The rendering of the skeleton had begun to change as a layer of skin wrapped around the skeleton to reveal the face of SHAMMI.

Raju was startled, shocked beyond comprehension. *What the fuck is this? Roy is Shammi?*

He slouched in his chair; every incident he could recollect of Sona and Roy together, now all of a sudden started to make sense. *It was the old fire that was back, but did Sona know? I don't think so. Otherwise she would have told me...or at least her father.*

Raju was at a loss of words, desperate to steer out of this. To claim what was his for which he had so diligently and patiently waited for all these years and now he was so close. *I won't let anyone take this away from me.*

He dug in the trash and took his pills out, quickly popping one.

He skittishly took his phone out and dialled a number. The 'confirm' box on the screen was still on, and Raju hovered the mouse and clicked the "Cancel" button.

"Publish aborted" displayed on the screen.

"Hello," Raju said as the person he had called picked up the phone.

The bright sunny Manhattan view from the twenty-seventh floor penthouse apartment was magnificent.

"We need to have a conversation about your new lawyer. He didn't even acknowledge me in court today." A text message from Monica lit up Roy's phone.

"We can look at remote monitoring." One of the men in the big living room stood up.

"How do you suggest we do that Owen, without breaking the law of course?" Mark Wolfe said.

"Well, we can do that the old fashioned way, warm tail, you know," Owen replied, taking deep breaths through his puffy cheeks with every sentence.

"We don't have time for this. This District Attorney is, excuse me for saying this," Mark nodded in respect in front of Thakursaab.

Thakursaab acknowledged. Mark continued, "But it looks like this guy is after Indians or anybody that looks like an Indian." Mark paused. "I mean the guy himself is Indian. I mean what the heck?"

"There is the Devika case." Thakursaab said, "You are right."

Owen raised his hand, like a good boy signalling to get a turn to speak. "We can buy drones." Everyone was suddenly quiet. "I mean, they are cheap. Two hundred thousand tops." Everyone was still quiet. "We can rent one too, you know."

Roy pulled back from the seat, "Stop it guys! We are over engineering this."

"Dude, with due respect, if we don't, you are in deep shit," Owen responded instantly.

"Your decisions about the lawyer and in general have not been helping much," Mark interjected.

Thakursaab looked at Roy and tapped comfortably on his shoulders. "It's not your stress to have, beta. I got this."

Roy was touched but at the same time his fury of being betrayed by Monica was still raging, even more now that he didn't care about her anymore and all he wanted was for her to suffer. "I know, Dad. But give me one chance. I think I can fix this rather quickly, now that I know who the enemy is."

Thakursaab sighed.

Roy said, "Let me just try it," and he picked his phone and dialed a number.

"Hi Srini. This is Roy."

"What's up dude? Now that you are a celebrity, you must be getting a lot of action, huh!" Srini replied.

Roy was confused. "You do realize that I am an accused in a criminal case, right?"

"Oh yeah. That is badass man. You are the bad boy. Girls love bad boys," Srini chuckled.

"Okay..." Roy was amused at his words. "By the way, I really needed a favour from you." Roy tried to infuse sanity into the conversation.

"Sure. But you have to promise me you will tell me how to become this bad boy." Srini spoke with childlike excitement.

"You got it, man," Roy replied.

"Cooool," Srini said.

"Remember you had that app that could talk to other apps?"

Srini replied affirmatively.

"*Cool.* Would you be able to activate that on a number?"

"Absolutely, my friend. What do you want?" Srini sat down and pulled his laptop screen on.

"I want you to turn on the voice recorder with every call," Roy said.

"Sure. And dude, I'll suppress the top status bar," Srini typed fast, pulling software zooming on the phone number.

"All I need to do now is, call this person," Srini said.

"I'd like to call," Roy intercepted.

"Sure, let me patch you through. Do you want your number displayed too?"

"Yes," Roy replied with a heavy voice.

Srini patched the call through. Monica picked up the phone while driving. "Hi, Baby."

"Hi babe, just got your message about the new lawyer." Roy said. "I wish all of this would go away."

"Oh baby. Me too. I don't think the new lawyer you have is the right one. I found out a few things about him. And they are not good. We need to meet to discuss it further," she said.

"Sounds good. By the way, I have something to tell you as well." Roy paused, took a deep breath, getting ready to lace the conversation with artificiality. "I have evidence that will vindicate me."

Everyone in the room exclaimed in panic. Mark gave him a "What the fuck?" look.

On the phone, there was a moment of pin-drop silence.

Monica pressed the brake and her car came to a screeching halt, right in the middle of the road. An incoming car swirled. In the chaos of blares of horns, Monica pulled to the curbside.

"I am sorry. I was on mute," replied Monica. "That is very good news. What is it?"

"It's a log of phone conversations confirming that there were other people in the firm who set up those firms – and set me up." Roy paused for a second and then continued, "It's in the server room. Remember where we use to meet?" asked Roy.

Monica didn't know how to react. "Do you know who those people are?"

"No, I can't access it. Can you get it to me? You know, since I can't get in the office," asked Roy.

"Absolutely." A smile appeared on Monica's face. "Actually I am on my way to the office right now. I can do it right now, if you want."

Roy gave an authentic location and kissed her goodbye on the phone.

He hung up the phone, threw in on the table and heaved a sigh, getting ready, for now it was his turn to wait and watch.

"What a childish thing was that?" Owen said. "You haven't done this before, have you? We need to get drones."

"Hold on! Give me some time. I haven't done this before, but I know her. I know what she would do," Roy replied.

Monica quickly took her phone and called Hilton.

"Hi Monica," Hilton said.

"You better give me more money now. Roy has a recording that will vindicate him and if it wasn't for me, you know who would have been behind bars?" She paused. "You."

"Relax. Tell me what it is," Hilton replied calmly.

"Roy called me to pick a recording; someone from our firm has given him a log – a recording of someone else who set up the accounts overseas. You are the only person who called me to get a status on those shell firms," Monica replied.

"Okay. So go get the recording and bring it straight to me. And let's handle this maturely, okay?"

Hilton waited for a response, but Monica was quiet.

"Well, we are in it together. So let's not flare tempers. We stay afloat together, we drown together," Hilton almost whispered.

"You said you could handle this. I shouldn't have been involved. This was all your bullshit idea." Monica was still mad.

"Are you mad about the whole pregnancy thing?" Hilton replied.

"No, I am mad because I am the one saving your ass all the time. When this is all over, I don't just want to be a partner...I want to be on the Board too."

"Oh well....of course...don't you worry sweetheart. Just get that recording first, okay?" Hilton replied affectionately.

$\mathcal{J}$t was past 8.00 p.m. The glittering meat-packing district was bustling with the young and the rich hobnobbing in the fancy high-end restaurants lined up along the cobblestone streets. The simple brick exteriority, Fig and Olive, was busy on the inside with the bar flocked by folks waiting for their entire party to arrive. It was one of those restaurants that wouldn't let you go to your table unless the entire party had arrived.

Sona and Raju sat on a plush booth overlooking the street.

Roy sat at the FBI office along with his attorney, Mark Wolfe. The lit up view of Manhattan was breathtaking and for once, Roy looked at it with a whimper of hope in his heart.

Moon sat in front of him. He played the voice recording of Monica on the phone. "We got them."

Cooper walked into the room and smiled. "In my twenty years of crime solving, this is the first case that I got wrong. Sorry kid. You are free to go. Go live your life like you were meant to."

"I don't know about that, Detective." Roy's tone was fatigued.

Roy and Mark stood up. Cooper shook Roy's hands and nodded. Moon looked at Roy and Cooper and shook his head, in a dignified gesture of triumph.

"You did good, Moon. How did you manage it?" Cooper asked.

Moon spoke with bright lit eyes. "I just met Monica at Da Vinci office and asked to copy her ringtone. Then I accidently played the voice recording on her phone."

"Ringtones," Cooper looked to the ceiling with his fingers foiled around his chin. "Huh. Smart. Then the phone becomes evidence. You did good, Moon... Ringtones? What is that, anyway?"

Moon smiled away.

"Apparently she was the one who travelled to all these places and set up shell firms. We have matched her travel dates to the date of registration for the shell companies.

"But wait, this gets bigger. As we speak, Hilton, the CEO of Da Vinci and Fox from Karara's office are being picked up as well," Moon said.

"Wow! I am confused now." Cooper was genuinely confused.

"Roy was just the fall guy, Cooper. This is much bigger. Hilton had been playing dirty for the last twenty years. Fox made a deal for all of it to go away for twenty-five million dollars and a high profile arrest with isolated fraud." Moon exuded pride as Cooper grappled with the shocking details of the case.

"I get why he asked for money. Why the arrest though?" Cooper thought out loud.

"You would think, right? Who would benefit from this?" Moon raised his eyebrows. "I'd say the guy who is thinking of running for a higher office...such as governor."

"Oh boy, on to that one now?" Cooper smirked.

Roy walked out of the room and into the lobby of the FBI building when his paths crossed with a cuffed Monica being taken for processing.

Monica looked at him for a moment and then looked away.

Roy stopped. "Was any of it true?" he asked.

Monica stood there quiet, without uttering a word, then as the officers nudged her to move for processing, she spoke up. "At times, to win a war, you have to lose a battle. Doesn't mean you didn't make sacrifices in the battle."

"But you lost the war too," Roy replied, looked straight at her, perhaps for the last time as he bid adieu to Monica's empty eyes, and slowly walked away.

The waiter had just finished cleaning up the plates after the main course. The dessert menu card was neatly placed in front of Raju and Sona.

"The meal was wonderful. Thanks Raju," Sona said.

"Desserts?" Raju asked.

"I don't know. I may need to skip it," Sona said.

"Try this new one. This is an Italian restaurant, but they have a very special edition dessert."

The waiter set the side table and gracefully put the symbolic dessert on it. The chef joined the waiter. The dessert itself was mystical – a soft creamy vanilla layer hiding ice cubes filled with dark chocolate and then entire dessert was wrapped around with a transparent dome of solidified syrup.

"The year was 1810 and Napoleon was to dine with his newly-wed wife, Marie Louise. In order to honor Napoleon, the wedding guests were served with a custom dessert that embalmed the essence of fire, ice and vanilla crème..." While reciting the story, the chef set the dessert on fire. Flames erupted from the syrup dome; the dome collapsed within seconds and the flakes of charred sugar spread all over the dessert.

The waiter served the dessert, took a scoop of vanilla crème wrapped around a melting ice cube and placed in on the table. He then took out a little hammer and knocked open the ice cube, rupturing the dark chocolate. A soft stream of vanilla and chocolate dripped out.

The entire staff of the restaurant clapped.

Sona was quite impressed. She took a spoon and dug in. The spoon hit something solid. She quickly cleared it and there it was – a princess cut five carat diamond mounted on a white gold band.

Sona was amazed, shocked, startled. Her mind was numb, thoughtless. It was difficult for her to comprehend whether the silence in the restaurant was real or a figment of her imagination.

Shyly, she looked up.

"Will you marry me?" Raju said in the sweetest humble tone.

The entire staff of the restaurant had gathered around the couple – a tradition that the upscale eatery had savoured for decades.

The ringing in her ears had staggered, scaling down notch by notch with every passing moment. She could now hear every beat of the sound of water gulping down her throat. Her quivering eyes had found solace in the pastor white fabric of the table cloth, hushing the tiredness of her eyes away in the blank stare. The sound of water had stopped; instead, the crackling sound of crushed ice had engulfed the silence with its Moroccan tune.

"He has waited a very long time," Sona's dad emerged from the crowd. The restaurant staff gracefully dispersed away, as a set of familiar faces had begun to gather around the table. The clandestine planning of the event left Sona dazzled.

Raju gently reached over and held Sona's hands. "I just thought before you took off to Africa...But, there is no pressure... If this is not the right time..."

Sona looked up to her dad. His shallow eyes were beginning to drown in a flush of mixed emotions. A moment he had wished happened when Sona's mother was alive, was a bit delayed, but it was finally becoming real. As he nodded to her to accept the proposal, the emotions burst out, raining tears down his face.

Sona looked at Raju. Everyone held their breath, like a nail biting finale of a cricket match. She lifted her hands and slowly dug it in the chocolate cake and took the ring out. She pulled her arms forward towards Raju. "Won't you put it on me?"

The silence of the coliseum had fallen by the sweet rebel of the excited crowd. The clapping echoed through the roof as the restaurant manager announced the name of the couple, bringing cheers from everyone in the restaurant and several dozen onlookers that had gathered around the glass walls. Sona smiled while her eyes were still locked in a raging fight against all the attention, fluttering away to a shy corner.

The dark closet illuminated as the lone bulb (tucked inside an antler semi rustic ceiling light) sparked to life with a pull of a string.

Sona looked around. The rack at the far inner corner of the closet was stacked with cardboard boxes. Shipping container labels from ten years ago were still intact on them.

Sona pulled down the string and opened up one of the boxes. A little worn-out notebook, a silver ring, and a diamond bracelet were neatly kept over the cushion of dusty soft toys.

Sona took the notebook out, flipping over the thin pages, some filled with dried rose petals, some had poems written in it, but all started with a smiley face. All the pages of the book had a happy smiley face, except for the last one.

There was no face on it at all.

The writing on the page had worn off; the month and date were scratched away.

The end of last of her teen years had brought her the drowning pathos, still fresh, deep in her heart. Or was it? For a while it had gone away. *I felt better. I had begun enjoying movies. Laughing, words of people around me had started to register in my brain as independent thoughts; the bias that everyone was not trustworthy had diminished away. Then, why the hell am I looking at this box? Why today? When I am about to get married in two weeks?*

Words and thoughts of Roy were circling in her thoughts inevitably.

Roy is right though, in helping me sail through this life. Everyone sails through, but his words have made me think that fate is stubborn, and we can fool it only if we look to the future. Past is like a sinful brat, trying to win a twenty dollar bet with the shy future, pulling all strings to emotionally destroy you to never look ahead. But the question is – is your life worth just that – twenty bucks? No!

Sona lay on her bed. Her arms drooped below the bed, lost in her thoughts she had fallen sleep. Her grip was loosening, slowly petals of dry roses began to drip out of the notebook, covering the hardwood floor with a dust of love and then the book fell as the hovering pages fell flat on the floor. The bed of dry roses lay on the floor, helplessly buried under the book, like a metaphor, under the burden of their own carrier.

Roy sat by the window, checking his phone every two seconds. Makhmal sat by Roy, right next to Mataji rocking on the plush leather chair.

"I know why you ran away from us," Mataji said.

Roy slowly turned to her. "Even I don't know why I did what I did, and for so long," Roy said.

"I quit alcohol the day you disappeared," Mataji said bringing tears in Makhmal's eyes.

"Not because I was doing a tapasya, but…" Mataji took a sip out of a Perrier sparkling water "…because we feel punished when we leave the things, people, we love the most."

Roy listened calmly.

"Love is a funny thing. It makes you tender in the heart but when it's ripped apart, it sticks to the soul, like a shadow, always reminding you, that no matter what and where you end up, just remember, you are in love." Mataji pulled back, closed her eyes as the soft sound of the rocking chair filled the air.

Roy stood up, smiled, kissed Mataji goodnight and retired to bed.

Roy woke up with the buzzing sound. In the living room, Makhmal hurriedly walked up and opened the door.

"Hi, I am Dr. Bhat." Raju introduced himself. "I have been treating Mr. Roy."

Makhmal pleasingly acknowledged Raju. "Yes sir. Please come in."

"I wanted to see Roy. To check if he is okay." Raju cleared his throat.

Roy walked out of the foyer into the living room. "Oh, hello doctor."

Raju pursed his lips. "Hello Roy. How is everything? I thought I should talk to you regarding the progress."

"Very well...Healing...Slow and steady..." Roy said.

There was an awkward silence. Raju signalled Roy to go outside to talk.

"Why are you here?" Raju furiously asked Roy.

"What do you mean, doctor?" Roy asked.

"Don't bullshit me. I know who you are," Raju taunted. "Shammi..."

"You are the filthiest man I have ever seen. All you ever wanted was a fuck. You never cared about her then and now what... you are having a midlife crisis that you have to walk right in when she is finally getting ready to move on?" Raju was unrelenting. "You didn't care about her....her family. For Christ's sake. You changed your fuckin' face to run away from her."

Raju stopped, still breathing heavily. Roy stood there, listening quietly. There was an eerie silence.

"We are getting married in two weeks," Raju said in a rather subdued tone.

Roy looked at Raju and acknowledged.

"She told me she wants to invite you, personally," Raju said.

"Don't worry. She will never know," Roy said. "If it was for me, you would have never known too."

Raju looked at Roy. His aggravated heartbeat was levelling off. He wanted to say something, but didn't. He just shook his head.

Roy looked up, took a deep breath, and looked away outside the window into the wilderness of the city.

The chilly evening was a consolation for Roy, as he slowly jogged in central park. His limbs were getting stronger. He didn't need crutches anymore.

A familiar sight stopped him. He tried to look closely. The person's face became clearer and a pretty Sona draped in sky blue polka dotted Versace dress appeared before him.

"Hi," Sona said.

"Hi," Roy replied with a fresh burst of energy.

"Well, I was in the area and…" Sona paused. "You know what, I am not going to do this…."

Roy halted and stood still, waiting for Sona to finish her thoughts.

"The truth is I have something to tell you…"

"And I have something to tell you as well…" Roy said. "But go ahead! I am dying to know what is so special that you came all the way to tell me."

"No, you go ahead first…"

"Ahh, my life is boring. I am not going to bring you tales like my girlfriend set me up for FBI," Roy was mocking his own life.

Sona smiled and shrugged it away. "Anyway, my life isn't exactly a bed of roses too."

"But, a weird thing happened yesterday. Out of nowhere, Raju gathered all the courage and…" Sona massaged her temple with her fingers, "He got twenty of my relatives and proposed to me at Fig and Olive."

Roy's poker face was devoid of any reaction, cheating his sinking heart that was roiled in the emotional upcharge.

"Fig and Olive, huh! That is very romantic. I didn't expect that from him."

"Well, you have only known him within the confines of the hospital," Sona replied.

Roy's lips pursed as he nodded.

"That's beside the point anyway." Sona looked straight in Roy's shy eyes. "I need to ask you something…"

Roy raised his empathetic eyes, spreading a comfort blanket for Sona, who was ready to let her demons out.

"You asked about my past, right? Here it is. Ten years and three months ago, the man who I handed over my soul to, ran away and took with him my spirit to live." Sona paused. They had walked onto a side and sat on a patch of grass. Roy's feet were aimed straight at Sona, his attention was undivided. "Raju has helped me since then. Like an angel, he has been there, pulled me out of the darkness I was falling into, but…I have…" Sona turned her eyes away from Roy and looked away.

"You have never loved him. You still love the man you loved ten years ago," Roy finished her thoughts.

Sona was emotional as she wiped her tears.

"Do you want my advice?" Roy cleared his throat. "Like what I would have done if I was you?"

Sona nodded.

"Well, I'll tell you this, and I may have told you this before – first love is puppy love. You will never forget it. Period. In my case it was my much older art teacher when I was nine years old."

Sona chuckled, still trying to fend off the emotions.

"As far as the ass that ditched you is concerned, don't pity him…or that relationship. That guy is unfortunate. And he is not unfortunate by design, he is unfortunate by choice. You think what is happening to you is bad? You have no idea that there is something a lot worse out there. And who knows it could be happening to someone right now, right at this moment." Roy paused. "I think life likes you; it has given you an angel-like path to wash away the not-so-good past and move on with a guy whom you have known for an entire lifetime."

Sona looked at Roy and smiled. "You make it sound so much better. But, what if he came back?"

"Has he come back yet?"

Sona shook her head.

"See. He will not come back. I don't think. Not now. Not ever," Roy said in a deep monotonous tone marred with apathy.

"How can you be so sure?" Sona asked.

"Well, you thought it was me." Roy looked at Sona, "and a guy who doesn't look a bit like your boyfriend from many years ago is going through so much shit, the guy who actually hurt a kind soul like you, can't get redemption with a little bit of repentance in just one lifetime."

"Don't say that," Sona said softly. "I don't wish bad for anyone, especially not him."

"Here is what you need to do." Roy stood up and turned to Sona.

"Stand up." He offered his hand.

Sona gently clutched on to his hand and stood up. "Now say with me," Roy said.

Sona took a deep breath.

"What was your guy's name?"

'Shammi," she replied.

"Ok. Now say after me…" Roy said. "I Sona Gill, on the solemn day of November fifteenth, cleanse myself of any lingering memory of my past with Shammi."

"What is all this rubbish?" Sona said.

"Trust me on this. Play with me like a joke, if you will," Roy said calming her down.

Sona hesitantly repeated the line. Roy's intimidating bug-eyes had forced her into going along with him.

"Not because I didn't love him, but because I loved him so much that even after ten years his memory lingered on. Having taken ten years of my life for a reckless person is a punishment in itself without any fault of my own. Today is the day that I shall move on."

Sona's voice was getting firmer with every sentence. She had forgotten where she was or why she was saying this.

Roy continued as Sona followed his words. "Today is the day when I'll leave behind the shadows of the past and step into the future, with my heart, with my soul."

Roy had stopped.

But he had set something in motion and Sona went on, pouring her thoughts out loud. "I will never forget you but I will forgive you. I had forgiven you the day you left me. My sorrows were my own. My tears were my own. You didn't ask to be loved. I chose to love you and I will always love you. I know I'll never forget you, but I'll try to carve a little place in my heart...it may just be enough to live the rest of my life....with someone else." The sound of words stopped, but her lips were still moving. She realized and turned to Roy.

She hugged him tightly. Roy looked up to the sky; his teary eyes were fighting hard to not give in.

"Thank you." Sona pulled out of the embrace, wiping her tears. "I don't know what is between us, but...thank you."

"You had something you wanted to tell me?" Sona asked.

"Nothing that can't wait," Roy said. "Nothing that is important enough to take you away from this solemn moment of liberation."

She took a deep breath, put on her infections smile. "You have to come to my wedding."

"I'll try. Life is beginning to get busy with Monica and all," Roy said.

Raju waved from many feet away as he strolled past the entrance and on to the walkway.

Sona smiled and waved back. She got ready to take off. Raju walked in and kissed her. She smiled and air kissed him with her puckered lips.

"Raju, do you know something about him?" she said as Raju got closer.

Raju was bewildered. "What?"

"He is saying he won't come to our wedding. Now you deal with him. I won't get married unless you get him to come to our wedding."

Raju secretly nodded.

"I'll be there." Soft words dispelled out.

Sona smiled. "Good. No matter what may come, and with a date. Promise?"

Roy looked at Raju and then at Sona. "Promise."

The quaint street in the affluent neighborhood of Garden City was bustling with festivities. The lighting, the color, the vibrancy, everything around the place was just perfect. The thematic setting of the wedding was breathtaking: there was a carnival set in the back garden, complete with a round-go-robin, photo booths, popcorn corners, a dance floor, a stage and an enormous clock counting down to 'the time' when Raju's decades-long wait would finally be over.

One adjacent house on a two-acre plot was recently bought by Raju and bulldozed to be converted to a parking lot for his wedding. Choppers flew in around the house, sprinkling rose petals bought fresh from Italy.

As the beautiful red sun simmered down the Atlantic Ocean, the twelve-acre drive shone with the crème de la crème of New York high society.

A shiny black Cadillac Escalade pulled up. Bumpy disguised with a thick moustache and beard got off the drivers' side while Roy gently climbed down from the passenger's side, making way for the tuxedo-clad valet to drive it away in the expansive parking lot.

Dressed in an all-black tuxedo and a designer black hat, Roy slowly walked inside the venue. The stylish black hat on his head covered the bandages around his head. *You can do this. All you have to do is smile. And do what you have been doing for the past ten years; get your coldblooded lizard out.*

"I can't believe that Kaju is where he is today," Bumpy was stunned to see the house, the decoration, the splurge.

"It is all karma, Bumpy. Karma is a gift, when you are!" Roy replied.

"And karma is a bitch, when you are!" Both said simultaneously, raising soft chuckles.

An announcement echoed. "Ladies and gentleman, please be reminded that the *varmala* ceremony will start in thirty minutes in the central gathering area." The central gathering area, right in the middle of the decoration, was precluded by an open air dance floor with live performance by Jay-Z.

"Do you remember Anuja?" Roy looked at a curious Bumpy. "She is actually happily married and is a Bikram Yoga instructor."

"Wow...really?" Bumpy was surprised. "How do you know?"

"I have cleansed a lot of my sins in the last ten years," Roy replied in a rather sombre tone.

"Do you remember? We crashed that wedding?" Bumpy tried to cheer him up. "The Nagin dance...The little fat uncle. And then the aunty caught us..." He looked at Roy and they both started laughing.

"Let's do it again," said Roy.

"What? Spot an aunty who can catch us?"

"Let's go back to how we were. Carefree...Dancing away..." Roy exhaled.

"Sure." exclaimed Bumpy while fixing his fake beard and moustache.

Upstairs, the master bedroom was swarmed by a host of girls as Sona sat in front of the dressing mirror. Everything about Sona looked perfect. Almost everything, except for her alluring eyes – like a gateway to her feelings buried deep in her heart.

"You have the most beautiful eyes, but they are also your giveaway. For some reason, they never lie." Her mother used to tell her.

"You mother would be very proud of you. She would have been very happy to see you like this," an older lady said.

"Chachi!" Sona turned around joyously. She stood up and gave her a tight hug.

"You look so beautiful." Chachi took a little black kajal out of her eyes and put a bit of it behind Sona's ears. "It will ward off the evil eyes from my beautiful princess."

"Let's go. Bhaisaab is waiting and so is the groom," Chachi said. "I see you have already taken over his bedroom."

Sona smiled. A hint of sadness still lingered as she spoke. "Nothing like that."

"Okay… Let's go. It's time for the varmala."

"I am right behind you. I just need some alone time before it all starts," Sona took a deep breath.

"That you definitely deserve," Chachi said with a sparkling smile. "Let's go…Let's go…" Chachi walked out of the room along with everyone, clearing the room in a jiffy.

Sona turned back and sat in front of the dressing mirror.

She took a lipstick out to cover a slight smudge on her lips when her mind relentlessly paced back.

A young Sona sat in front of a mirror in her teeny bedroom. Her cheeks had sunk in. Her skin had paled, her persona robbed of all happiness. The splashes of rain through the window had sprinkled her room wet, but she was oblivious. Her mother had come inside the room. "What happened, beta?" The dreary of her daughter was unbearable. Nothing she said could change Sona, but the persistence of a mother never gave up.

"One man cannot take you away from us," and tears started flowing down her Mom's cheeks.

"I'll be there, Mommy. Just give me a minute." Words out of her mouth were just that…words.

Sona took the lipstick out and stared at it. The worst part for her was that she didn't know why this had happened to her. Her helplessness was brewing a storm of rage inside her, fighting her for her own survival.

She ran the lipstick crisscross on the entire mirror with scratching lines all over it, trying to scratch away her own reflection... the reflection of despair, the reflection of loss.

The bride Sona took a deep breath; clearing her mind, she stood up and walked towards the door when a buzzing sound stopped her. She stopped and looked around trying to locate the source of the sound. As she got closer to the side table, the sound intensified. She opened a drawer and found Raju's pager buzzing non-stop.

She looked at the message: "CODE RED: Patient getting seizures again." With professionalism running in her blood, she held on to the pager and ran outside the room. Nobody was there. She peeked outside the window. Raju dressed in a heavy exquisite *sherwani* was walking towards the varmala *mandap.*

Damn it. Let me wrap it myself. She took her phone out and dialled the number.

"Hello, Dr. Bhat is not here. But tell me what is going on."

"Yes, Dr. Gill," the electronic voice resonated outside the phone.

"Patient is Joshua Becker. He is a diabetic..." The voice on the phone started with the medical history.

"I don't have the patient's records," Sona looked around. She walked up to the walk-in closet and in the well-designed closet found the laptop bag. "Hold on. I got the laptop."

She pulled the laptop out of the bag and threw it on the bed. "Do you have access now?" The voice on the phone echoed in emergency.

"Give me just one sec..." Sona was typing fast on the keyboard. The screen on the laptop got filled with multiple popups. "Got it," Sona said.

"Alright. This is what you do..." and she went on to explain the procedure and medication in great detail, patiently waiting as the nurse followed through the instructions and applied to the patient.

"Got it, Dr. Gill. The patient seems to be stabilizing. Whoo! That was scary!" The voice paused for a few seconds. "Yup. The patient has stabilized. We are good. Thank you very much and my deepest apologies."

"No worries. Trust me, I'd rather be doing this than getting married," Sona said.

"Uh oh. Don't you run on Dr. Bhat! He has been on to you for an entire lifetime." Both Sona and the nurse chuckled.

"Alright now, Doctor. I'll let you go, and many congratulations!! May god bless both of you." The nurse hung up the phone.

Sona sighed. The conversation was a lifesaver, for it broke a smile on her face. She pushed down the screen of the laptop when something caught her attention.

She slowly pulled the screen back up. In the clutter of patient names on the system, as Sona read the folder name of a small yellow folder, she felt a shivering chill down her spine – The folder name was Roy (Private) – and it was updated less than a week ago.

The big clock shone on the pole in the middle of the decorated backyard, counting down to the *muhurt* of varmala. The festive atmosphere was in full swing as the clock ticked down to 4:59.

The hip-hop beats of *Dirt off your shoulders* blasted out. The berserk well-dressed crowd had let loose, cramping and stomping up the dance floor. Roy in his trance-like state stumped, and danced away, even as Bumpy stood at a distance, helplessly looking at the mockery of fate bestowed upon Roy.

An ecstatic Raju flanked by family members looked back to the paver walkway leading up to the house, waiting for Sona to appear. The reward for his honest deep love was to culminate; today was the day he was to wed his soulmate, a culmination to the journey that started ten years ago.

Sona's father was getting visibly worried. "Raju beta, do you want to check on Sona. We are less than five minutes away from the muhurt time."

Raju humbly nodded. "Yes, Papa. Let me go check." Raju waved to his friends signalling that he will be back in a minute as he walked down the paver path into the house.

Sona's trembling hands opened the folder. The screen transformed and many little files started opening up, tiling one after the other. A video file appeared on top. With bated breath, Sona clicked on the video, with the fear that her worst nightmare may spring back to life.

The white space in the video got filled with a picture of Roy. Sona sunk in the chair. The skin peeled off Roy's face, the image bared down to the skeleton, rotating three-sixty degrees. A few breathless moments later, the rendering of the skeleton had begun to change as a layer of skin wrapped around the skeleton to reveal the face of *Shammi*.

Raju rapidly ascended up the spiral staircase, with his chin up and a smile covering his entire face.

Tears started flowing through Sona's cheeks as the 'before' and 'after' picture appeared on the screen. The transformation was real, medically validated, as Sona clicked through dozens of supporting files.

She pulled an image, the image sprung up a newspaper article some ten years ago. The headlines – "Ivy League Kid Survives a Murder Attempt".

She leaned closer to the screen, reading through the gruesome details of the incident. She touched the laptop screen with her bare hands, feeling Shammi's picture. Just then, she noticed a blurry line of medical diagnostic. She hovered on the mouse, and pulled out the results. "Acute Cerebral Hemorrhage Syndrome" in the footprint of the report jumped out to her, and Sona sprung on the chair just as Raju walked into the room.

The black hat on Roy's head was stuck like a sticky pad. The sweat from the dancing was beginning to seep out to the surface of the head. Roy stopped for a second and wiped the sweat off his forehead. He could feel that his head was unusually moist. He put his hand inside the hat, slowly pulled it out; his hand was covered with blood. The worrisome smile appeared as he looked around. Bumpy spotted him.

Raju's eyes locked with Sona's. One look at the baffled expression on Sona's face, and Raju knew that something was wrong. Sona looked outside the window. The crowd was swarming near the dance floor.

She pulled her dupatta down, lifted her *lehenga*, and ran towards the staircase, and down to the floor. Raju jogged in and looked at the laptop. A spine-tingling sensation ran through his entire body. This was the end of it all – His life with Sona and his career as a doctor. He had crossed the ethical line the moment he had concealed medical facts about Roy. He held his head in despair, then turned around and paced right behind Sona.

Sona climbed down the spiral staircase, as the conversation with Roy echoed in her head bringing a blurry visual flash of Roy's words for Shammi in front of her eyes.

"*...Don't pity him or that relationship. That guy is unfortunate. And he is not unfortunate by design; he is unfortunate by choice... A guy who actually hurt a kind soul like you, can't get redemption with a little bit of repentance in one lifetime...*"

Tears were flowing down her cheeks, taking with them the kohl that had lined her eyes beautifully just a few minutes back.

"*...You think what is happening to you is bad? You have no idea that there is something a lot worse out there. And who knows it could be happening to someone right now, right at this moment...*"

The smiling face of Roy dissolved as Sona ran towards the backyard.

The crowd had gathered around Roy as he lay unconscious on the ground. Bumpy held him in his lap and screamed, "Somebody help! My friend isn't moving."

Sona pierced through the crowd, located Roy and kneeled on the floor. She looked around and screamed, "Somebody, call 911…"

Raju emerged at the forefront of the gathered crowd. The big countdown was fast ticking down from five…four…. As Sona's screams muted through the crowd, a dark cloud was beginning to engulf Roy's consciousness, resting his years of agony, converging his charade of humane to its singular reward – death. But the feeling of death wasn't what he had feared; far away from the pain, a feeling of cool air whistled through his head. The smile on his face scaled back, as the counter ticked three…two…one…, and the smile had dissipated away. The counter struck zero, and a barrage of fireworks triggered all around the house – commemorating the deliverance of darkness that had prevailed in Roy's heart and body.

The sound of the drip resonated in the eerie silence. Sleepy eyes woke up with a soft flutter of eyelashes.

The blurry images around him started to clear up with every blink and the bright sparkle of Sona's face shone in his eyes.

Sona clutched his hands, trying to control a blizzard of emotions storming out of her eyes. "You wanted to leave without letting anyone know...again...." An emotion of anger and care uncontrollably came out of every word. "What did I do to deserve this? All I did was to love you...Why am I always the last person to know? What right do you have to do this to me?"

Roy smiled bleakly. "Because I knew you would scold me," he said softly.

Sona clutched his hands tighter, stooped down and gave him a tight hug.

"Your husband will be jealous," Roy said softly.

Raju appeared from the back. "To be jealous, you would have to marry her first, Shammi...Roy... Good luck for the future."

His eyes were shying away from Sona. "I know you make the most lovable couple."

He waved goodbye to everyone, turned around and walked out of the room. Thakursaab followed him and gently patted him on his shoulders. "Thank you beta. If it wasn't for you, I don't know what would have happened to Shammi today."

Raju smiled. "I have done enough harm. It was time for my sworn duty, sir. Maybe this way I can one day look into my own eyes again."

"What are you saying beta. Only you had the expertise to perform this complex surgery. May god fulfill all your wishes." Thakursaab choked with tears.

"Some wishes are best unfulfilled, sir." Raju slowly walked away.

"Raju told me what happened when you came back to India. It wasn't you silly. It wasn't your fault." Sona kissed Roy's hands. "Your guilt was so pure that you didn't even bother to clarify...if your guilt was so pure, I can't even imagine how pure your love is."

The rustic thousand pound weight had been craned off his chest. Roy choked on his own words as his eyes gushed with a tsunami of tears. Sona bent and hugged him really tight. A smile appeared on Roy's face.

A convertible Maserati raced through the empty highway lanes of I-95. Raju helmed at the drivers' seat, memorializing a montage of his time spent with Sona. He felt different today. The void of Sona in his life had been created in permanence. But perhaps, it was time for him to come to terms with it. He glanced at the prescription pills on the passenger seat. He smiled, then took the pills and threw it out in the wilderness of the tall green trees running along the highway. Hip hop beats blasted out of the car stereo as words of the Eminem style rap song echoed –

"...And then the lady said, didn't your heart just break?
I went to a party, I think was a rave
Masquerade and people with rage
They looked at me funny, at my bare face
I snuuck in, hiding in a devil's mask,
Snaked in, to the center of the stage
I stood there, like in the eye of the storm
There was silence everywhere

A faint hum broke the gate, I heard choir sing my name
I got mad… asked them… what the heck
And then the lady said, didn't your heart just break?
And then the lady said, didn't your heart just break?"